THE
DEATH
OF A
FALCON

THE
DEATH
OF A
FALCON

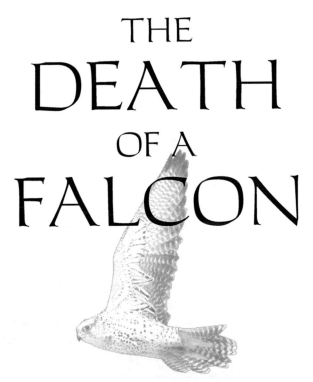

A Muirteach MacPhee
Mystery

Susan
McDuffie

Liafinn Press

Cover Design by Jennifer Quinlan at Historical Editorial
http://www.historicalfictionbookcovers.com

Interior Design and Formatting by

www.emtippettsbookdesigns.com

Published by Liafinn Press
ISBN Trade Paperback: 978-0-9847900-9-8

THE MUIRTEACH MACPHEE MYSTERIES
BY SUSAN MCDUFFIE

A MASS FOR THE DEAD

THE FAERIE HILLS

THE WATERGATE, a Muirteach MacPhee novelette

THE STUDY OF MURDER

THE DEATH OF A FALCON

ACKNOWLEDGMENTS
AND
DEDICATION

I owe sincere thanks to all the many people who have helped me with this effort. Thank you to Diane Piron-Gelman, my editor, whose work greatly strengthened the book. I am also very grateful to Jenny Quinlan at Historical Editorial for her fantastic cover, and to E.M. Tippetts Book Design for the beautiful interior formatting and design. I am so fortunate to be able to work with all of you.

My family offered encouragement, and the cats helped, providing editorial assistance and numerous typos, hopefully now removed with Diane's aid. Donna Lake, Donna Thomson, and Robin Dunlap read the original manuscript and made helpful suggestions; I feel very lucky to have good friends who know the vagaries of horses and gardens, and are willing to share. Sharron Gunn's help with Gaelic continues to be very much appreciated. Thanks also to the Santa Fe Raptor Center for their inspirational hawks, most especially to Gandalf, and to Margaret Evans Porter for timely help with autumnal flowers. A vendor at the flea market sold me a piece of fossil walrus tusk and Alvin Calavaza carved a gyrfalcon, which kept me inspired during this lengthy process. Ann Chamberlin encouraged and advised me to stick with the longhand.

My sister, Judie Churchill, generously helped ensure this book would see the light of day. I am so thankful to have you in my life!

Salvador helped with everything, keeping me fed and driving me here and there while I pursued this project. This book is for you, Salvador, you are my very own much-loved Gudni.

CAST OF CHARACTERS

Muirteach MacPhee, Keeper of the Records for the Lord of the Isles

Mariota, his wife

John MacDonald, Lord of the Isles

Henry Sinclair, Baron of Rosslyn

King Robert II, king of Scotland

Queen Euphemia, his queen

Lady Isobel, one of the queen's ladies

Sir Johann Drummond, a knight of the court

Lady Ingvilt, his wife

Magnus, their young son

Peter Leslie, Drummond's squire

Agnes, Ingvilt's red-haired maid

Morag, another maid

Robert Cruickshanks, captain of the king's guard

Fearchar Beaton, Mariota's father, a physician

Duncan Tawesson, captain of the *Selkiesdottir*

Malfrid, his daughter

Gudni Skraelingsson, his foster son

Gybb Saylor, his mate

GLOSSARY

Gaelic

Amadan (feminine: Amadain): Fool (ah-mah-dan, ah-mah-deen)

Birlinn: Scottish galley, varying in size from a few to many oars (bur-leen)

Brat: mantle (brat!)

Ceilidh: A social gathering with music and singing (kay-lee)

Lèine: Shirt made of linen; "saffron shirt" is lèine cròch

Mo chridhe: Literally "my heart", an endearment (mo CHree-yuh)

Selkie: A seal man or woman

Sgian dhubh: Small dagger, literally "black knife" (skee-an doo)

Uisge beatha: Whisky (literally, the water of life) (oosh-kuh beh-ah)

Inglis (Scots):

Aweel: Well then

Bairns: Children

Dochter: Daughter

Dreich: Dreary or bleak

Kerch: Kerchief

Puir: Poor

Wynd: Narrow alleyway between two buildings

Other

Cameline: A sauce flavored with cinnamon and other spices.

Cotehardie: A long, close fitting over-garment for men or women.

Daggotted: A garment with a bordered edge shaped as tongues, scallops or leaves.

Flummery: A sweet custard.

Garderobe: A privy, also refers to a closet or wardrobe.

Groat: A silver coin worth four pennies.

Gyrony: Term used in heraldry; divided into eight spaces (gyrons) by straight lines all crossing a single point.

Helluland: A western land in the Norse sagas, "Slab Land", possibly Baffin Island.

Herber: An arbor or shady bower in a garden, also an herb garden.

Houppelande: A robe for men or women, full and belted at the waist, usually made from ornate fabric.

Hvítramannaland: (Norse) A fabled land to the west, said to be populated with folk with white skins and hair, also sometimes referred to as "Greater Ireland".

Manchet bread: Fine grained white bread.

Marchpane: Marzipan.

Markland: A forested land to the west in the Norse sagas, possibly Labrador.

Mazer: Drinking cup.

Pattens: Thick-soled wooden shoes worn outside.

Posset: A drink of heated milk combined with wine, ale, or spices.

Reresoper: A late meal or snacks served in private rooms to a few people.

Rewarde: The table to the right of the dais in the hall.

Saker: A species of falcon.

Skraeling: (Norse) One of the indigenous native peoples of the western lands, also used to refer to the Greenland Inuit.

Sotelty: A surprise dish served at the end of a course, often very elaborate.

Targes: Smaller round shields.

Tercel: Male falcon.

Tormentil: An astringent herb, *Potentilla Tormentilla*.

Vinland: A land to the west in the Norse sagas; possible locations range from Newfoundland to New England.

Wadmal: A coarse, undyed woolen fabric woven in the Norse lands, a major trade item from Iceland and Greenland.

CHAPTER 1

Edinburgh, Scotland, 1375

"They say the folk there have green skin, and drink salt water."

I snorted. "And you are believing that?" I strove to control my horse, which gave his own snort in response to my efforts.

Mariota laughed, but shot me an irritated glance as she rode next to me, her blue eyes brilliant in the late morning light. My wife sat her horse easily. "I'm not sure that I'm believing it, Muirteach, but I am certainly wanting to see the truth of it for myself."

A brisk breeze blew the smell of salt water towards us long before we reached the port of Leith. It was a fine day for riding and His Lordship had mounted us well enough for the jaunt from Edinburgh Castle to Leith, myself on a roan gelding and my wife on a smaller grey palfrey.

We had accompanied the Lord of the Isles to Edinburgh on business with the crown, and had already been at court for some days. But on this day word had reached the court of a trading vessel in port from the far northern lands—Greenland—and my master wanted a gyrfalcon. So did his liege lord, Robert II, King of Scotland.

"I'll send my man, Muirteach here, down to the port for you," the Lord of the Isles had offered to the king earlier that morning as we concluded some of our business. I busied myself putting pens, ink and parchments into my satchel while my lord and his sovereign conferred. "He'll check into it, right enough, and see if what they have merits my royal father's attention."

The king's bleary eyes lightened a bit. "Aye, that would be a fine thing. I thank you, my son, for the thought." King Robert's daughter was His Lordship's own wife, and although not the closest family, the canny lord had no hesitation in reminding King Robert of that fact when circumstances offered. Although he himself was close in age to his royal father-in-law.

"And I will send another man along with you," King Robert continued, "someone familiar with the area." The king motioned to a brown-haired noble who stood with some other courtiers at the far corner of the king's solar. "This is our own well loved Henry Sinclair, Baron of Rosslyn. He is somewhat familiar with the northern tongues, as his mother is from

Orkney, and has served us at King Haakon's court in Bergen, as well as in other matters. The baron has a good eye for birds. And he speaks Norse. Christ only knows what tongue these traders speak. He can accompany your man. Muirteach, is it?"

I nodded that indeed I was Muirteach, and of course agreed to my lord and my king's request, as did Henry Sinclair.

And so, late that morning, several of us had set out from the castle that perched high on the mount. My wife wished to join the party, she would not be gainsaid, and a groom accompanied us as well. The Baron of Rosslyn rode a spirited black horse while the groom sat astride a plump mare. The road measured but a few miles from the Edinburgh into the port of Leith, and a cool breeze blew little fluffy clumps of white clouds, like young lambs, quickly across the blue sky on this mild September day. While we rode I smiled a little at the thought of lambs frolicking in the heavens and caught my wife's eyes.

"What, are you laughing again at my fancies, Muirteach?" Apparently she had not quite forgiven me for my earlier comment.

"No, no, *mo chridhe,* just some fancies of my own." My horse stepped restively and I brought him under control while the breeze blew a faint scent of the sea towards us, underlying the scents of earth and warm horse dung on the road.

Neither Mariota nor I had ever visited court before, although I had met the king once, at Urquhart Castle the year before, at Easter-tide. The royal court, now at Edinburgh, proved to be a strange new world, full of folk dressed in finery, prattling away in Inglis and sometimes in Norman French. Although we had been here only a few days I sensed murky intrigue that made our own lord's main hall, at Finlaggan in Islay, look like clear stream water in comparison. His Lordship planned to remain here for some weeks, and I relished the chance to see more of court life.

I turned in my saddle to our companion trotting along on my other side. The Baron of Rosslyn, a broad-chested man, had hair of warm chestnut, and hazel eyes that missed nothing. The groom followed a few paces behind on his plodding mare. "So you have travelled to the north?" I asked our companion.

Sinclair nodded and smiled at me in a friendly fashion. "Aye. The Orkneys. And I have visited Bergen, in Norway, several times. When I was younger, just a lad really, I found myself betrothed to King Haakon's young sister, but the *puir* wee lass died before anything came of it. It would have been a fine match, that."

I nodded. Who would not wish to wed a princess? But it was not my marriage we spoke of; I was married to Mariota, and happy enough, I told myself. Although she had proved, that last year in Oxford, to have a knack for disregarding my wishes at times.

"Your father is from Orkney?" I asked to change the topic.

"The lands there should be mine, by right," Henry declared, not immediately answering my question. After a moment, he continued. "My father is the Earl of Ross, but my grandmother, Marjorie, was sister to Queen Euphemia, King Robert's wife. My grandmother married Malaise, the Earl of Orkney. Their daughter is my own mother and it is through her that the Orkneys should have come to me. King Haakon sets my cousin master there for now, but the lands will come to me someday, be sure of it."

"And so now you serve the King of Scotland?" I asked, feeling that the topic of the Orkneys was perhaps best left alone for now.

"I am Scottish, but Norway holds the Orkneys. What of it?"

"It is hard to serve two masters."

Henry shrugged, reining in his horse easily as we neared the city gate of Leith. "We all serve two masters, I think. Ourselves, at the very least, and our lords. And our wives," he added with a smile, "if we are married men."

Mariota flashed Henry a grin, she had overheard. I smiled back at her, and nodded my own agreement to Henry as we entered Leith by the Edinburgh Gate. Carts loaded with merchant goods, drovers and their livestock, and pedestrians, as well as others mounted on horseback crowded through the gate and down the narrow road inside the city walls, the main way between the busy port and the burgh of Edinburgh.

"Come, the docks are this way." Henry motioned, and we followed him through the crush. I struggled a bit to control my horse as we threaded a path through the busy traffic and bustling townsfolk down the roads that led towards the harbor.

I smelled the sea and the docks before I saw them. The scents of the harbor overwhelmed the usual odors of town life as we neared the docks. The area bustled with merchant cogs unloading and loading amidst a noisome babel of tongues. Large vessels, whose sweating crews unloaded casks of wine from Bordeaux and Burgundy, bales of brocade and velvet from the Italian ports—Venice, Luca, Genoa—silks and other cargo from as far away as Constantinople, the eastern boundary of the Christian world, mingled with cogs from the north and smaller fishing boats smelling of their catch. I caught a whiff of spices, mingled with the scent of the salt ocean, as we passed a larger vessel where a merchant, perhaps the owner, stood on the docks, richly dressed in velvets, berating some sailors who worked at lowering some chests with rope pulleys into a smaller boat for transport to the land. I could have gawked all afternoon but we had a mission to perform.

Henry found the ship we sought, the *Selkiesdottir*, easily enough. Few ships put in from the far northern lands. A small vessel, she sat at anchor tucked between a Flemish trader and a merchant cog from Bremen. Mariota's grey palfrey shied nervously at the clamor of the docks, and she gentled it while Henry and I hailed the ship.

"We're seeking the captain of this vessel," I called up. A few men, whose skin looked of normal hue, not greenish at all, heaved bales of what seemed to be furs above decks from the hold below.

"He's below," one old sailor indicated, in fair enough Inglis.

His companion, dark complected and short, did not speak, just gestured below also. A slightly built youth—or perhaps a lass, for although clad in a boy's tunic and hose, she wore her blonde hair in two long plaits down her back—yelled something down the hatch in Norse. After a moment a man stuck his grizzled head through the hatch door and clambered onto the deck.

"And what is it I can be doing for you?" he called down to us in Inglis. From the faded lilt in his voice I judged him once to have been a Gaelic speaker.

"We're here from the king's court on business," Henry responded. "Our lord is desirous of a gyrfalcon. We heard you might have some to sell."

The captain surveyed us a moment before he answered, taking in Sinclair's fine horse and raiment, the attendant groom, and myself and Mariota. "The king, you said?"

"Aye, the King of Scotland himself. And for my master, The Lord of the Isles," I put in.

"And you are?"

"Muirteach MacPhee. Of Colonsay, and His Lordship's scribe," I answered.

He considered. "I might have some birds, for a price," he admitted at length, "although they could be promised already. It is not difficult to sell gyrfalcons, although it is hard enough to catch them." He paused. We waited until he spoke again. "Well, best come aboard then. We'll speak more comfortably in my cabin."

We dismounted, leaving the groom waiting on the docks to hold the horses, and one of the crewmen above threw a rope ladder over the side of the ship. Henry went first. I looked to see if my wife needed my help, but Mariota hiked up her blue skirts and climbed the ladder with no problem. I confess that I enjoyed the glimpse of her shapely legs, encased in knitted stockings, as she made her way on board. I have always admired my wife's fine legs. I made the ascent well enough, without any help. I have strong shoulders and arms that do well enough for climbing rope ladders despite the limp that plagues me, the result of a childhood fever.

The captain, a tall lean man with the weathered face of a sailor and grizzled hair showing his age, watched us closely as we came aboard, but he proved courteous enough. I think the richness of Henry's garb impressed him. The three of us soon found ourselves ensconced in the captain's small cabin, actually nothing more than a rough tent on the deck. The captain offered us seats on bundles of packed goods, sent the young lad to fetch some ale from below decks, and we got down to the business at hand.

"I am called Duncan Tawesson," the captain said, introducing himself while we settled ourselves on the bales.

"You have the accent of an island man," I observed. "A Gaelic speaker."

"Not the islands, but close enough to them. Your ear is good, sir. My family owns lands near Kilmartin, but I'm a younger son, and one cursed with wanderlust as well. I've not seen Kilmartin in years. Your companions?"

Henry spoke up, confident and assured. "I am Henry Sinclair, Baron of Rosslyn. His Majesty King Robert II of Scotland himself sent us to attend upon you."

Duncan raised an eyebrow at this but said nothing.

"And this is Mariota, my wife." I introduced her and Mariota smiled at Duncan.

"So you're a trader? And captain of the ship?" my wife inquired with interest. Duncan's demeanor softened a bit.

"Aye. And owner of the ship as well. The *Selkiesdottir*. My own sweet beauty, she is. I trade between here and the northern lands, and sometimes run to Bergen as well if I can avoid those Hanseatic bastards. Think they own the ocean." He spat eloquently on the deck.

"And where have you been trading this year?" I asked.

"The northern lands. Greenland, mostly. Although the market for walrus ivory and wadmal is not what it used to be, and the trade not so profitable as some years back. But despite it all I have managed to secure some fine furs." Captain Tawesson paused a moment before he continued. "White foxes, and even white bearskins, among others."

"And yet we hear you have gyrfalcons among your wares." Henry came back to the point as the dark lad returned with a pitcher and some cups. Duncan poured the ale and served us himself. I took a swallow gratefully; the salt air had made me thirsty.

"Aye. You heard right. I have three birds. Two sisters and

one brother, and they're beauties. I myself caught them, along with Gudni here." Duncan gestured towards the dark lad, who had returned to stacking the bales brought up from below decks.

"In Greenland?" Henry asked.

"No, a land further to the west. Helluland, the Norse call the place. A rocky land, cold and snowbound, that holds little of value. But fine birds breed there, if you are brave enough to make the journey."

"I have heard somewhat of those lands, in Bergen. We must speak more of that sometime," Henry interjected, his hazel eyes lightening with interest. "But where are these falcons? We would see them, if we may."

Tawesson nodded to the deck. "Just there. Go and have a look. Gudni will take you." He summoned the lad over to us.

The dark boy, who did not seem given to much talk, led us to the further end of the craft, where some cages sat near bales of rough woolen cloth. The cages, covered with other stoutly woven fabric, kept the occupants in darkness. The lad made an odd crooning noise and removed the covers.

I had seen falcons before. My Lord of the Isles has several, a peregrine and a saker among them. He even has a golden eagle although he cannily had not advertised that fact at the king's court. Golden eagles, along with gyrfalcons, were commonly reserved for kings and emperors. But on the islands my Lord of the Isles did pretty much as he willed. My previous experience with birds, however, left me unprepared for what I now saw.

Three magnificent falcons perched on wood blocks. Golden eyes glared balefully at us, as the birds adjusted to the sudden light. They flapped their wings and shrieked, until the lad made some singsong sounds and they gradually gentled a bit.

The two largest birds were nearly pure white, one with a few darker feathers. The smaller of the birds, the male falcon, the tercel—although I judged him to be near as long as my own forearm—had somewhat darker plumage.

"The two white ones, those are the females," said Duncan, who had approached behind us.

"They are truly amazing," whispered Mariota to the captain, who gave her a smile.

"Indeed, they are," he replied. "Well fit for a king."

The boy re-covered the cages, the birds settled, and we returned to our own seats and worked out some arrangements. Besides the falcons, Tawesson's cargo consisted of some fine furs—lynx, marten, white fox, and others, as well as wadmal cloth and other items from the north. We agreed that Duncan would bring the falcons and a selection of his finest furs to the castle in Edinburgh the following day. Henry Sinclair, acting as King Robert's agent in this matter, agreed to send some carts the next morning, at first light, to carry the goods to the palace. He explained to the captain that King Robert was desirous of inspecting the raptors himself. For my part, I devoutly prayed that the king and my own Lord of the Isles would not covet the same bird.

"We've something else that might be of interest to the court," offered Duncan as those arrangements were concluded.

"And what would that be?" countered Henry Sinclair. I expected the captain to say a unicorn's tusk or something of that ilk and was surprised at his reply.

"Tumblers."

"Tumblers?" I asked, confused.

"Aye. Here, lass." Duncan summoned the girl with the plaits. She came readily, followed by the stocky, dark boy.

"This is Malfrid, my own daughter. And Gudni. They're tumblers."

"Really?" I felt the same skepticism that I heard in Henry's voice.

"Aye. Malfrid it was who started it all. She ran wild when she was a lass and had little company. Except for Gudni, here. Her foster brother."

I looked at the two youngsters. They seemed of about an age with Seamus, my young friend on Colonsay—that would be about fourteen or fifteen years. At first somewhat shy, the both of them stared at the wooden decking until Duncan said something to them in Norse. At that the girl looked up and smiled—she had a beguiling smile, and vivid green eyes that lit up her face—then she lightly ran a bit, turned a cartwheel and vaulted into the lad's arms. He held her up triumphantly and flashed a smile of his own, his teeth white against his dark complexion. Then the lad got out some little leathern balls and set to juggling them in a creditable manner, while the lass assisted him.

Mariota clapped, we all did, and Henry finally agreed that the court might well enjoy watching a performance. So it was agreed that they would accompany the gyrfalcons to court tomorrow, along with Duncan, who would present his goods to the king. Our plans concluded, we left the *Selkiesdottir* and returned to our horses, remounting for the trip back to the castle.

"So Malfrid is Duncan's daughter?" Mariota observed to me as we followed behind Henry Sinclair and the groom on the ride back. "And what of that boy Gudni? He looked odd."

"No green skin, though," I joked, although the lad did not look like anyone I'd ever seen before, with his dark skin. Yet his face was not as black as that of a Moor I had once seen in Oxford. "Well, perhaps you can ask him tomorrow, *mo chridhe*," I added. As we approached the castle gate I turned in my saddle back towards Leith to admire the view for a moment. The castle sat on a high mount overlooking the burgh and from this vantage point there was a fine view both of the town and the harbor beyond. From someplace I heard the shrill cry of a hawk. Thinking of gyrfalcons and faraway lands, I faced forward again and entered the castle, following my wife and Henry Sinclair.

CHAPTER 2

At supper that evening Mariota and I sat together at a lesser table, along with some minor nobles and others not deemed sufficiently important to sit at the high table. The court dined in the Great Hall of the newly completed tower, started by David II and brought to completion by his successor. The hall boasted a richly painted vaulted ceiling and elaborate tapestries hung against the walls, which did little to muffle the diners' noisy discourse.

King Robert and his queen sat at the high table, along with my own lord and his wife, Margaret, King Robert's daughter by his first wife who had died some twenty years earlier. His present wife, the Queen Euphemia who was Henry Sinclair's own great-aunt, seemed to me a pleasant woman, calm, tall and dark-featured. The queen chatted pleasantly with her stepdaughter and her powerful son-in-law while the evening meal progressed. The meal ended with a dramatic *sotelty*, an immense castle complete with crenelated turrets, all created from pastry and gilded a shining golden color by some chef's artistry. The cook himself proudly brought his masterpiece into the hall on a large silver platter and set it before the king and queen with a flourish.

One woman in particular among the diners caught my eye. Dressed finely in a red brocade gown trimmed with dark marten fur, she sat at the table opposite us, across the hall. Her golden hair gleamed, although whether its hue was real or assisted by some artifice I could not be sure. Her vivid green eyes and dramatic dark eyebrows could not help but draw my attention. She wore her hair braided in the elaborate fashion that appeared popular at court, intricately plaited on either side of her face, crowned with a circlet and filmy veil of silken stuff, as though she herself was royal. She sat at the upper end of the table, well above the salt, deep in conversation with a young man seated near to her who seemed most attentive. They both largely ignored the older knight seated beside her. I attempted to put names to many folk in the crowd, and thought to ask Henry Sinclair of the lady after the feast was over and those still present milled around the hall.

"Oh," replied Henry, glancing in her direction. "That is the Lady Ingvilt, married to Sir Johann Drummond."

"And that would be the young man she is speaking with?"

Henry laughed. "No, that is Peter Leslie, her own husband's

squire. Sir Johann is over there," and he indicated the same older gentleman I had seen, now in some grave discourse with other elders of the court. Sir Johann reminded me a bit of Mariota's father and I said as much to her, before my wife turned aside to greet another lady of the court she had made some acquaintance with.

"He is a minor knight, with some lands in the north, near Aberdeen, but he is well regarded by King Robert, and by the former king as well," Henry concluded. "I traveled with him to Bergen some eight years ago, which was when he met Ingvilt. She was high in King Haakon's favor and in fact King Haakon did much to encourage the match between them."

The talk turned to other subjects but not before the lady, seeming to sense our words, glanced our way and smiled elusively.

"Och, you've caught her eye, Muirteach," jested Henry. "That dark hair of yours, and those grey eyes. You'd best watch out."

I tried to laugh, feeling flustered. I know I am not handsome although others, my wife and aunt among them, disagree. But I am slightly built and find it hard to forget my limp in company, especially such exalted company as I found here at court. "I am happily married," I protested, "as is the lady herself, no doubt." Henry raised an eyebrow but did not reply, and just then Mariota, done chatting with her new friend, rejoined us.

"Lady Isobel has told me of the queen's own herb garden,"

enthused Mariota. "She waits upon Queen Euphemia here at court, and says she will ask the queen if she may show the gardens to me." My wife grew fine herbs in her own garden, back on Islay, and I said as much to Henry Sinclair.

"Oh, so you are knowledgeable of such things?" Henry asked Mariota with a smile.

I could not at first tell if my wife was annoyed or embarrassed, as she flushed slightly, but she answered Henry pleasantly enough. "My father is Fearchar Beaton, a noted physician of the Isles. And I strive to learn all I can of his art."

"A fine thing," Henry replied diplomatically. "Of course, everyone has heard of the Beatons, such fine healers as they are. I am honored to meet one of such a distinguished family."

Mariota's flush deepened. "My father is quite skilled," she said. "I thank you, sire."

Just then a hush fell on the crowd as the king and his queen prepared to leave the Great Hall. The crowd drew back, leaving the way clear for their passage. As the royal procession neared us I noticed the Lady Isobel whisper something to the queen, and now the queen and her royal lord stopped before us. I bowed and my wife curtseyed deeply.

"My lady Isobel tells me you are a healer," the queen said to Mariota.

"Indeed, for my father is Fearchar Beaton, and he taught me a little of his skill," Mariota replied modestly, her eyes downcast.

The queen smiled, her own brown eyes friendly. "We have

heard much of your father from my daughter, Margaret, the wife of your own lord. She also has spoken highly of your talents. Please visit us tomorrow, and I will show you the herber, if you would like."

Mariota nodded, pleased, and the royal personages continued through the hall, followed by my own lord and his wife.

"Well, you shall get your wish, *mo chridhe*," I said to Mariota as the royal party left the hall and folk began chattering once more. As we returned to our own lodgings, my wife spoke excitedly of the palace gardens, while I thought, less excitedly, of the scribing I would do for the Lord of the Isles.

❖   ❖   ❖

I found myself still unfamiliar with the ways of the court, as did my wife. It seemed a lot of overdressed fops, all chattering like noisy magpies in Inglis, with smatterings of French thrown in. John MacDonald, my own Lord of the Isles, might have agreed but he kept his thoughts to himself as he and the king attempted to hammer out the number of *birlinns* and fighting men the king could call upon if needed, in return for a grant of lands in Knapdale. The talks lasted most of the next morning and I think both men were glad of the chance to quit negotiations and go and see the gyrfalcons—although they might both compete for those as well. The large white falcons easily cost a king's ransom.

Henry Sinclair already stood in the hall when I arrived

with my lord from the king's private solar, where we had been negotiating. My wife also had arrived, along with the queen's ladies, returned from the visit to the gardens. My wife waved to me gaily and continued her conversation with Lady Isobel. Other courtiers and their ladies milled about, chatting and craning their necks to see, while Duncan and Gudni unloaded the carts outside the hall and hefted the cages and heavy bales of fur inside, for the fine mizzle of rain had made the courtyard too muddy for either furs or tumblers. I greeted Henry and we watched the proceedings.

Mariota rejoined me as Duncan Tawesson began laying out his goods, below the dais and the king's own high seat. All the other tables had been taken down save for one, placed in front of the dais, and on that Duncan spread his wares. In three large cages to the side, close to two feet tall, perched the gyrfalcons. They sat regally, sullen, hooded, exuding latent power. Although I had seen them the day before my breath still caught in my throat; I could see why kings and emperors squabbled like toddlers to possess them.

Duncan unbundled some furs, large black ones and two pure white pelts, which he claimed were bear, as well as martens, white foxes and lynx, and spread them out on the table. With a few words and a deep bow, he described his wares and invited King Robert to inspect them. A long horn caught the king's attention and Duncan explained it belonged to a sea unicorn. People hung back until after the king and queen made their initial selections and then came closer, eager to see the fine furs and to marvel at the gyrfalcons.

The hall grew quite crowded; most of the folk at court crammed their way inside, courtiers as well as any servants who had managed to escape their duties. The castle folk craved some novelty on this grey day, and the air inside grew somewhat close with the crush of people. The scents of pomanders and perfumes mingled with the smell of the hides and furs.

Duncan did brisk business, showing furs to various nobles, including Queen Euphemia, who seemed much taken with some white fox pelts. I saw one of her servants carry several of them off. The king meanwhile conversed with his falconer in front of the gyrfalcons, discussing the merits of the birds, I assumed. My Lord of the Isles stood with them.

After folk had looked a bit and some purchases were made, servants cleared the space in the center of the room. The steward invited members of the court to sit on benches set up along the walls, while others, servants and attendants for the most part, crowded behind. Chairs were set up for both the king and queen, who sat on the dais at the end of the hall with a few others of the high nobility, my own lord and his wife among them.

We had all piled onto the benches in no particular precedence and I found myself seated with Mariota on one side and the Lady Ingvilt, accompanied by the young squire I had seen the previous evening, on the other. A young boy of about six years of age or so, dressed in fine clothes, sat on Peter Leslie's lap, with another woman, a red-haired maidservant

I assumed to be the child's nurse, on the far side. Despite a somewhat obdurate look to his face the lad was obviously Ingvilt's get. He had her blonde hair, but something of the look of his father in the set of his jaw and in his brown eyes. I presented Mariota and myself to the Lady Ingvilt. She smiled in return and in sweetly accented Inglis introduced her companions. The child's name was Magnus, the maidservant Agnes.

Seated next to the squire, Agnes made constant attempts to engage Peter in conversation. He alternated his attentions with ease, seeming to flirt and jest with her, and then raptly conversing with Lady Ingvilt. I noticed the red-haired maid pout a little as Peter spoke with his mistress. I gave the maid a smile, and she smiled sweetly back, her pout forgotten. After a short time the squire turned back to her and Lady Ingvilt began to speak more with me. She asked me where we were from and engaged me so in conversation that I nearly forgot my wife, sitting on my right side. However, at that point the herald blew a horn and the show commenced.

Malfrid and Gudni appeared, both dressed in parti-colored tunics of green and blue. Malfrid wore a youth's garb with a short cotehardie and hose, but her long golden plaits hung down behind and there was no mistaking her for a lad.

"Kind and gentle lords and ladies," announced Duncan, "here, come from the far and frozen North, the very land of Greenland itself, the furthest outpost of Christian souls, the veriest edge of the world, I present, for your pleasure and your marveling, my own daughter Malfrid Duncansdottir and her foster brother, young Gudni Skraelingsson, whom I found abandoned on an ice floe as a mere babe, left to die by his heathen parents and wrapped only in a pelt of skin."

Folk murmured at that. Gudni flashed a confident smile, white teeth gleaming against his dark skin, and Malfrid smiled as well. They both bowed. I sensed the Lady Ingvilt beside me tense with anticipation, as did we all, for just an instant before the tumblers commenced.

Gudni began the show, leaping forward with three somersaults and one backwards flip, then landing on his feet. Malfrid, graceful as a swan in flight, entered the area, performing a series of four cartwheels. Then, scarcely pausing, she vaulted atop Gudni's shoulders and balanced there precariously a moment, then flipped off backwards.

The performance continued and we marveled at their agility. Malfrid balanced again on Gudni's shoulders and then leapt to the earth, as swift and graceful as a swallow, somersaulting in the air to land on her hands, and then, after a final vault, gracefully stood upright. Gudni got out some colored balls and set them flying in the air, juggling, while Malfrid assisted. The act culminated as they balanced several stools one atop the other, and Gudni climbed up and balanced upon the stools. Malfrid then ascended and stood, balanced on Gudni's shoulders for one long moment.

I heard Mariota catch her breath as the lass surveyed the crowd like some goddess from an old story. Then she dove to the ground, turning a double somersault in the air and landing lightly on her feet to stand, triumphant, while we all applauded wildly. Gudni followed with a single cartwheel and the crowd roared its approval.

I watched as Gudni embraced his foster sister. She returned the embrace for one lingering moment, then stepped back and smiled at the lad, flushed and proud. Then she kissed the lad on the cheek while folk continued cheering.

"Perhaps they're foster brother and sister, but who's to say that is all there is between them—" I heard a voice say from the crowd, in a nasty tone. It might have been Peter Leslie; I could not be certain.

Mariota, next to me, made a face. "Och, they are but children," she replied, to no one in particular. "Surely that was innocent enough."

I saw many silver coins dropped in the wooden bowl Malfrid passed around after the performance. She and the lad bowed one final time and then mingled with the audience that surged into the center space, chattering about the show and milling around Duncan and his furs once more. Business looked to be even better than before the acrobats' spectacle, folk perhaps wanting some kind of souvenir of the afternoon. Lady Ingvilt smiled at me, then excused herself, and went to speak with the performers as well as examine some of the remaining white fox furs on the table. Just then His Lordship called me over to where he stood observing the gyrfalcons. Although I'm not knowing much of falconry, my uncle Gillespic on

Colonsay does keep a hunting hawk or two. Duncan saw our interest and, leaving the furs to Malfrid for the moment, also approached, followed by Gudni.

"I caught them myself, me and Gudni here," volunteered Duncan. "They were but fledglings, all three in the nest together. Two sisters and one brother. We had to scale quite a cliff to get to them. Gudni came near to falling, did you not, boy?"

Gudni nodded and quietly reached out to gentle one of the birds.

"He's got a way with animals and birds. It comes from being Skraeling, no doubt," continued the lad's foster father.

"Skraeling?" I asked. I'd not heard the word before, although I remembered Duncan had called Gudni "Skraelingsson".

"Aye, the heathens who live in Greenland. Sail in funny skin boats, they do, and they're masters with them. They shoot seal and even whales from those small craft, with harpoons. Those are spears on a line," he explained. "The cold don't bother them none. They are people of the ice, dressed all in furs."

"And the lad?"

"It's as I said, I found him, abandoned in the snow. Wrapped in a sealskin hood, as if a selkie had birthed him and then left him on that desolate shore. The tide would have taken him, had I not seen him. The heathens must have put him out to die. Just a wee thing, near to newborn he was. So I took him, not having a son of my own. And he was close enough in age to Malfrid, my own daughter by blood. Her mother still suckled her at that time. She gave him suck as well."

"So the lass is your own daughter?"

"Did I not just say so? My own dear daughter, indeed."

"And what of the lass's mother?" I found myself curious about this strange family group.

"My Astrid." Duncan's eyes took on a faraway look for an instant, as he remembered. "A Norse woman from the west of Greenland. A widow when we met. She lies dead now, buried where the dancers light up the sky above her grave during the long nights."

"What happened?" I asked.

"The harvests had grown smaller and the weather worse. I returned from a voyage of some months, and discovered my sweet Astrid had died. I found Gudni and Malfrid barely alive, trying to live by eating the few goats left, along with whatever Gudni could catch. So I brought the children away with me and we left that place."

"A sad tale. And what of the farm?"

"Abandoned, now. That land had never been mine, it belonged to Astrid's first husband who died many years ago. They'd birthed another, older daughter, but she is gone now as well. I suppose the land could be Malfrid's, should she ever wish to go back and claim it."

Our discourse had veered far from gyrfalcons. I turned and saw Queen Euphemia approaching at a stately pace, accompanied by a few of her ladies, including the Lady Isobel and Lady Ingvilt. I saw nothing of the latter's son and guessed his nurse had charge of the lad whilst his mother attended on the queen. Queen Euphemia smiled at the Lord of the Isles. Son-in-law though he was to her, they were close enough in age, I guessed.

"What think you of the birds, my lord?" she asked, her dark brows arching as she spoke.

"They are the equal of your own noble lord and yourself in their majesty," replied the Lord of the Isles in a courtly manner. "The kings and queens of the kingdom of the birds."

She laughed a little. "Indeed. Yet as his son-in-law, you might well covet them."

"Tempted, of course, my queen. I would have to be insensate were I not."

"Well, there are three birds," the queen responded, somewhat ambiguously, and turned from him to examine a white bear's pelt that lay nearby on the table. After a moment she turned to me. "Your wife has healing skill," she remarked.

"Yes, Your Majesty. Her father is Fearchar Beaton and she has learned much from him."

"I have an interest in herbs and healing myself," the queen said with a smile, still lightly running her fingers over the white pelt. "Your wife is welcome to attend upon me in my chambers at times while you remain here in Edinburgh. Until my son-in-law's business is completed. I have told her this, also."

"An honor, my lady," I replied with a bow, feeling a little awkward. "We both thank you for your kindness." Queen

Euphemia nodded in reply. Then she left the white pelt, and left me as well, continuing down the hall with several of her ladies, stopping and chatting here and there with other courtiers in the crowd.

Lady Ingvilt approached the cages and reached out as though to touch one of the falcons. Gudni quickly moved towards her and reached out, grabbing at her arm, saying something sharply to her in Norse. The woman stepped back abruptly, almost bumping into me. I caught a whiff of some exotic perfume before I excused myself.

"What did he say?" I asked her after a moment when she did not move away.

"Just that they are not entirely tamed yet, and not to be trusted."

Duncan Tawesson turned towards us and bowed to the lady. "Indeed, my son spoke truly, my lady. You take careless chances. One could easily rip off a finger."

"They are magnificent. I reached without thinking." Lady Ingvilt smiled. "The lad did right to stop me."

"He was but concerned for your safety, and for that of the birds."

"A worthy concern. The boy is chivalrous." She smiled again, directly at Duncan. "He is your foster son?"

"My son in all but blood, my lady. As I was telling Muirteach here, I found him left to die, abandoned like a selkie's child on the shore."

"Well, he was a lucky babe indeed on that day."

"As was I, my lady. A better son no man could want."

"I have kin in Greenland, and spent time there myself as a child," Lady Ingvilt continued. "Perhaps you and your children would sup with me this evening in my apartments—mine and my lord husband's. It will be a small gathering, just a simple *reresoper*. We have invited just a few folk. And you of course, as well, are welcome," she added, including Mariota and myself. "It would be a pleasure to speak of the old days, and to make new friends as well."

We all agreed to come and received directions to Lady Ingvilt's lodgings, in one of the old buildings near the summit of the castle mount. As Mariota and I left the hall I glimpsed Malfrid conversing with a young squire, the same Peter Leslie who had sat next to Lady Ingvilt at the tumbling show. Both seemed to be enjoying themselves, despite the ridiculous way the lad was dressed. The squire stood inches away from the girl, but she seemed pleased by his proximity, smiling up at him. The boy certainly seemed to have a way with the lady-folk, and I wished for an awkward moment that I were as practiced at the light conversation so common here at court. Young Malfrid certainly seemed entranced, and for an instant I felt some concern for her virtue. Ah well, I said to myself, if Duncan didn't care to discipline his daughter I had no cause to worry over it.

I'd seen some of English fashion the time we'd spent in Oxford, but these court fashions far eclipsed student wear in foolishness. The lad's shoes came to a fashionable point near the length of his forearm and he wore a parti-colored houppelande with slashes to show the rich velvet underneath. Fine clothes indeed for a squire. Malfrid appeared taken, either by his finery or by his visage, which even I realized, as I watched him lean possessively close to her, was not unpleasant. She backed away a bit and blushed, but he reached out to caress her cheek before the lass finally turned and walked away towards her father.

CHAPTER 3

The king had expressed a desire to see the gyrfalcons fly, so later that afternoon, after the rain let up and the dinner ended, a party made their way down the castle mount to the tilting grounds below. The greens spread out on the southern side of the flatter lands below the crag, a bit removed from the growing burgh that crowded around the steep road leading up the east side of the mount to the castle entrance. His Lordship of the Isles was of the party, along with King Robert, Queen Euphemia, Henry Sinclair, and many other nobles and ladies. Their rich robes and mantles gleamed against the grey clouds on this dreary day. Many rode horses down the mount and the harnesses and tack jingled gaily, while others made the journey down to the tiltyards on foot.

Mariota and I, among the latter group, watched as Duncan

Tawesson and Gudni, following the king and mounted nobles, maneuvered the cart carrying the caged falcons down the steep track to the horse greens and the tiltyards, where grooms exercised the king's horses and knights clashed in stately tournaments. But no tournaments had been planned during our time here, and a great pity that was, I thought. I would have delighted to see one. Still, the sight of so many finely dressed nobles and their ladies thrilled me and made me think of the stories I had read of Sir Gawain, and other knightly romances.

A cool brisk breeze from the Firth began driving the clouds ahead of it, bringing a faint scent of the sea. Although the view was not so grand as the other side of the mount, at times I actually glimpsed patches of pale blue sky despite the few stubborn raindrops that splattered on the ground, refusing to give way to the promise of better weather.

The cart lurched to a halt when it reached the level greensward. The mounted knights and lords and ladies stopped as well, as did our own monarch and his queen. They waited while those of us following on foot arrived, crowding behind to get a better view. I watched Gudni and Duncan open the cages and take out the hooded falcons, Gudni cooing and singing that same strange air that seemed to pacify the majestic birds.

"Malfrid, do you have the lures?" I heard Duncan ask. Malfrid, now dressed again in respectable women's garb, nodded and brought out a worn leather bag from the cart. Duncan un-hooded the largest gyrfalcon and removed her from the cage. She flapped her pure white wings a bit, blinking in the light. Duncan fought to keep his arm steady as the snow-white bird settled on his wrist, her head reaching up well past the man's shoulders.

Malfrid removed the lure from the bag—two crane's wings tied together to resemble a dead bird, fastened to a cord—and handed it to her father. Duncan moved down the green, a bit away from the crowd. He loosed the gyrfalcon and then, holding onto the cord and swinging it in a circle about him, he loosed the lure. The bird swept into flight, soaring over the green below, her wings glinting against the clouded grey skies. Then she dove for the lure.

On her first pass she swooped past Duncan, who deftly swung the lure aside. The falcon circled again, far, far above the castle and the watchers standing on the green. I wondered what we all looked like to her as she flew so high above. Duncan continued to swing the lure, calling to the bird. At length she returned and this time plummeted like a stone on the lure. He quickly gave the falcon a scrap of meat after she landed, distracting her, and retrieved the lure. Gudni ran to the bird and, still making those soft singing noises, gathered his charge up and re-hooded her.

King Robert watched, shading his eyes with a richly gloved hand. Henry Sinclair whistled in approval and I realized I had been holding my breath as I watched. I let it out now in a deep sigh and glanced at my wife next to me. Her blue eyes shone as the breeze whipped her plaid mantle around her shoulders.

"Well done," pronounced the king and my wife murmured, "Beautiful." I spied the gleam in my Lord of the Isles' eye and I hazarded a guess that we would be negotiating with Duncan for one of the birds before too much longer. It did not take the Sight to guess that.

In their turn both the second falcon and the tercel flew, each performance equally spectacular. Duncan and his children had trained the birds well. The rain stopped sputtering and began pouring down with more force. As the group broke up I saw Malfrid speaking heatedly with her foster brother while they waited by the cages for Duncan to return with the tercel. Perhaps they argued over the birds, for I saw Malfrid adjust the cover over the whitest falcon's cage, just as her father approached with the third bird. Duncan and Gudni quickly put the tercel back in his cage and checked the birds were secure. Then they loaded the cages back in the cart, and the entire party made its way back up the castle mount.

❖   ❖   ❖

The main meal had been served at noon and although most folk supped in the Great Hall, I had to confess that I found the thought of a special supper in Lady Ingvilt's quarters enticing. She and her husband, Sir Johann, had several rooms in one of the older buildings on the castle mount, in what was called the Old Queen's Lodgings. It was a wooden and wattle three-story building and several apartments had been carved out of what, at one time, had been the queen's royal solar and withdrawing rooms. Since the New Tower, begun by David II and recently completed by King Robert, now held the royal lodgings, the living spaces in these old buildings had been doled out to courtiers. Henry Sinclair had told me that Sir Johann had lands in the north, near Aberdeen, but when in attendance on the king, he and his wife had rooms here.

Mariota, fussing over her appearance, finally decided to wear her new blue woolen houppelande over a green tunic, with her plaid mantle. After watching the falcons that afternoon, my wife had abandoned me to wait upon the queen with the Lady Isobel, and had just now returned to our chamber. I watched as my wife combed out her blonde hair and then braided and arranged it under her linen coif in a somewhat different way, a new style no doubt inspired by the fashions of the court ladies. For myself I put on a clean *lèine* and wore a wool doublet over that, and arranged my own mantle over it. I smiled at my wife as she smoothed her coif one final time. "You're looking fine tonight, *mo chridhe.*"

"As are you, Muirteach." Mariota adjusted the silver and cairngorm pin on my own *brat*, her touch soft, and then she gave me a lingering kiss before we left our apartment—really more of a closet next to His Lordship's quarters. We counted ourselves fortunate to have that much privacy here at the court. At least the room had a small window and a door we could close. After another kiss we proceeded towards Lady Ingvilt's apartments in the building across the way.

When we arrived we found Duncan, Gudni, and Malfrid

there before us. Sir Johann and Lady Ingvilt's quarters were luxuriously furnished. Bright woolen tapestries hung on the walls and soft cushions had been spread on benches for the guests to sit on. The room filled with pleasant conversation and the aromas of spiced wine and savory foods. A trio of musicians played crumhorns and recorders in one corner of the room. In another corner I spied Henry Sinclair, now deep in converse with Duncan Tawesson. Gudni sat, stiff and awkward, on a bench glowering across the room to where Malfrid sat. I watched Malfrid chat animatedly with that same young fop I'd observed her with earlier in the day.

I glanced around the room, looking for our hostess. I did not see the lady at first, just her husband and Magnus. I thought the child must be close in age to my own half-brother Sean, who was now safe and happy on Colonsay. A dark-haired maid hovered behind them. Sir Johann caught my gaze and gestured in welcome.

Just then the door to the apartments opened and our hostess herself appeared, breathless and flushed. The lady gave a few orders to another maidservant nearby, that same comely red-haired Agnes we had met earlier. The maid took her mistress's cloak, and then our hostess turned to greet us with a welcoming smile, breezing across the room in a flood of exotic scent and scarlet brocade.

"You must excuse my tardy greetings," she said. "I was called away, a matter dealing with the queen that could not be deferred. How goes it, sire?" she asked her husband, glancing at the boy who stood beside him. Without waiting for his reply, she turned to her son. "Magnus, you are still awake?"

"He wishes to stay and join in the party, my dear," replied her husband mildly.

Lady Ingvilt smiled and patted her son's yellow hair affectionately. "My young son has no wish to go to bed, he wants to stay and watch his elders make merry. And so you shall, my dear, for a time." The red-haired maid had reappeared from the inner rooms, and Ingvilt gave her some orders concerning the lad, then turned back to us.

"A handsome boy," Mariota observed.

"A rascal, but we dote on him," his mother said, with a fond look backwards to where Magnus had seated himself upon a bench, the red-haired maiden hovering distractedly nearby with a dish of sweets. Sir Johann, standing close to his son, chuckled and took a goblet of wine from a servant, giving the boy a taste.

Mariota exchanged a few more words with our hostess, while the dark-haired girl followed and quickly handed each of us a glass goblet of wine—Rhenish, I think it was—spiced with fennel and cardamom. I savored the fine taste as the sweet liquid slipped down my throat like the softest velvet. Our hostess turned away with a smile and moved around the room, setting the other guests at ease.

My wife began to speak with Duncan Tawesson and Henry. I stood awkwardly a moment or two watching the goings-on and sipping at my wine. I felt a light touch on my elbow and turned, surprised to see the Lady Ingvilt standing next to me again, looking like some empress, I fancied, from ancient days. She wore a ruby red houppelande of fur-trimmed brocade over a kirtle of scarlet satin. Amber beads hung around her neck and I noticed some delicate gold filigree rings at her ears. Her intricately braided hair was barely covered by a coif of the finest silk. I caught a whiff of her exotic perfume, although I could not tease out all the notes—rose perhaps, some spices, civet—

"My lady," I said, wishing the Rhenish wine had lent my tongue more eloquence. "Your hospitality is most gracious. This is a lovely evening, in every way."

"Oh, it is indeed my pleasure," she replied, gazing into my eyes in a way I found pleasantly disconcerting. I forgot both my lowly status and my limp as she looked at me. "It is so seldom I get the chance to hear news of my home."

"So you speak of Norway? Or Greenland?"

"I was born in Greenland, but left when I was quite young."

Just at that point Henry Sinclair approached. "My lord." Lady Ingvilt nodded graciously.

"The lady was just speaking of her early years in Greenland," I added, hoping to hear more of the story. Lady Ingvilt did not look to have green skin, nor did her goblet contain salt water, but surely she came from a far-off and mysterious place. I yearned to hear more of it.

"Ah," said Henry. "But we first met in Bergen. At court."

"Yes, I was young then," said Ingvilt, smiling into Henry's

hazel eyes. "As were you. And nearly wed to that little princess, Florentia, although she had but six years."

"Poor wee mite. She was a bonny little girl, and that was a bonny time. Was it not, Ingvilt? But the *puir* thing died early, of some flux or fever, long before we actually would have wed," Henry explained to me. "It was but a betrothal, as I've already told you. Still, I made a good enough match later with the Halyburtons. Jennet brought a fine dowry and we deal well enough together."

"And how does your lady wife?" asked Ingvilt, a teasing lilt to her lips. "We are sorry she is not with you." From the appraising look Ingvilt gave Henry, she did not seem to me to be sorry at all.

"Lady Jennet has just given birth to our son, so she recovers at Rosslyn," said Henry, a bit stiffly. Both the lady and I gave him our congratulations.

"So you were at King Haakon's court in Bergen?" I continued, turning to Lady Ingvilt, wanting to hear more of faraway Greenland. Or even of Norway, for that matter. Truth be told, I'd have enjoyed listening to the lady discuss almost anything. Her voice was deep and resonant, unusual, and the faint Norse accent gave it an exotic tinge that fell pleasantly upon one's ears.

"Aye. I was. It was Ivar Bardsson, the Norwegian king's agent, who brought me with him from Greenland when he returned to Bergen. I was just a poor orphan, dependent on his kindness, but I found good fortune at Haakon's court. I met my first husband there. But the poor man died—he was elderly even when we wed, and plagued with poor health besides. And then I met my good lord here, when he journeyed to Bergen a few years back, on Scots business for King David. We married, and now I am here."

"A far traveler."

"Indeed. But we Norse enjoy seeing new sights. And meeting new folk," the lady added, again meeting my eyes in that appraising and disconcerting way. Her eyes, I noticed, were green like the northern sea, but with little golden flecks.

I broke from her gaze and scanned the room, seeking my wife. I saw her seated on one of the benches, speaking with Gudni and Duncan. The musicians stopped their playing.

"And now it is time to dine," announced Lady Ingvilt, summoning the servants and making sure our glasses were refilled.

The servants scurried to set up a trestle table and lay a cloth, and then proceeded to bring dishes after we had seated ourselves. Lady Ingvilt and her husband of course sat at the head of the table, and on Sir Johann's left, Henry Sinclair. Mariota sat to Henry's right, then myself, and on my other side sat the young fop, Peter Leslie. Across the board on the right side sat Duncan, Malfrid, and Gudni. Magnus, who had been allowed to join the adults, sat sandwiched in between Gudni and Agnes at the low end of the board.

Plates of silver, not bread trenchers, sat at each place. The feast commenced. Magnus needed frequent prompts from his nurse to speak quietly and not with a mouth full of food, but perhaps his behavior was no worse than that of most children his age. I smiled across the table at him, thinking again of my own half-brother, but the lad, intent on pouring syrup over the sauced quinces on his plate, did not smile back.

"Do you think the food comes from the royal kitchens, or did she get it at a bakeshop in the town?" Mariota whispered to me in Gaelic as we commenced eating.

I cared not where the food originated. I was hungry and the dishes tasted fine. The servants brought turbot in honeyed sauce, eel in a pie, and some fine pheasants and partridge and grouse. That course ended with a flummery of almond milk and exotic dates cooked with currants. The sauced quinces that Magnus had preferred remained on the table, and the servants poured more Rhenish to go with all of it.

Our hostess, I noticed, spent much of the meal conversing with Duncan Tawesson and Mariota spent much of her time talking to Henry Sinclair. I listened idly as the young squire to my other side, oblivious to the glances Agnes gave him, focused his attention and his conversation on Malfrid, seated across from him. Henry and Mariota spoke of some book, a record of a journey to the far north, that a crazed monk had made some twenty years earlier. It was a curious conversation but the tantalizing tastes of the second course stole much of my attention from their talk. I savored the mushroom pastries, the herb fritters in honey sauce, and the tiny game birds, served in a cameline sauce. At length, all of us well fed and well watered, the servants cleared the board.

After the feasting the musicians entertained again with some ballads sung in Inglis—*Graystiel* I remember, for its length if nothing else—and then the fop played the lute for a time and we all sang such songs as we knew. Mariota and I sang a song in Gaelic, our contribution to the *ceilidh*.

Magnus, somewhat excited, wanted to play blind man's bluff. Peter Leslie and Agnes dissuaded him from this desire with some difficulty. The lad began yawning and finally fell asleep on one of the benches while the musicians sang of the exploits of the Bruce. The maids then served us hippocras, along with some candied nuts to nibble on and shortly after that the evening broke up. Lady Ingvilt sent servants with torches to accompany us back to our lodgings, while Duncan and his party made their way back to sleep near their stores in an outbuilding, near the Royal Mews.

❖   ❖   ❖

After the party, as we settled into our chamber near the larger quarters assigned to His Lordship, I watched Mariota comb out her hair, enjoying the play of the candlelight against the pale sheen of her locks.

"It was kind of the lady and her lord to include us in her gathering," I commented.

"Especially as we are not Norse," retorted Mariota tartly, "but she certainly seemed taken with you, all the same."

"And Henry Sinclair, and every other man there," I

answered, ignoring the frisson of excitement I felt at Mariota's remark.

"Aye."

From the tone in my wife's voice I thought it best to speak of other things. "And what were you and Lord Sinclair and Duncan speaking of so seriously?"

"Och, a book, just," Mariota replied. "Duncan was speaking of a journey he made some years ago, to the furthest northern regions. Further north even than Greenland. Some wandering friar wanted to go exploring and Duncan crewed for him. He spoke of the strange wonders they were seeing on the journey. Were you knowing, Muirteach, there are places where, in the summer, the sun does not set at all? It is bright even in the mid-hours of the night. And yet the ice does not melt there, it remains frozen and cold throughout the year."

"That's odd," I ventured. "You would think with all that sunshine the ice would melt."

"Duncan said the friar wrote a book describing the journey. The *Inventio Fortunatae,* he called it. And Baron Sinclair is most desirous of seeing it."

"I wonder why? Does Duncan have a copy? He does not seem the literary type. Can the man even read?"

"Well, I am not knowing if he can read or not, Muirteach, but he has a copy of the book. The friar left it with him. But he has no wish to part with it. There, at last—" Mariota combed the last tangle out of her hair and turned to face me in her linen shift, the long tresses like a pale golden waterfall over her breasts. "I wonder how my hair would look, plaited as our hostess wore hers?"

"Come to bed, *mo chridhe*," I said without answering her question, and I took her into my arms, inhaling the elderflower scent she wore as we kissed. Then I snuffed out the candle.

CHAPTER 4

The next morning a pounding at our door woke me from a sound, deep sleep. It must have been very early; the palest light came though our one window, barely a lightening in the sky. I roused myself, wrapped my mantle around me, and opened the door, surprised to see Gudni and Malfrid on the landing.

"You come," Gudni said in halting Inglis. "And your wife. We need healer."

"What is it? Who has been injured?" cried Mariota, sitting up in the bed in alarm.

Gudni and Malfrid looked at each other a moment, then burst into an excited babble in Norse, both speaking at once. Mariota, not understanding a word but hearing their urgency, threw her dress on over her shift and saw to her laces, while I also hurriedly dressed.

"The birds—you must come," Gudni repeated over and over, and he and Malfrid led the way.

We followed them down the wooden stairs that led to the ground floor of our lodging and outside, back towards the kennels and the mews, to the storehouse where Duncan, Gudni and Malfrid had slept guarding the furs and the gyrfalcons. We entered the shed, which was lit only from the open doorway. In the growing light I saw Duncan standing abjectly in front of the birdcages. One sat empty, the door to it flung open, the bird vanished. In the second cage perched one of the female birds, her wing hanging at an odd angle. The third cage held the tercel, his eyes wide and feral.

"They've found you," Duncan said, turning towards us. "Praise to Saint Christopher. It is you, Mistress Mariota, that I've need of."

"What is it?" asked my wife.

"A foul thing. And I'd happily murder and gut the bastard that has done this. But I'm hoping you can be of help, as you've some skill in healing, I hear."

The pure white female, the most beautiful and largest of the raptors, perched, her eyes dull with misery, silent in her pain. She tried to raise her wings. Shocked, I saw her left wing flop weakly as she fought to move it.

"Och, the poor thing. How was this happening?" demanded my wife as she approached the cage.

"We found her like this when we woke."

"But surely you'd have heard—"

Duncan shook his head in answer. "Nothing. We heard nothing."

"And what of the other bird?" I asked.

"Vanished," Duncan replied.

"But how could that have happened?" It would not be easy to steal birds such as these, I thought, nor to hide them once taken.

"It might have been done while we were at the supper. We had covered the cages when we left. And it had grown full dark when we returned. We were all a bit in our cups and did not want to alarm the birds, so we did not uncover them. I curse myself for a blind fool, for leaving them so, and not looking in on them. But all seemed peaceful. It wasn't until Gudni went to feed them this morning that we discovered what had occurred."

"And the missing falcon? Surely it will be hard to hide such a magnificent bird," I said.

"I hope so. I pray we find her unharmed. But the damage is done, here, all the same." He looked at the wounded gyrfalcon. "This one's good for nothing now. A falcon that cannot fly."

"And worth a great deal of money," I observed.

"Aye, there's that. But more than that. We climbed the cliffs, Gudni and I, to get these birds. Trained them. Raised them to eat from our hands. Just look at the lad—"

I did look. Gudni's slumped posture displayed his misery as he tried to stroke the raptor's back. The bird, equally miserable, snapped at his touch.

"We'd best alert the castle guard," I said, "and let them know of the theft."

"Perhaps this one's wing can be healed," said my wife, gazing intently at the injured bird. "May I touch her?"

"Best to wait a bit," said Duncan as Gudni gestured towards Mariota. "Let him hood her first." Gudni hooded the gyrfalcon and took her from the cage. She flapped her good wing angrily while the left flopped, impotent. I could see some red, and a thin white bone protruding from the white feathers. At length the falcon settled while Gudni held her, crooning to the bird.

"Now, mistress," said Duncan. "See what you can make of it."

Gudni continued to hold the bird while Mariota gently felt the injured wing. "I'm none so versed with birds," she admitted, "but at least this one bone is broken, most likely more."

The bird squawked in protest, a little rough, harsh sound, and attempted to move her wing as Mariota examined it again. Gudni soothed her, still making those odd noises and gently petting her with his fingers while Mariota softly touched the injury.

"Yes," Mariota continued, "it feels as though at least two bones are broken. The wing could be set and splinted, but whether the bird will fly again I am not sure."

"She'll not be worth the money," said Duncan. "Although I'm somewhat loath to say it, it might be best to get rid of her now."

Malfrid interrupted, speaking urgently with Duncan in a torrent of Norse, while Gudni flushed and responded to both his sister and foster-father, his speech choppy and harsh. He gestured angrily, which upset the bird he held even more. It seemed to me that Malfrid attempted to intervene, her tone placating. After a few moments Duncan seemed to relent and nodded. Gudni let out a deep breath and the taut muscles in his face relaxed.

"Ah well, we can try it. But there's little room on a trading vessel for an injured bird." At that Gudni, who perhaps understood more Inglis than he let on, muttered something under his breath in Norse.

"No now, son," said Duncan, "I've said you may try and so you may. We'll be here some days now and if the bird makes progress perhaps she can be saved."

Gudni said in halting Inglis, "The lady, she will help." He pointed with his chin to Mariota.

"Indeed I will," agreed Mariota, without, I thought, being fully cognizant of what would be involved.

"He is saying you will help him with the falcon, *mo chridhe*."

"Aye, I thought it was something of the sort," my wife replied. "And I'd be happy indeed to try. Although I've more skill with humans, I used to nurse injured birds as a child. It is a beautiful bird and would be a shame indeed to have to kill it." I smiled a bit at the thought of my wife as a wee girl, tending to injured sparrows and crows. She continued speaking, ignoring my look. "First we must find a splint for it." She turned to Duncan. "How well does your son speak Inglis?"

"Well enough I think, my lady," offered Duncan. "And he learns quickly, and has a good ear. What do you need for the splint?"

"Some thin boards, not too wide. And bandages to tie them tight. Here, I'll go with the lad to search for them. We'll deal well enough together, I'm thinking." She and Gudni left on their errand and the space seemed suddenly emptier.

Duncan stood disconsolately by the cages after the pair departed. The hooded gyrfalcon, her wing hanging awkwardly, mirrored the trader's pain.

"Come," I said, my voice tight. "There's no more we can do now. We'll alert the guard to the theft, and raise the hue and cry. If we search for the second bird perhaps we'll find her. She'd be damned hard to hide." Duncan nodded dumbly. "Malfrid," I continued, summoning the girl closer, "you'll stay here, will you not, and watch the birds until my wife and your brother return?"

The girl nodded tautly and I saw her wipe at her eyes. The cruel and vicious attack might have been intended to hurt the pockets of Duncan Tawesson, but it seemed to me that the blow had sorely wounded the hearts of the captain and his little family as well. And that made me burn with anger.

❖   ❖   ❖

Duncan and I left the shed and as we walked down

the mount I saw, with some relief, Henry Sinclair walking towards the Great Hall with some other men of the court. Henry no doubt knew the captain of the guard, although I did not. I hailed him and he waited for us while the other men continued into the hall. "How goes it today?" inquired Henry as we approached him.

"Not well," I replied darkly. Henry's eyebrows rose with curiosity. Duncan told him about the maimed and stolen birds and I watched Henry's face flush red with fury.

"That's a sin!" he exclaimed. "Such incredible birds."

"Aye. I took them as fledglings from a cliff in the northern lands. Raised them by hand, did Gudni and I. They could just as well be my own children, as much as Malfrid and Gudni—" Duncan laughed a short and bitter laugh. "Not to mention the money they'd have brought. No one will buy the one now. Even if her wing heals, I doubt she'll fly. And the other—"

"It's a foully done crime," Henry repeated. "Come, let us tell the castle guard of it. I'll take you to them."

He walked rapidly towards the guard tower, built into the castle walls close to the main entrance gate. Duncan followed close behind. I struggled just a bit to keep pace with him, and not for the first time I cursed the childhood illness that had left me with this limp.

"Robert! Robert Cruickshanks!" Henry called as he pushed open the heavy wooden door and we entered the guardroom.

I peered around, my eyes adjusting to the dimness. The place reminded me somewhat of the sheriff's rooms I once had occasion to visit in Oxford Castle. A table, scarred with knife cuts, sat in the center of the room with a chair behind it and some benches to the side. Some smoky torches cast a little light and round targes and other shields hung on the walls. A brazier smoldered in one corner, giving off a little heat. I smelled the heavy fragrance of smoke, mingled with the metallic scent of oiled mail and leather, and stale ale, although the room looked well enough kept with nothing out of order.

A tall man entered the room from a door to the back. Mainly sinew and muscle, he carried little fat on his lank frame, yet although he was so lean he looked fit enough, wiry and strong. The man showed no signs of any limp, I thought with a moment's envy, despite his name. He wore a quilted linen gambeson; his greying hair cut short, with a trimmed short beard.

"Henry Sinclair," the captain of the king's guard greeted us, when he saw who had called him. "What brings you here, sir?"

Henry and Duncan told him of the stolen falcon, and the attack on the other bird. "I'll send some men to look around the castle. But what will they be looking for, a grand birdcage?" Cruickshanks asked, with a sad attempt at humor. I watched Duncan's face tighten. A muscle in his cheek twitched and I thought he had not appreciated the poor joke.

"A bird like that could fetch a great deal of silver," Henry cautioned Cruickshanks. "And the king himself wished to buy the falcon."

Cruickshanks grunted. "Aye, I saw her fly. A bonny bird, indeed." He turned towards Duncan. "You dinna think she just flew away? Perhaps the cage was left open?"

"Hooded as she was? And left a tercel behind, and another gyrfalcon with a maimed and broken wing?" Duncan snorted and shook his head. "My falcon has been stolen," he insisted, glaring at the captain of the guard, "and the other grievously wounded. Sir," he finally added, with little grace, as he saw the stone in Cruickshank's expression.

"Aweel, if the king wanted the bird, we'd best be about it, then." Cruickshanks called out, and four of the guard emerged from the back room. He gave orders and the men left the guardhouse to begin the search.

"And what of His Majesty?" Sinclair demanded of Cruickshanks, after the guard had left. "Won't he be needing to know of this?"

"Och, let us see what the search turns up, first" retorted Cruickshanks. "We dinna need to be stirring trouble before it comes to boil. I've set my men to searching the outbuildings, the stables, the kennels, and the old lodgings. You two," he said, gesturing to Duncan and myself, "can help me search the Tower."

❖   ❖   ❖

We searched, and although I admit I found the glimpses of life in the Great Tower intriguing, full as it was with fine tapestries and rich furnishings, we found nothing of the missing gyrfalcon. Neither a jess nor a single feather. Henry Sinclair accompanied us. I wondered cynically if his friendly concern rose from avarice and if he, as well as the king and my own master, coveted a gyrfalcon, although his care seemed genuine enough. However, after some hours of fruitless searching, we returned to the guardhouse, discouraged and frustrated. We found the other men already there, with nothing to report. Duncan sat nervously, drumming his fingers on the table while he listened to the guards' reports.

"Well, there's little more we can do here. Let us know if anything else is found," Henry told Cruickshanks.

"Aye, I will. Indeed, His Majesty won't be pleased with this when he hears of it. Especially if it was a bird he was wanting for his own mews. If it's not the damned English and their spies, now it's disappearing falcons," I heard Cruickshanks mutter as he turned and gave orders to his men to resume the search. We shut the door of the guardhouse behind us and walked across the castle yard through lowering clouds interspersed with faint sunshine.

"None of us have eaten," Henry observed. "Come to my rooms, I've some ale at least that we can share."

Duncan did not seem eager to stop searching, but we did not know where else to look. And I was ravenous. So we made our way across the yard to Henry's lodgings, in a building near to the New Tower and Great Hall. Once we arrived he gave some orders to his manservant and we were soon settled at his table with drinks in our hands. Sinclair's man procured a loaf from someplace, and we shared that as well.

"I should go looking for my bird," Duncan said, restless.

"Aye, but you've not eaten yet this morn. Drink a bit first, then you can search again. And eat some bread, here. Cruickshanks will have it in hand. You can leave it with him for a time."

Duncan finally nodded assent, but did not relax, nor did he eat. Instead he perched on the edge of his seat on a carved and painted bench and held tightly onto his leather mug.

Henry took a swig of his own small ale. "Where did you get the birds?" he asked after a moment. "Greenland?"

"No, from Helluland—rocky lands to the west of Greenland," Duncan answered. "No one lives there, just Skraelings. But it is a short sail, a few days only from the Western settlement if you have a good ship."

"And your voyage with that friar some years ago, was that to this Helluland?"

Duncan took a drink of ale. "On that trip we sailed further north. I was younger then, although I had already been at sea for some years. Close to the time Malfrid was born, some fifteen years ago, it was."

"Tell me more of these lands," Henry asked, curious. Or perhaps he hoped to distract Duncan from his difficulties. I did not know, but I also listened intently to the captain's answers. I found his stories of these mysterious lands fascinating.

"In the summer the sun does not set. You can see clear to

mend a sail at midnight. But the ice and snow never melt away there. The dancers—the lights—play in the sky most every night. And there are white bears that live on the ice. They are good swimmers, and fierce beasts, indeed. They catch seals, mostly. You saw the pelt I had, did you not?"

Henry and I both nodded. I had heard of those white bears, but had never seen their pelts before.

"Are there other lands to the west?" Henry asked.

"Yes, great lands. There is Markland, rich in timber and furs, and somewhat further south a land called Vinland. And beyond that it is said there is a mysterious settlement called Hvítramannaland, white man's land, although that place I have not yet visited. But I hear Skraelings dwell there as well, as they do in Vinland."

"Skraelings?"

"Aye, folk that dress only in skins. Heathens. Poor wretches. But their arrows are sharp enough for all that."

"But I thought you said Gudni was a Skraeling," I put in. "And he is from Greenland."

"Aye, but the Skraelings in Vinland are different."

"And you have a book that tells of these wonders?" asked Henry. "I would love to see such a text."

"The friar wrote it. A very learned man, always writing he was, even when his ink would turn to ice. He would hold the ink bottle under his robes, warming it with his own body, until the ink thawed, then write of the marvels we saw. He made a fair copy of his stories once we returned to Bergen. Although on that journey I made with him we went only to the furthest northern lands. We did not go to Markland, nor to Vinland, on that voyage."

"Who was the friar?" asked Henry, intent.

"Nicholas of Lynn, he called himself. From England."

"He travelled a long way from home," Henry observed, and Duncan nodded assent.

"And how did you come to own the volume?" I asked. "Books are valuable." I had learned that lesson in Oxford, to my sorrow, the year before.

"He gave it to me, in exchange for the use of my ship. It was the *Selkiesdottir's* first voyage. And I kept it, thinking my daughter might enjoy the tale someday. She knows how to read," Duncan added, somewhat defensively when he observed our looks. "I saw to that."

"You yourself can read?"

"Aye. I was well enough brought up in Kintyre. But I was a younger son, with wanderlust in my feet, and took to the seas once I had the years to."

"You've no wish to sell that book?" asked Henry, a trifle wistfully.

"I've no wish to. But with the loss of the falcons, I may have to. And I should be searching for my bird now. We've wasted enough time." Duncan rose from his seat.

A knocking at the door interrupted us. Henry's manservant

opened it to find one of the king's guard, and ushered the man into the room.

"You'd best come with me," the guard ordered Duncan. "They've found your falcon."

CHAPTER 5

We followed the guard out of Henry's lodgings and over to the small graveyard, near the little chapel dedicated to Saint Margaret. A young guardsman with a downy beard stood by the chapel. And there, thrown on a mound of dirt in the far-most corner of the small chapel graveyard, by the stone wall around it, we found the falcon.

Her pretty white neck had been twisted and someone had slashed off one of the great white wings. I saw no sign of the wing anywhere around, just the bloody stains on the white body of the bird, and a little blood beneath it. The corpse had been tossed on a newly mounded grave not far from the chapel, the dirt still fairly fresh. I shuddered. My guts chilled in the face of this wanton cruelty. Who would kill such a magnificent bird—and one easily worth an emperor's ransom? And who would defile a graveyard with the corpse?

I saw Duncan's tanned face pale as he looked at the maimed body. He swallowed as if trying to keep from retching and I fought down a tide of sour bile myself. Henry looked solemn, his hazel eyes keen yet sad. I shuddered again. The pale late morning sun did little to warm me in the face of such evil.

Just then Cruickshanks arrived from the direction of the guardhouse. He took in the scene and questioned the guard. "And so the bird is found," he said at length. "I am sorry for it."

"I'd want to keep this from the *bairns*," Duncan said, his words coming slowly, as if from very far away. "They should not see this."

Cruickshanks agreed and the guard hastily buried the bird outside the chapel yard. But why take one wing, I wondered, as I watched the dark dirt cover up the pure whiteness of the feathers. What devil's work was that?

❖   ❖   ❖

Duncan returned to the storehouse to break the news to Gudni and Malfrid. He also spoke of trying to arrange things with the steward so they might stay a bit longer. He had no wish to travel, even into Leith, with the one bird injured, and he wanted justice for the slain one. I had business to attend to with my lord and the king and left Duncan to see to this.

Neither His Majesty nor my Lord of the Isles took the news of the stolen gyrfalcon equably. King Robert sent for

Cruickshanks, who made his own report. My lord and his royal father-in-law conferred, while Cruickshanks and I both stood by awkwardly in the solar, watching the pale afternoon sun make its feeble way through the mullioned windows. In the end, the king charged me with helping Cruickshanks in his investigations, and also gave orders that Duncan and his falcons stay at the castle until the culprit could be apprehended. Although, in the way of powerful men, the king and my lord also then commanded me to remain with them that afternoon and make a record of their own negotiations. The conference between them took most of that day and I had no chance to speak further with Duncan.

Mariota, forsaking the queen's bower, had spent most of the day with Duncan's children and the remaining gyrfalcons. When she returned to our chamber late that afternoon, she told me that Gudni and Malfrid had taken the news hard. Malfrid had sobbed the whole afternoon. Gudni, she related, had been more stoic. "Yet his eyes also were red, Muirteach. He said little, but he feels it deeply. I know." My vows to find the slayer of the falcon failed miserably to lighten my wife's heavy mood, and I saw nothing more of Duncan and his family until the next morning.

❖   ❖   ❖

At court folk broke their fast simply in the early morning, on bread and ale set out at a trestle table in the Great Hall. Many chose not to eat at all, and saved their appetite for the main meal at noon. And although some people think it a sign of weakness to break your fast early, I have always been hungry in the morning. People who did choose to eat took what they wished and sat where they pleased as well.

When I went to break my fast the next day, I passed the young cockscomb who had flirted with Malfrid the night before, sitting at one of the benches with the other squires. His eyes brightened but he quickly lost interest upon realizing Malfrid was not with me.

I saw Duncan and Henry Sinclair sitting next to each other. I made my way to their bench in time to overhear Duncan say, "Let's speak of it in a week or so, once we see how the *puir* bird does."

"Speak of what?" I asked, curious.

"I am wanting to buy his book," admitted Henry. "The *Inventio Fortunatae.*"

"And I've no wish to sell it, as I've said before. But I might be forced to."

"How does the injured bird this morning?" I asked. Mariota had gone to see to it on first arising, but she had not returned before I'd left to break my fast.

"Your wife splinted the wing, and when I left she and Gudni were changing the dressings. But the bird has not eaten yet, despite the meat we offer it."

"And what of your plans?" I asked. "The king has ordered you to remain here."

Duncan nodded. "For now we must bide here, and cannot

leave as quickly as I wished. Not until you find that murdering thief. I think folk have heard of our losses, perhaps they pity us. Or perhaps they just hope to buy more furs." Duncan grimaced, as though he had a bad taste in his mouth, took a drink of his ale and then continued. "Perhaps they think I'll sell them cheaply now. It is a shame to miss the last good sailing weather of the year. But if we must winter here in Scotland, perhaps I'll take the *bairns* over to Kintyre—that's no so far— and see my brother and whosoever is left of my family."

"Gudni also?" Henry asked."

"He'll go with me. He is my son, now, in all but blood. Since Malfrid's mother died, some eight years ago, both the *bairns* have traveled with me."

At this point I looked up to see Malfrid walk into the hall. Duncan's daughter saw us, waved, and started towards us, but the young swain I had seen speaking with her that other day, Sir Johann's squire, approached her as she gathered her bread. She seemed hesitant and glanced at Duncan, whom I noted glowering at her. The single glance must have been enough, for she shook her head, motioned towards us and then walked our way, her admirer following somewhat reluctantly behind. Duncan gestured to an empty seat on the bench next to him and Malfrid sat down obediently.

"Father, this is Peter Leslie," Malfrid said, her voice soft. "He is Sir Johann's squire. You met him two nights ago, at the party his lord and lady hosted."

"Aye, so I did. And how are you this morning," inquired

Duncan, glaring at the youth, who had the courtesy to flush a bit. The squire's attire today looked only slightly less foolish than his party clothes had been; he sported a doublet short enough in the back to nearly show his buttocks, although his sleeves, long and scalloped, nearly touched the floor in front. Malfrid wore a plain green kirtle over her linen shift, modest enough, her long hair hanging down in two simple plaits. Although her sea green eyes were a bit puffy, perhaps from her tears of yesterday, she looked lovely.

"I'm well enough, sir," Peter replied with fortitude, obviously set on charming this crusty old man.

"Fancy dress for a squire," commented Duncan.

"I will change before I see to Sir Johann's horse."

"Those sleeves would get in the way, no doubt," huffed Duncan. Henry and I watched in amusement as Duncan continued to grill the lad. Finally Malfrid said something in Norse to her father. I did not know the words but they had a pleading tone and Duncan evidently relented. He stopped questioning Peter, at any rate.

Malfrid said something else to her father and he replied, also speaking Norse. They seemed to have a bit of an argument. Finally Duncan appeared somewhat appeased, for Malfrid smiled a bit.

Duncan eyed the squire. "My daughter tells me you wished to show her the palace pleasure gardens."

"Indeed, sir, there is nothing that would please me more."

"And how many other maids have walked with you there?"

Peter took this well in stride but did not answer the question directly. "It is a pleasant place, and one favored by many in the court." He smiled reassuringly at Malfrid, who shyly smiled back.

"She could not go un-chaperoned. And we have need of her help this morning. Perhaps later in the day I could allow it." Duncan turned to me abruptly. "Would you and your wife like to walk in the gardens this afternoon?" he asked.

"I am sure my wife would love to see the gardens," I said. "Although I believe she has already seen the herber."

Malfrid's face fell.

"Oh no, sire," Peter put in. "These are the pleasure gardens, not the herber. And they are indeed lovely, with a flowery mead, and many plants that will be of great interest to your wife, I am sure."

At length I agreed, more to assuage the concern in Malfrid's face than out of any great desire to see the gardens myself. Almost nothing thrilled Mariota more than a garden, although I fail to share this fascination.

"Good, that's settled, then," returned Duncan. "You and your wife can accompany Malfrid and this young squire this very afternoon."

Malfrid had been listening intently, and her young face brightened like the morning sun gently touching a rose bud. The happiness in her face went a far way towards overcoming the irritation I felt with her father. And Duncan did look relieved. I imagine, were I to have a daughter of that age, I would share that anxiety. Peter flushed again, professed contentment with this plan, and so we made arrangements to meet later in the day. The lad made an elaborate bow and prepared to leave, saying something about impending duties. Henry Sinclair and I tried hard not to laugh as we watched him walk away.

"I'd best go and see to those birds," said Duncan. "And you will come with me, lass. Your brother has been there by himself long enough."

Malfrid followed her father obediently, although I saw her flash a parting smile at Peter Leslie.

Henry rolled his eyes a little after Duncan and Malfrid departed. "I have three *dochters* of my own—I shudder to think of what's in store for me someday." He picked up another piece of bread, took a bite and chewed thoughtfully.

"Och, she's a good lass," I replied in Malfrid's defense. "This is surely different from shipboard life. You can't expect that her head would not be turned by a pretty face and fine raiment."

"And hopefully her heart won't be broken as well," came a familiar voice. I looked up and saw my wife smiling at me. "The lad seems to have an eye for pretty girls."

"And so the birds are seen to?" I asked.

"Aye, as comfortable as we can make them. Gudni's aye there, crooning to them still. The boy has a fine way with them. And I promised Lady Isobel and Her Majesty that I would wait upon her this morning for a time. I must join them very shortly."

"Are you not hungry, *mo chridhe*?" Mariota had taken just a small piece of bread. I watched her nibble at it, leaving most of it at her place.

"No, I've no appetite this morning."

I let that be. His Lordship waited upon me to review some agreements made with his royal father-in-law pertaining to a land grant in Knapdale, and I needed to speak with Cruickshanks as well, before seeing those powerful men. Perhaps something new had been discovered that might improve the tempers of those mighty lords. I kissed my wife on the cheek, took my leave, and left her sitting in the hall with Henry Sinclair.

CHAPTER 6

Later that day, after the noon meal and His Lordship's business had concluded, Duncan Tawesson accosted me as Mariota and I left the hall. "Are you ready, man?"

"For what?"

He scowled. "To walk in the pleasure garden with Malfrid and that fancy lad of hers. She's been mooning about all day, and badgering me continually, asking when she may go—"

Indeed, I had forgotten all of it, my mind having been absorbed by the killing of the falcon and wondering who might be at fault, and in my Lord of the Isles' negotiations with the king; the numbers of galleys, oarsmen and gallowglass His Lordship owed to the crown, in return for grants of land in Knapdale. I quickly explained the situation to my wife. She smiled.

"It could be fun, Muirteach, to walk in the gardens. The last two days have not been cheerful. I mislike caring for maimed birds; such cruelty makes me melancholic. And if a walk in the pleasure gardens with a handsome lad diverts Malfrid I am happy to go along, for she also has been sad. If they are as fine as the queen's herber, they will be grand indeed."

"Aye," I agreed, unaccountably irritated with our roles as chaperones.

But the gardens glowed in the September light, and the afternoon indeed looked a lovely one. The sun shone on fruit trees, where apples, pears and quince hung heavy on the boughs. The leaves had just begun to turn from green to yellow and scarlet, and fall flowers bloomed in the beds. Lush green grass interspersed with blooming Michaelmas and ox-eye daisies, heart's ease, and even a few late mallows filled the space—the flowery mead. Beds of lavender, thyme and other aromatic herbs bordered neat garden pathways, strewn with a few early colored leaves just fallen from the trees, and the herbs' sharp scent mingled with that of the ripened fruit and the sweet perfumes of the flowers.

Although Mariota and I stayed fairly well back, Peter behaved with courtly courtesy. We only had to clear our throats loudly the one time; the pair had wandered ahead of us behind a yew hedge and both Mariota and I coughed, loudly, before we rounded the corner to see Peter and Malfrid, with a tinge of rose staining her cheeks, standing just a few careful feet from each other.

At length we could wander no more. The shadows lengthened and we left that lovely place. Peter bade Malfrid a courtly farewell that caused the lass to smile and flush prettily again, then he bade us a polite goodbye as well. We walked with Malfrid a bit further and then said goodbye to her as she took the path towards the shed where she and her family stayed. Then we entered our own lodging and went upstairs to our chamber to relax for a time before the evening meal was served in the Great Hall.

❖   ❖   ❖

At supper I noticed Duncan sitting down the benches from us, alone. I could not see Malfrid, and at first assumed the lass remained with Gudni in their lodgings, watching over the injured bird. Before we came to supper Mariota had checked on the falcon, and I had accompanied her. The raptor's splinted wing hung awkwardly, but she had torn into the flesh Gudni fed her.

"She does well enough, it seems," Mariota had said with a smile to Gudni, and he smiled back, a little shyly. I sensed my wife had completely won the lad over. We did not see Malfrid then, but I had thought little of it, thinking her busy on some errand with her father before supper, leaving Gudni behind to watch over the falcons. However, I wondered at it now, when I did not see her with her father at supper.

"Where is Malfrid?" I asked Duncan as we caught up to him when the meal ended and the diners dispersed.

"I was just about to ask you the same. Is the lass not with you?"

"No, we left her headed towards your lodgings."

Duncan's face turned ashen beneath his seaman's tan. "When was that?"

"Some time ago. Well before the supper."

He turned, his eyes scanning the crowded hall. "She's not here. I thought her to be with you."

I tried to push away the guilt that rose up. Malfrid had not had far to go, and had assured us she was returning straight to her lodgings near the mews. If the lass had been disobedient, and run off to meet with her squire again, surely we could not be blamed for that.

Across the hall we saw Peter Leslie joking with a few other young men. Pushing his way through the crowd, Duncan broke in on them abruptly. "Where's my daughter?"

"Sir, I know not," Peter replied, turning to face Duncan while the other squires continued their chatter. "Is there anything amiss?"

"Well, she is not here. And was last seen with you."

"No, I left her with her chaperones." Peter gestured towards Mariota and myself.

"And you've not seen her since?" demanded Duncan.

"Indeed not, sir. They will vouch for me." He glanced at Mariota and myself. "And I've been at my duties here, in the hall, since I left you after our walk."

"We'd best go and look for her, then," said Mariota, her

voice practical and calm. My own heart thudded rapidly, despite my wife's sensible words. "Doubtless she just wanted some time alone to daydream, and is now back, tending to the falcons," Mariota continued.

"I'll come help search," Peter offered, and our party left the hall and started in the direction of the mews, which were located out beyond the Old Queen's Lodging, towards the kennels. Nearby the mews stood the shed where Duncan had stored his goods and his family had slept, close to the birds' cages. When we arrived the shed was empty, except for the caged birds and Gudni.

"She's not here," Duncan announced flatly. Gudni said nothing when he heard of Malfrid's disappearance but his brow furrowed. Mariota also looked more concerned.

"Where could the lass have gone to?" she whispered to me in Gaelic. I had no idea, and began to feel sick deep in the pit of my gut. My wife continued, in a louder voice, in Inglis. "Perhaps she thought to walk around the castle walls. Or went back to the gardens."

"Well, wherever she has gone to, she had best be found quickly," her father said, his face stern. "For I will be beating her within an inch of her life for this disobedience."

Gudni said nothing, but from the tense set of his face I could tell he also was worried. Peter, familiar with the castle, led the search. We all looked, splitting up as the twilight deepened to search the mews, the outlying buildings, and the grounds. But it was Gudni who found Malfrid at last.

CHAPTER 7

A howl sounded through the dusk. The noise, inhuman and eerie, chilled me to my heart's marrow. I stopped, frozen, as Duncan and I neared the Old Queen's Lodgings after searching the mews for Malfrid without success.

"What was that?" Duncan asked, and I shook my head. A moment later Peter Leslie rushed towards us in the dusk, breathless.

"Muirteach, Duncan, they've found her—"

"Thank God," Duncan breathed, but I did not feel so sanguine. I followed Peter and Duncan the short distance to a narrow *wynd* between the Old Queen's Lodgings and another building beside it. The slight space between the two structures formed a little alley. There, somewhat down the alley, and partially hidden by shadows, we saw Malfrid, slumped against the wall, her face grey and pale and still, her eyes closed. Gudni and Mariota knelt by her side.

We walked the short distance to join them, although it felt like leagues to me.

"What is it? What has happened?" Duncan demanded. Mariota shook her head grimly. Duncan stopped short a few feet from them, staring at the unseeing face of his daughter in the dim light.

"Is she hurt?" I asked my wife. Again Mariota shook her head, her own face ashen.

"What has happened to her?" Duncan asked again, somewhat more quietly. I think he knew already what he would hear. I bit my own lip to stop it from shaking.

"I fear," Mariota paused and swallowed. It seemed my wife had been struck dumb. "I fear," she repeated, but once more could not finish. Finally she framed the words. "Duncan, I fear your daughter is dead."

"But she is not ill." Duncan stepped closer and reached toward his daughter.

Again Mariota shook her head. "No, Duncan, the lass was not ill." I watched her swallow. "Malfrid has been slain."

Gudni, pale under his dark complexion, sat against the wall in the shadows, cradling his sister in his arms and stroking her hair gently.

Duncan stepped closer, a dumb, uncomprehending look on his face. He reached out towards her but then stopped, as if afraid to touch the lass. "My daughter? Murdered?"

Mariota nodded. I could see tears spilling down her cheeks.

"How?"

"A wound. Here." She pointed to a spot on the girl's left side, along the ribs. Duncan came closer and squatted down in the muck of the alley. He took his daughter from Gudni, and held her in his arms. As he moved the body we could all see the place on the lass's side, the bloodstain dark against the paler green of her gown, where the knife must have entered her flesh.

No one spoke for a moment.

"It was you," Duncan suddenly burst out savagely, looking at Peter Leslie. "You tried to force her and she resisted. I see the way of it, now—"

"Upon my honor, it was not," protested Peter, his face white and his voice shaking. "I left her at the gardens with Muirteach and his wife. I had my duties to see to, before the supper. I did not see her again. I wish I had, indeed, I wish I had been there, to have protected her from whatever monster did this to her."

"We must alert the guard," I interjected, "and raise the hue and cry." I could not stand to see the lass lying there dead. So, coward that I was, heartsick at the scene before me, I fled to call the watch.

❖   ❖   ❖

I returned, bringing Robert Cruickshanks and a number

of the castle guard at the run few moments later. A few folk crowded together, gathered outside the entrance to the wynd, speaking together in hushed tones, but they made way for the watch. I noticed Lady Ingvilt and her husband, who must have been returning to their lodgings after supper, as well as some of the other courtiers who lodged there, milling about the broader area in the main street that faced the Old Queen's Lodging. Some craned their necks to see what took place in the darker alleyway. Lady Ingvilt saw me and murmured something I did not catch to her husband, and then she made her way through the crowd towards me.

"What has happened?" she asked in a concerned voice. I caught a whiff of her exotic scent as she gently touched my arm.

"It's a bad business," I replied, unable to tell her immediately, as if not saying it would make it not true.

The guards already had entered the alcove. Cruickshanks spoke with Duncan, who still slumped against the stone wall of the building, cradling his daughter's body. Gudni stood nearby, as did Mariota. I watched a moment as my wife began to speak to Cruickshanks, telling him what had transpired. Finally I answered the lady.

"It's the young lass, Malfrid. The tumbler. She's been slain."

"But that is terrible!" Ingvilt's eyes widened in shock.

I nodded.

"Who saw her last?"

My guilt rushed to the forefront. "My wife and I, I think.

We had walked with her and your squire a bit in the gardens. Peter left to see to his duties and we accompanied her as far as our own lodgings. Then we left her; it is but a short walk to the shed where she lodged with her brother and her father. But Gudni and Duncan said she never returned, and she did not come to supper. That is when we began to search for her—and found this horror, as you see."

"Was any one about? Did anyone see her? Or her slayer?" Ingvilt's voice sounded sharp with fear and concern.

I shook my head. "I think not. But we will ask." As I spoke these words I realized I had already sworn to myself that I would bring the poor girl's killer to justice. I continued speaking to Ingvilt, thinking out loud. "Most folk would have been in the Great Hall, at supper. There were few folk out."

"Oh, what a sad thing," Ingvilt said, and I saw tears in her lovely eyes. Sir Johann also looked grave, but he said little.

"What of the hue and cry?" asked Ingvilt after a moment.

"The guards are here. Robert Cruickshanks will know what to do," interjected her husband.

"But we could all be in danger," Ingvilt cried. "If the killer is mad—"

"Don't worry, sweeting," her husband reassured her. "You're in no danger. You'll be safe enough with me. The lass should not have been out alone." His words did nothing to decrease my guilt.

A stir from behind me made me turn and the crowd parted. I saw the king, accompanied by several of his nobles, including my own Lord of the Isles. Lady Ingvilt and her husband stepped back respectfully, as did I, and we all made obeisance.

"Sire," I said as the party approached and started to pass us, the king speaking to his guards.

"Muirteach, what's all this?" the Lord of the Isles asked in Gaelic when he came close by to me.

"It's the lass from the tumblers. Malfrid. She's been slain," I replied in the same language.

"Who do you think killed the lass?" my lord said.

"Sire, I've no way of knowing. Not yet."

"Well, find out, Muirteach." Indeed, I had every intention of unmasking this killer. His Lordship's orders acted as a goad to an already quickly running horse.

It had grown full dark now and servants lit more torches. King Robert observed the situation, spoke briefly to Cruickshanks, and then the royal party departed. But Duncan remained sitting in the muck of the alleyway, cradling his daughter's body to his chest while the alley grew darker and the torches guttered in the breeze.

At length Mariota convinced Duncan to let go of the corpse. Some of the guards removed the body, decently covered now, away on a stretcher to Saint Margaret's chapel to lie overnight while arrangements could be made for a burial and a mass. Duncan and Gudni followed behind, as did Mariota and myself, in a sad procession.

The guards laid the corpse on a bier before the altar. For

all that they were burly men, they handled the body with great gentleness. The priest, looking shocked and sad, brought a pall and he and Mariota softly laid it over the remains. Then Mariota and I convinced Duncan and Gudni to leave the chapel.

I walked with them to our small chamber. Upon arriving Duncan wailed loudly while Gudni sat stolidly on the wooden flooring, staring into the dark night. Mariota rummaged in her medical bag for valerian and other herbs to make some kind of soothing draught, as both men seemed deranged with grief. While Mariota went to get some hot water from the kitchens, I had an opportunity to speak with Duncan, who finally quieted enough to speak to.

"First your birds, then your daughter," I said abruptly as Duncan paced our small room, crossing it in a few steps, then re-crossing the tiny space. He seemed unable to sit still. "Who could have done this? Have you any idea? Is there someone here with a grudge against you?"

Duncan sat down abruptly on the bed, then glared up at me like an angry bear. "It's little enough I know of Edinburgh and Leith, and nothing at all I know of the court. Why would anyone here wish me harm? And if they did, why not kill me? Not my poor Malfrid." He collapsed into sobs again, like a bladder ball when the air escapes from it.

Gudni said little. I asked him who might have had reason to hurt his sister, but he just shook his head, his dark eyes red-rimmed in his strange face.

At that point Mariota returned with her remedy and we accompanied the two men back to their sleeping quarters, near the remaining gyrfalcons in the shed. Gudni immediately removed the injured bird from her cage while the tercel watched our doings with unblinking eyes. Crooning and singing to the both of them, Gudni sat huddled against the wall of the barn, stroking the bird, hand feeding her bits of flesh. He did not look at any of us, just kept his eyes fixed on the bird as his hands gently stroked her back. Mariota watched, her own eyes sad and troubled.

"Are you wanting me to stay with you?" I asked Duncan.

"Nah, there is no need. They've ripped my heart out the now. There's nothing more they could do to me."

We left the two of them then, alone, after they drank Mariota's remedy. Duncan drank a good bit of *uisge beatha* besides. The queer sound of Gudni's crooning lingered in my ears after we returned to our chamber and I slept but little that night. Neither did my wife.

❖   ❖   ❖

The next morning I met with His Lordship and the king after breakfast. The stated purpose of the meeting was to iron out the final details of their agreement regarding the grant of the Knapdale lands, and the fighting men and the number of *birlinns* the Lord of the Isles was expected to supply to the king if called upon. That quickly disposed of, I started to rise, intending to quit the private meeting chamber and make a fair copy of the agreement, when my Lord of the Isles stopped me.

"Muirteach, stay a bit. We've something else to speak of with you."

"My lord?"

"A terrible thing, the murder of that girl."

I nodded.

"And coming as it does on the tail of the death of the gyrfalcon. Another sad thing."

For a moment I wondered which event my lord found worse, but I attempted to dismiss that thought as unworthy. The Lord of the Isles continued, "I was telling His Majesty, my own royal father, more of your previous experience solving these sorts of things."

"Yes, my lord." I guessed what was coming, and felt an eagerness, like a great dog on the scent of some quarry.

"His Majesty was wanting you to help the guard in solving this sad mystery. Seeing as you've experience."

"Indeed, it would be my greatest pleasure." In that I indeed spoke truly. My blood ran hot at the thought of the poor girl's murder and I ached to bring to account the butcher that had knifed her. And the guilt I felt at having left the poor lass alone before her death only hardened my resolve.

"Here." His Majesty called to one of his men, who stood ready by the carved wooden door. I recognized the man as he stepped forward. "This is Robert Cruickshanks, captain of my guard," His Majesty informed me.

"We have already met, sire," I reminded him. "Over the

matter of the slain bird."

"He'll assist you. I'm hoping the two of you can bring the foul criminal who did this deed to justice. And find the thief who killed the falcon as well."

"As I said, it will be my greatest pleasure."

King Robert rubbed at his reddened eyes and nodded approval.

"Your Highness?" I asked. The king motioned for me to proceed. "My wife has some experience in these matters also."

"Aye," put in His Lordship, his grey eyes keen. "The woman's father is my own physician. She's got a good pair of eyes on her and is wise for a woman."

"Yes, of course. Let her assist you as well, if that is helpful," the king replied, then turned his attention to an equerry who had entered the withdrawing room on some sort of court business.

I thanked His Majesty and retired from the royal presence, along with Robert Cruickshanks. Saying I would meet further with him in a few moments I left the captain of the guard in the hallway, and went to seek my wife.

I found her in the mews tending to the birds with Gudni. The lad still sat in the same spot. Perhaps, I mused, he had not moved all night. The wounded gyrfalcon, however, now sat aloof in a corner of her cage and refused to eat at all. She snapped at Gudni's hand when he reached in to offer her the raw tidbit but did not taste the offering. Small bits of refused morsels of flesh and a few feathers lay forlorn on the floor of the cage. Mariota stood to one side, holding a pot of unguent. She looked up, a worried furrow on her brow, as she heard me enter the room. Her face lightened a little when she saw me.

I took her aside and explained the charge the king had given us. She nodded and excused herself. I doubt Gudni even noticed, so intent was he on the bird. Duncan Tawesson lay asleep in a corner of the room, on his pallet. I saw an empty flask near him, knocked over on the floor.

"He took to the drink, poor man. Meager consolation though it is. Gudni says he started in again as soon as he woke this morning," Mariota explained to me as we left the sad scene.

Outside, we made our way through a bright sunny morning to the guardhouse where I had agreed to meet Cruickshanks. I introduced him to my wife, although they had in fact spoken the night before. Accompanied by another guard, the three of us then made our sad way up the mount, past the New Tower and Great Hall, to the outside of St. Margaret's Chapel. The normal daily clamor of castle life bustled about us yet I felt we walked alone. Finally we reached the small grey stone chapel and hesitated outside for a moment.

"Mariota, will you examine her?"

My wife nodded grimly and we entered the chapel, accompanied by Robert, who ordered the man at arms to stand watch outside. Inside, the body of Malfrid lay before the altar, covered by a pall, as we had left it the night before. I saw the priest kneeling at the altar in private prayer but he stood when he heard us enter. Robert spoke with him, and after some troubled exclamation and discussion with the king's captain the priest left the building. We were alone with the dead.

The few candles and the faint sunshine coming in through the slit windows yielded but dim light. I glimpsed fine paintings on the walls, of the life of Saint Margaret on one side, and the Assumption of the Virgin on the other, but my eyes took a bit of time to adjust to the darkness and beyond an initial glance I paid the paintings little heed. Robert took a candle from the altar and brought it to where we stood near the corpse.

With Robert holding the candle close we removed the pall and viewed the body.

I heard Mariota draw in a sharp breath and I felt my own breath catch, harsh in my throat. A shift clothed the body, just as Mariota had left it the night before, decently covered. Mariota touched one arm and I could see that the stiffness after death had fully set in. Malfrid's other clothing, the green dress and mantle, lay piled beside the bier, neatly folded. Carefully Mariota pulled up the linen shift to view the fatal injury. I saw an ugly wound, dark with a smear of dried blood against the pale white of the girl's flesh. I thought of her beauty as she had vaulted through the air, like some wild falcon herself. That grace now lay vanquished, vanished, gone.

"It looks as though the slayer drove the knife into her side," Mariota said, as she probed the wound with a narrow stick she had pulled from her medical pouch. I often wondered what my wife carried in that bag, and was sometimes surprised by what emerged.

"And sank it in deeply," my wife continued. "The wound is about as deep as a dagger, not a small table knife. Most likely it went straight through the lung and to her heart. She would have died quickly. And not have bled too much."

"So the killer could have escaped without getting much blood on him," Cruickshanks said.

Mariota nodded again.

"There's nothing else?" Cruickshanks pressed.

"You mean was she violated?" I fancied I heard an odd tone in my wife's voice. I glanced at her but she kept her eyes stonily fixed on the body as she examined it. "No. And she was virgin," Mariota said after a moment.

"There are no bruises?" Cruickshanks asked.

"I see none."

"So whoever struck her, did not grab her forcibly. She must have known and trusted the person, to let them get so close."

My wife nodded again but did not raise her eyes. I thought I glimpsed tears. "I will just examine her clothing," Mariota finally said, her voice thick. "Perhaps there will be some clue there to help us."

Cruickshanks and I nodded, and we looked over the poor pile of clothing. The garb seemed strangely forlorn with its wearer lying close by, still and cold. We examined the green kirtle, stained with dark blood and cut from the knife thrust. And the girl's mantle, but we found nothing much of import until Mariota emptied the girl's bag onto the refolded kirtle.

There, along with a wooden comb and a blue ribbon, lay a fine ring, glinting where it caught the candlelight.

"What of this? I do not remember her ever wearing such a thing," my wife wondered, holding the ring up to the light. After a moment she handed it to me, and I examined it as well.

"Nor do I. I have never seen it on her," I admitted. "Although her father will know better. Perhaps the killer gave it to the lass." The ring sat innocently in my hand, gold, with a chalcedony stone set in the middle. "But you'd think, if it was the killer's, he'd have made sure to take it with him."

I handed the ring over to Cruickshanks. "I'll inquire," he said.

"Perhaps it is that Peter Leslie's. He might have given it to her as a token."

"And killed her as well," put in Mariota with a bitter edge to her voice. "Well, I'm thinking there is nothing more to be learned here."

"Then let us leave her here with the saints to watch over her," said Cruickshanks to Mariota in a kindly tone. "And ask the lass's father when he'd like the priest to perform the burial mass." We must have looked confused, for he turned to me and explained. "Queen Euphemia has ordered masses to be said for the wee thing. It will cost her father naught. She's a fine Christian woman, our queen."

As we left the chapel I thought to confer with Mariota but she surprised me by leaving abruptly. "I told Gudni I'd help him with the birds. At least they're still living," she added bitterly. I would have followed her but she turned and stopped me. "Too much noise, he says, is bad for them. We'll talk later, Muirteach."

CHAPTER 8

Which left me with Robert Cruickshanks to discuss the murder. We stood together in the courtyard before the chapel. The coolness of the morning, after the coldness of the chapel, with Malfrid's corpse resting inside, made me shiver and I drew my *brat* more tightly about me as a gust of wind swirled around us.

"So," Cruickshanks mulled, running his tongue over his front teeth for a moment before he continued, "the slayer most likely knew the lass, for her to let him get so close."

"Unless some madman just grabbed her," I put in.

"Unlikely," he scoffed. "Our guards keep good order here." I had forgotten, for a moment, that I spoke with the head of the castle guard. "But the girl was a stranger. Whom did she know? What acquaintances had she made in her short time here?"

I enumerated. Of course she knew her father and foster brother. Peter Leslie. Mariota and myself. The others who had been present at Lady Ingvilt's *reresoper*. Henry Sinclair. Many folk had seen her perform two days earlier, but she had not known them to speak to.

"What happened before Gudni found her?"

"At the supper hour her father awaited her in the hall. And her foster brother stayed with the two remaining falcons, to care for the injured bird and guard them both. My wife and I saw him there, before we ourselves went on to the hall to sup." Another gust blew some dried leaves about us and I watched them dance in the wind for an instant before they fell to the ground, released.

"And what of Peter Leslie?" asked Cruickshanks sharply, interrupting my sad reverie. "He is known to have a bit of a temper, common enough in young men. He's been in more than one brawl."

"He swears he remained busy with his duties in the hall from the time he left us, after our visit to the gardens."

"Left you and your wife. And Malfrid was with you then?"

"Aye. We parted with Peter close to the New Tower and Great Hall, then the three of us continued up towards Mariota's and my lodgings. We left Malfrid close to the mews—at the spot where the path branches between the old lodgings and the path to the mews, the shed and the kennels," I explained.

"That should have been safe enough."

"Aye. But it proved not to be." I watched another dead leaf blow across the yard.

"And you say the three of you had been with Peter before that, walking in the gardens?"

I nodded. Cruickshanks continued. "Doubtless they made plans to meet later. He tried to have his way with her and knifed her when she would not submit."

"That is hard for me to believe," I protested.

"I will check with the other squires," Cruickshanks continued. "Perhaps Peter is not such a dedicated servant as he would have us all believe. And as I said, he's hot tempered. He could easily have slipped away, or arranged to meet the lass later. Women are licentious, you know."

"But would he have knifed her?" I asked. "He seemed caring, solicitous, and he helped us search for her."

"I'm sure it's as I said. She teased him, then refused him, and in his lust he knifed her. And why not help search; he would know well enough where to find her body."

I muttered something under my breath, feeling my jaw tense. I hated to think that of the lass. Or of the lad. Peter might be a fop, and perhaps he had a temper, but this just did not ring true.

"That maid was jealous, the red-haired girl," I mused, thinking out loud. "She seemed envious of the attentions the squire paid to Malfrid."

Cruickshanks shook his head. "Jealous enough to knife the lass? It does not seem like a woman's crime. And wasn't she busy with her duties at that time?"

"Perhaps."

"What of Baron Sinclair?" Cruickshanks asked.

"He was already seated in the hall when Mariota and I arrived. And what motive would he have to slay the lass?"

Cruickshanks shrugged. "The same as the squire. He's a man, after all."

I scoffed. "He's a wife at home who has just given birth."

"What matter would that make?"

"He strikes me as ambitious. And canny. I doubt he'd chance all to satisfy a moment's lust."

"You may indeed be right. The king thinks well of him." Cruickshanks shrugged his shoulders again, as if to toss Henry Sinclair away from him. "What of the lass's father? Were they on good terms?"

"You've seen him, seen his grief," I exclaimed, aghast. "Think you he killed his own daughter?"

"It happens. If she's disobedient, most folk would not blame him."

I shook my head in disbelief. "No. I don't see it. Not her father. He loved her dearly."

"Well, what of her brother? The dark lad."

I shook my head again, mulishly. "Nor her brother. He adored her."

"He's but a foster brother."

"What of it?"

"He's no Christian soul, from the look of him, with that

dark complexion. Dark as the devil himself. I'd not put it past him," Cruickshanks declared.

I almost laughed while another gust blew about us. "But what reason would he have had? To stab his own foster sister?"

"Could the lad have been jealous?"

I thought back. An image bloomed in my mind—Gudni embracing his sister after their performance for the court.

"I don't know," I answered slowly. "He's at that age when lads take love hard."

"Well, find out, Muirteach. Find out. I'll ask among the squires, and set a man to watch Peter Leslie. You speak with that boy. And watch Henry Sinclair."

I nodded, although I doubted Gudni had had anything to do with his sister's slaying. But what madman could have killed a lovely young girl?

❖   ❖   ❖

I left Robert Cruickshanks to his other duties, at first intending to find my wife. The path led past the gardens where we had walked just yesterday afternoon. I felt ill at ease, with the murder and Mariota's reluctance to discuss it with me, and with her abrupt departure.

And where was the knife?

It had not been found at the site of the killing. Rather than seek out Mariota I decided to check the area again. Perhaps the daylight would reveal something we had overlooked in the dark last night.

The narrow alleyway led between the two old buildings on the castle mount, known as the Old Queen's Lodgings and the Old King's Lodgings. These structures now lodged others, noble perhaps, but not kings and queens. King Robert and Queen Euphemia had moved into the New Tower some years ago after its completion.

I imagined the muddy ground between these two venerable buildings had been trodden beyond recognition, with the crush of folk the night before. That surmise, at least, proved correct. Few recognizable footprints remained that I could see, just a trodden mass of muck.

Malfrid had not been a foolish girl. What had possessed her to follow someone to this place, where she had met her death? The promise of a kiss from Peter Leslie, or something else? Some stolen moments of lust in a dark alley?

I thought of the grieving Duncan Tawesson and felt a fleeting moment's gratitude that the Lord had not yet blessed Mariota and myself with children. If this was the pain they brought, with their foolish, stupid choices…

Well, such thoughts gave me no help. I had just neared the entrance to the alley, with a mind to search it more thoroughly, when a party exited the lodgings on the left. I glimpsed the Lady Ingvilt, along with several other ladies, her maidservants, and Peter Leslie. They came down the path, heading my way. I did not see the red-haired maid, however. Perhaps she was with Ingvilt's son. The group stopped when they saw me.

I hailed them. So much for an unobtrusive look at the

murder place.

"Ach, Muirteach," Ingvilt greeted me, her intriguing Norse accent making her voice a little throaty. "And what is it that you are about on this fine morning?" A breeze blew her veil around her and caught at the edges of her cloak.

I explained. Ingvilt looked distressed, while the other ladies twittered like sparrows in the background, discussing the sad events of the night before, no doubt.

"Can you not wait a bit? We were just off to the gardens. Although it is still cool the sun promises to appear. It should be a fair day."

"No, my lady," I replied. "I fear I cannot."

"Peter has a lovely voice and we thought to have him entertain us," Ingvilt continued as though she had not heard my words. She looked into my face with a little smile and again I noticed the flecks of gold in her eyes. "You would be welcome to accompany us. Although I fear Peter also is not in a happy mood today. These sad events have touched him sorely."

"And so they should," I replied, perhaps a little priggishly. I glanced at Peter, who in truth looked grave and as though he had slept but little. "Not even a day hence he walked in those very gardens with her."

Ingvilt nodded. "A lovely girl, was she not? So graceful, like a flying bird. A soaring falcon, like those she helped to train." Her face looked suddenly sad, and I felt my own melancholy return as I saw her pain.

"Indeed," I replied. "Her poor father is most distraught.

As are we all. And there is also the fact that someone slew one falcon and maimed the other. You heard of that, did you not?"

"There was talk of little else, the day it happened," Ingvilt said. "Who could do such a thing? Who could be so cruel?" She fixed her lovely eyes upon me and I found myself wishing I had courtly manners, and did not limp.

"Well, I hope that shall soon come to light," I said. "His Majesty has charged me with finding the murderer. Along with Robert Cruickshanks, of course." Ingvilt's eyes widened and I continued. "I have investigated similar matters, both at home in the Isles and even in Oxford."

"Oxford? In England?"

I nodded. "I will tell you of it sometime, if the tale is of interest to you. But this murder. I feel at fault. I should not have left her—we should not have left her."

Lady Ingvilt looked sympathetic. "It was not a great distance, and the king's own castle should be safe enough. No one could fault you. Doubtless your wife was fatigued."

"No, that was not the case. We just did not think anything would happen. I thought she could safely walk that short distance alone."

The lady nodded, again in sympathy. A cloud passed overhead, obscuring the faint sun, and her green eyes looked suddenly colder as well, all the gold in them vanished in the changing light. "Indeed it is most distressing. Well, you must do as you think best. You must pursue that fiend and bring him to justice. We will miss your company, though."

I took my leave, then stood and watched the party walk down towards the gardens, wondering if I should have seized the chance to question Peter. But Cruickshanks had said he'd see to the lad and I had other sad duties to attend on. So I let the party pass and turned my attention again to the alley that ran between the two lodgings.

The place had a sour muddy smell to it, and the stink of piss overlaid that. Most likely the alley frequently served as a handy urinal for courtiers on their way home, too drunk to find the latrines. I saw blood on the wet earth, the dark clotted red of it mixed with the mud where Malfrid had been knifed not far down the alleyway. Perhaps the murderer had departed through the back of the alley, leaving some footprints there. Picking my way carefully I made my way down the dank close.

It took my eyes a bit of time to adjust to the dimness. A small amount of light filtered through between the several stories of the two buildings; on occasion a sharp shaft of light pierced the gloom. The stench grew a bit less; it seemed the palace folk were not overly modest when they needed to take a piss. I nearly slipped in the wet mud and cursed my bad leg.

Towards the end of the narrow space some slates lay in a jumble, perhaps fallen from the royal roofs above. If the killer had passed this way, I reasoned, he'd have wanted to discard the knife before emerging onto the area behind the lodgings—a path that led towards the smithy. I looked at the slates and pushed one or two aside without seeing anything. They all sat presumably as they had fallen, in a jumbled pile. Odd that they would fall mainly in this area. Or perhaps workmen had thrown them down when making a repair. I moved another few slates and thought I caught a glimpse of a darker, metallic grey down below. I shifted the final slate.

Beneath it lay the dagger.

CHAPTER 9

I picked it up. An old, workmanlike dagger, with a handle of worn walrus ivory, and a much-used blade. Someone, the owner I supposed, had carved a gyrony of eight on the handle. Dried blood still stained the hilt and blade, and I did not doubt that I now held the knife that had slain the lass. And my heart plummeted to my guts as I examined it. I recognized it, and the carved design on the handle. It looked to be Duncan Tawesson's knife.

I took up the knife, wrapped it lightly in the free end of my mantle, and went to seek out Robert Cruickshanks.

I found Cruickshanks in the guardhouse near the main gate of the castle, just down from the newly completed tower. He sat at a trestle table, sharpening and polishing something, a broadsword, I realized as I approached. A few others of the guard also lounged around the room, all similarly occupied.

"Cruickshanks!" I called out. Robert looked up, his lean face darkening as he read my expression.

"What is it, Muirteach?"

I let the mantle unroll, spilling the dagger onto the table with a clatter.

"This. I found it at the end of that close where Malfrid was murdered. The killer had hidden it under some slates. And I fear I know the owner as well," I continued, less willingly. "I've seen Duncan Tawesson with this knife."

"But he'd not kill his own daughter," Cruickshanks responded evenly. "You yourself said so."

"You'd not think so, would you?" My frustration at Malfrid's senseless murder got the better of me and I heard my voice rise as I replied. "Nor did I, yet here is the knife."

The other men in the guardroom had left off of their polishing to come and stand in a circle around the table. The bloody dagger lay on the wood surface like an accusation.

Cruickshanks sighed. "Well, best to go get him and take him in. He'll talk. We'll make him."

I took a deeper breath, and another thought occurred to me. "Perhaps someone stole it from him and planted it there," I suggested.

"Perhaps, but it damns him all the same," returned Cruickshanks, his thin lips set, as he gave orders for the men to fetch Duncan from the mews.

❖ ❖ ❖

It took but a short time for the men to return with Tawesson. He looked in a full rage, his face red with choler. His hands had been tied behind his back; his eyes, bloodshot and bleary and wild, gave him the look of some battle-maddened stallion, or the dreaded fierce water horse, the kelpie.

The guards holding Duncan hustled him to the table and stood next to him in front, facing Cruickshanks where he sat. The dagger still lay on the trestle table, a silent and bloody condemnation. Cruickshanks stared at Tawesson, who stared back until he glanced at the table before him. Then he stared at the dagger.

"Well, man, is this yours?" Cruickshanks demanded.

Tawesson looked at it again. He nodded. "Where did you find it? Someone stole it from me two nights ago."

"Muirteach found it where you hid it, at the end of the alleyway where your own *dochter* was slain," retorted Cruickshanks.

"I never hid it there," protested Tawesson, the choler in his face ebbing, leaving paleness under his sea tan. "I've not seen it since the night my birds were stolen and maimed."

Cruickshanks cocked an eyebrow and rolled his brown eyes, as though he did not believe one word Tawesson had spoken. "Indeed?"

"Yes, you must believe me," Tawesson insisted. "You

remember, Muirteach, do you not?" I heard a pleading tone in his voice. "It was the night the bird was attacked. I could not find it the next day. The dagger, I mean. I had left it off before we went to Lady Ingvilt's that night and then, when we found the birds the next morning, all else went from my mind. I did not note that it was gone until much later that day."

"You did not speak of it to me," I said, my heart like a lump of lead within my chest.

"Christ's teeth, man, I had other things to think of, with one bird maimed, the other dead, and my poor daughter flaunting herself like a harlot. I did not even notice it had vanished until later in the day when I went to use it."

"Indeed?" Cruickshanks repeated, a skeptical edge to his voice. "And why would someone steal your knife?"

"For the same reason they would cripple my birds and kill my own daughter."

"And that would be?"

Duncan said nothing, obstinately silent, and finally shook his head.

"Hold him," Cruickshanks ordered. "He admits to it being his knife, and it was found in the alley where the poor lass died."

"But when could he have stabbed her?" I wondered out loud. "We all saw him at supper in the Great Hall."

"He must have knifed her and then gone on to dinner."

"I do not think so," I protested. This felt just too easy, a facile settling of the crime with no castle-folk involved.

"Then who else could have attacked the lass, Muirteach?"

"That's what we must find out," I retorted. "We were charged with finding the slayer, whoever he might be. We were not charged with settling the matter for the ease of the court, and wrongly accusing an innocent, grieving man."

I saw a flush spread up Cruickshanks's lean face and watched his mouth tighten. "Are you saying His Majesty's justice is faulty?" he demanded.

"No, but I am saying we have the wrong man."

I saw his arm tense and his hand start to form a fist. For a moment I thought he would strike me. But I saw him take a breath, and he mastered himself. I let my own breath out in a rush of relief. I did not want to fight the captain of the guard.

"Think for a moment," I persisted. "What cause would Duncan have to kill his own daughter, and slay and maim his own falcons?"

"Aweel," Cruickshanks said, thinking, "it will still do no harm to hold the man here. And when you find the right man, Muirteach, we'll let Tawesson go." I heard the emphasis on *you*. "We have Duncan's knife. You found it yourself; you recognized it. He's the murderer."

I felt sick as I heard Cruickshanks's words. Tawesson stood, listening and struggling a bit at the two guards holding his arms, as we argued. Eventually he wrenched one arm free and lunged towards Cruickshanks. One of the guards slugged him and he fell down in front of the table, groaning and clasping his eye.

"Who else could have done it, Muirteach?" repeated Cruickshanks when some order was restored. "What other suspects have you found?"

"Peter Leslie, for one," I replied. "If Malfrid would not yield to his advances."

"You saw them together. Did it seem his style to drag her off to an alley and stab her like a whore?"

I thought of Peter, his good looks and his foppish clothing. I did not truly think he could have done it either, but I felt sure Duncan had not. "I do not know the lad well. You yourself said he was a brawler. Perhaps."

"And how would the lad have gotten hold of Duncan's dagger?"

I had no good answer for that. Just then I heard the sound of running steps and Mariota and Gudni burst into the guardhouse.

"Muirteach, what is all this? Gudni was saying they've come and taken Duncan—" My wife scanned the guardroom, seeing the bloody dagger, Duncan on the floor with a bruised and bloody face, and myself and Cruickshanks standing nearby.

"Muirteach, what's all this?" Mariota repeated more slowly. "Tell me."

"I was on my way to speak with you, *mo chridhe*, but then I thought to look in the alley where the lass's body was found. And I found this, hidden under some slates. Duncan's own dagger."

"Which proves perhaps that his is the knife that killed Malfrid. It does not prove her father dealt the blow. *Amadan*!"

My wife calling me a fool in public did not improve my own temper, although she had used the Gaelic and doubtless none of the men there understood her words. She continued in the same language. "Muirteach you cannot seriously believe that Duncan would be killing his own daughter!"

"What of the knife? That's proof enough to damn him. At least, that is what the captain of the guard believes."

"Anyone can be stealing a knife. What does Duncan say?" my wife retorted.

At that point Cruickshanks interrupted. "What is she saying? Speak in Inglis, mistress, like a civilized person." Mariota bristled at this but nodded and I answered her previous question in Inglis.

"Duncan claims the knife disappeared the night the birds were injured. And in his distress and confusion at the time he did not remark upon it at first."

"Indeed. And just when do you think Duncan stabbed his own daughter? He was in the hall before we came to supper that night, and in plain view of many people."

"Yes, but the dagger is his. He admits as much," put in Cruickshanks.

"And he claims it was stolen," continued my wife, on a rant. "Plus, if we're speaking of proofs, there are other things to consider. What of that ring we found on the lass this morning?"

Gudni, who had been listening to all the previous

conversation, pushed forward to look as Cruickshanks produced the ring from a small chest on a side table.

"Is this ring your sister's?" Mariota asked the lad.

Gudni emphatically shook his head no.

"Is it your father's?"

"It is not hers. And not my father's. I have not seen it," Gudni said. "Never."

"Perhaps the killer gave the ring to her," Cruickshanks said.

"And was fool enough to leave it on her person, pointing straight to him?" Mariota said. "I think not."

"He might not have had time to retrieve it. Perhaps someone approached and he had to leave quickly," I added.

"Aweel, at any rate, we must try and find the owner of it," answered Cruickshanks. "Best to start with Peter Leslie."

Cruickshanks sent some men at arms to fetch the squire who soon arrived, dusty and sweaty from practice in the tiltyard. He did not look such a fop today. Peter took one look at the ring and paled.

"Yes, the ring is mine," he admitted readily enough when questioned. "I lost it some days ago. But that does not mean I killed her. Rather the opposite. If I had killed her, surely I'd have taken it back from her."

I nodded my head and looked at Cruickshanks. "If you had time. Or knew where she had hidden it."

"Still, that reasoning seems sound enough," the captain said. "Why even give the bauble to the lass, if he intended to slay her." He turned to Peter. "Where did you lose the ring?"

"I wore it three days ago, and lost it during the day. Perhaps it fell off my finger while we stood on the green, when we watched the falcons fly. I did not notice, to my sorrow, and only realized I did not have it when I prepared for sleep that night."

Cruickshanks looked somewhat convinced; I felt sure I saw relief on his face.

"Perhaps poor Malfrid found it on the grass as she returned to the castle," Peter added.

"It could be possible," the captain of the guard conceded. "Just. But you, lad, are known to have a temper. What of that quarrel you had, just a few weeks ago?"

Peter did not reply. I saw his jaw tense and his handsome face flush.

"What was all that about?" Cruickshanks persisted. "Didn't you near break the other boy's jaw? And knock out a tooth?"

"Yes, sir," said Peter, looking more and more concerned.

"It was not chivalrous. In truth, I am surprised Sir Johann did not dismiss you."

"But that has naught to do with," Peter finally protested. "It was but an argument—"

"Over what cause? A wench?" Cruickshanks demanded.

"No, sir, not that."

"Then what? What do lads fight over, besides women?"

"It is a question of honor, sir. I cannot tell you."

Cruickshanks turned to me. He spoke in a sarcastic tone.

"You see, Muirteach, it is a question of honor. *Certes* the lad is blameless."

"But where would the lad have gotten the dagger?" Mariota put in.

"Perhaps he stole it when he crippled the birds," I answered.

"For what reason?" Cruickshanks scoffed. "To impress the girl's father? I think not."

I shrugged. Truth to tell, I could see no reason anyone would have had to maim the gyrfalcons, unless it was to get back at Duncan for something. But mention of the birds had agitated both Gudni and, I was surprised to see, my wife.

"Muirteach," she said in Gaelic, and I could tell she was close to tears. "I must go with Gudni. He is wanting me to change the dressing on the poor bird's wing. And after that I promised Lady Isobel I would attend upon Her Majesty."

"Aye, well enough," I muttered, annoyed. What with Mariota's constant care of the falcon, and the time she spent waiting upon the queen, I barely saw my wife here, and that rankled. But I now had my own worries and concerns for both Duncan and Peter. Gudni and Mariota swept out of the room together.

"And so are you going to keep both Peter and Duncan under guard for murder?" I questioned Cruickshanks.

"I think not." I noticed Peter's face relax somewhat as he heard these words. "As you say," Cruickshanks continued, "the fact that the girl had Peter's ring does not prove he killed her, rather the reverse, as both your wife and Peter himself have pointed out most stridently. So we shall let him go." I heard Peter exhale in relief, and Cruickshanks heard it too. "We will be watching you, knave," he admonished the squire. "So mind yourself."

Peter made a hurried bow and quickly left the guardhouse. "But what of Duncan?" I persisted. "He would not have slain Malfrid."

"His dagger was used to slay the lass, his own *dochter*. The man stays here for now."

"Are there assizes?" I asked. I was somewhat familiar with the English manner of trials from our time in Oxford the year before, and of course I knew the Celtic law of the islands. But neither of those would stand at the royal court in Edinburgh.

"There'll be a Royal Assize when His Majesty sees fit to call it," offered Cruickshanks. "Murder is a capital crime." Which gave me scant comfort. Things did not look good for Duncan Tawesson.

CHAPTER 10

I slammed the heavy guardhouse door shut behind me, and my eyes adjusted to the daylight of the castle yard. As I stood there I wondered if anyone had thought to send word to the crew of the *Sellkiesdottir* about the murder. For certain Duncan, now a prisoner of the castle guard, would not be able to do so. And in the depths of his drunken grief I doubted he had sent word previously. As I walked away from the guardhouse I resolved to question Gudni about that, and set off towards the mews where I expected to find Gudni and Mariota.

As I passed the New Tower I heard my name called and looked up to see Henry Sinclair. I smiled at the sight of a friendly face. My day had been none too pleasant so far. And Duncan's arrest reminded me all too much of another occasion, the year before in Oxford, in which an innocent man nearly died for a murder he had not committed.

"So, Muirteach," Henry called to me. I waited for him, watching his large frame cross the courtyard towards me. "What is the latest news?"

I told him of finding the dagger and the ring. And of Duncan's apprehension by the guard. Henry's hazel eyes looked troubled.

"'Tis ridiculous," he scoffed. "Duncan would never have murdered the lass. He fair doted on her. Anyone could see that. He had no reason for to slay her."

"But who did have reason? She was but an innocent."

Henry's eyes narrowed. "Well, there is Peter Leslie."

"The captain thinks him blameless." I scowled. "Although the lad has a temper and has been chastised for brawling, Cruickshanks is quick to look for guilt among strangers. Not so quick to see it among his own folk."

Sinclair nodded. "Where are you off to, Muirteach?"

I told him and he said he was heading towards the farrier's, to see about a horse he was having shod. The farrier's workshop lay in the same direction so we walked together towards the mews and the smithy.

"Who else could have wanted to harm the girl?" Henry wondered. "Didn't I see her quarreling with her brother, that day we saw them fly the gyrfalcons?"

I thought back and remembered the incident, the heated exchange between the two, although I had not been close enough to hear what they had said.

"Out on the green?'

"Aye, that was it."

"And he's but her foster brother. The two were close. Perhaps he grew jealous of Peter Leslie."

"He does not seem the type to murder."

"But he'd have ready access to his own foster father's knife."

"But why murder Malfrid? Why not murder Peter rather than his foster sister?" I said, unconvinced. "Think you it could have been random—some drunken courtier wanting his way with her?"

"Then what of the knife?" countered Henry.

That was true. No random drunkard would have had access to Duncan's knife. But if Duncan had not slain his daughter, which I refused to believe, then someone had sorely wished to incriminate him. And who, I wondered, could that be? Besides Peter Leslie? Surely not the maidservant Agnes.

The path branched at this point and Henry started in the direction of the farrier's. "Oh, Muirteach?" he called back to me.

"Yes?"

"What of Duncan's book? That book about the northern regions. The *Inventio*?"

"What of it?'

"Have you seen aught of it? Perhaps I could look at it while he—while he is in custody."

I shrugged. "Best ask Gudni." We took our final leave and

I headed towards the shed near the mews. I found Mariota there, tending to the injured falcon. It cocked its head and glared at me miserably as I approached. Mariota, intent on examining the splinted wing, did not raise her eyes until she had completed her inspection. I saw no sign of Gudni.

"Hello, Muirteach," my wife said. She did not appear overjoyed to see me. "What brings you here?"

"I was looking for Gudni. As well as you," I added, coming close to her and giving her a little kiss, despite her expression. I felt her stiffen a moment then she softened in my embrace. "Do you know if the lad has sent word to the *Selkiesdottir* of what has transpired?" I asked her after a time.

I felt my wife nod her head against my shoulder. "He went down to the port himself, just a short time ago. After we returned from the guardhouse. The crew may well be wondering if anything's amiss, with no word from their captain these last few days. Although no doubt they're enjoying the taverns and whores in Leith."

"And they will not be happy to hear the news he brings them now."

Mariota nodded again, and pulled away from me. "But Muirteach, it is ridiculous. Cruickshanks can't truly believe that Duncan murdered his own daughter!"

"He is certainly loath to accuse Peter Leslie. And Duncan is an outsider," I pointed out.

"Aye, there's that. But who could have done these things? Someone with a grudge against Duncan—and such a grudge it must be! To maim his birds and slay his daughter. It could be Peter, I suppose, although I'd not have thought it of him. He seemed a pleasant lad," my wife said.

"Cruickshanks said the boy fought with another lad awhile back, and blacked his eye. He has a temper beneath those fancy clothes."

"Well, perhaps you should speak with him, Muirteach. Or others who know him. Wasn't he flirting with that red-haired maidservant, Agnes?"

"I did think of her," I responded. "She seemed very envious of the poor lass. And Agnes and Peter serve in the same household. She might have something to say, indeed, although I doubt she would have killed out of jealousy."

"Don't discount jealousy, Muirteach," my wife said. "It is powerful, and a deadly sin."

"Perhaps," I said, and thought for another moment. "But she would have no reason to hurt the falcons. Can you think of anyone else who could have slain the lass?"

We stared at each other, stymied. We knew of no one else, really.

I remembered my conversation with Henry Sinclair. "Gudni?" I suggested.

"Gudni! Muirteach, have you taken leave of your senses?" My wife's voice rose a notch, shriller, and she stepped back, staring at me as if I were possessed.

"I saw him arguing with his sister that day after their performance," I persisted. "As did Henry Sinclair. And she's but his foster sister. Perhaps Gudni became jealous of Peter Leslie."

"But what of the birds, Muirteach? Gudni would never hurt these birds. It cannot be him."

"Perhaps a different person injured the birds."

"Or Gudni himself is a madman. No, Muirteach, I'll not believe it of him. He's but a lad, and one with a kind heart."

"Still," I persisted, "he could have wanted his foster sister, been jealous of her attraction to Peter and stabbed her in a fit of jealous rage."

My wife looked singularly unconvinced, but I was relieved to hear her voice return to a more normal range. "I am not believing a word of it, Muirteach. There must be someone else here with a grudge against Duncan."

"But he's never been here before. No one knows him here. Who could have a grudge against him?" I asked.

"Or perhaps not a grudge, so much as wanting something of his. A gyrfalcon."

"Then why maim and kill them?" I retorted, my own voice hard.

"Or that book," Mariota suggested. "The *Inventio*." Our time in Oxford the year before had sadly shown us what some folk would do for books. "It has gone missing, Muirteach," my wife added when I did not immediately reply.

"What has?"

"The *Inventio*. Gudni searched for it and could not find it. He said he wanted to show it to Lord Sinclair, as he had been asking for it the other evening."

"Perhaps Duncan hid it someplace. It is a valuable book."

"Perhaps." Once again my wife sounded unconvinced. "Or perhaps Lord Sinclair himself stole it."

"Then why ask for it? That makes no sense. Perhaps is on the *Selkiesdottir*. Mayhap Gudni will find it when he's on the ship."

Mariota said nothing and returned to the bird, beginning to feed it. The bits of meat bloodied her fingers.

"Have you more to do here?" I asked, now out of charity with her and somewhat annoyed with her stubbornness.

Mariota nodded. "I told Gudni I would remain here until he returns, to watch over the falcons. Someone might try to hurt them again."

"That could be some time if he went into Leith," I observed.

"I don't mind, Muirteach. Go on if you wish. I must then attend upon the queen but I shall meet you in our quarters before supper."

So I agreed and left her, thinking to myself that women were waspish creatures.

❖   ❖   ❖

I walked from the mews towards our lodgings feeling somewhat out of sorts. I thought to see if His Lordship had need of me but before I could go and seek him out I spied Lady Ingvilt and her two maidservants. From the posies and daisy chains the maids carried I assumed the party was returning from their outing to the gardens.

"Muirteach!" Lady Ingvilt hailed me.

"My lady," I said, making a little bow. She was richly dressed in green brocade and as I bowed, I saw the rich white fur trim of her sleeves. Ermine, I supposed, or white cat's fur.

"And how are you this afternoon?" she inquired, coming closer. I caught a whiff of her exotic scent. Civet.

"I am well enough," I answered.

"And your search?"

"We have found the weapon—her father's own knife."

Ingvilt's ladies murmured in horrified fascination at this news, like the wind rustling through the trees.

"How shocking!" said Ingvilt. "Muirteach, we are just about to take some refreshment. The sun shone warm in the gardens and our voices grew dry from singing. Won't you join us in my chambers? You could tell us all of it. My maidservants would find it most interesting, the silly things do not realize the horror of it. But I do have some good wine from Gascony if you wish some. Do you thirst?"

Suddenly finding His Lordship seemed less pressing to me. I did thirst. And felt weary and disheartened from the events of this sad day. "I accept with pleasure, my lady. Please, lead on."

Ingvilt's pleasantly appointed chambers seemed a world away from the guardhouse and wounded falcons. Agnes appeared with Magnus, who clamored noisily about his mother for a few minutes before settling himself by the window to play with some carved wooden horses and men at arms. I did not see Sir Johann and surmised him to be out about his business.

I gratefully accepted the goblet of wine Ingvilt offered me and nibbled on some dates stuffed with almond paste, served from silver plate, while Ingvilt's ladies twittered about. I found it a pleasing change from having one's friends arrested, examining the bodies of murdered lasses, and searching in mucky alleyways for bloody daggers. I sipped the wine, savoring the rich taste on my tongue, relaxed against the embroidered cushions on the bench and closed my eyes a moment, wanting to erase the image of Malfrid's cold corpse from my mind.

I felt a stirring next to me, and a gentle touch on my arm.

"Are you tired, Muirteach? You look done in."

"Not as tired as that, my lady," I replied, feeling faintly embarrassed to be caught with my eyes closed, "but the day has been long, and—"

"Trying?" Ingvilt finished my sentence. I could smell that intriguing civet perfume she wore and feel the fur trim of her long sleeves as they brushed against me when she refilled my glass. "It is such a very sad thing," she murmured.

"Yes," I agreed. "It is such a very sad thing." My own guilt at having left the lass alone added to my grief, but I did not share that thought with my hostess.

Agnes, the pert young maid with the red hair and wide-set hazel eyes, offered me a plate of little cakes. I took one, enjoying the flavor of caraway and the crunch and sweetness of it.

"Sir, I have heard that the *puir* lassie's own father killed his *dochter*," Agnes said as she handed me the cake. She did not look guilty to me, just somewhat morbidly interested.

"His knife was found all bloodied and mired in gore," put in another of the girls, Morag, the one with dark hair.

"And so close to here," shuddered Agnes. "We might all be murdered in our beds."

"Oh, ladies, I am sure you are not in danger," I replied, attempting to act the courtier. "You have many strong men about. What of the squire? Is he not strong and skilled with the sword?"

"He is too busy making sheep's eyes at whatever pretty girl passes by," Agnes said, offering me another caraway cake, "and adjusting his pretty sleeves."

"I heard you say you thought him handsome!" Morag chimed in as I bit into the cake.

Agnes scowled. "Not I!"

I put down the cake. "But surely, fine feathers or not, he is a strong fighter," I said. "I heard he knocked out another squire's tooth in a brawl."

"Aye," Morag said. "He did. At least he bragged of it to me."

"And what was the fight about?"

"Indeed, and I've no idea whatsoever," the dark-haired maid replied. "Agnes, you are just annoyed because he walked in the garden with that *puir* murdered lassie."

"Och, I'm never jealous," Agnes retorted, "and certainly

not of that popinjay. But the thought of a killer amongst us makes my blood run cold."

"I am sure you ladies are safe," I asserted.

"Well, so long as there is someone valiant to protect us," put in Ingvilt, who had been watching me speak with her maids. "Morag, fetch more wine for us," she ordered.

"Surely there is no shortage of strong knights and lords here," I replied. I drained the last of my wine and thankfully accepted the refill that Morag brought. "What of your own husband, dear lady? Is he not a champion?"

"Indeed," replied Ingvilt in that husky voice of hers. "He is a brave warrior and won many tournaments in years past, when he was young."

"Or I shall protect you, Mama," Magnus chimed in, looking up from his game. The ladies all laughed. Ingvilt patted her son affectionately, and dropped a kiss on the top of his blonde head.

"How did you meet Sir Johann?" I asked my hostess after Magnus went back to his playing. "The lad takes after you both."

"We met at the Norwegian court, in Bergen." Ingvilt sat down on the bench beside me. I heard the brocade rustle as she settled her skirts about her.

"When was that?"

"Close to seven years ago, now. How the time has flown! King David had sent my lord to King Haakon's court on business. Lord Henry Sinclair accompanied him. That was before our good King Robert took the throne, of course."

I nodded. I knew who King David was. "And your match was made there?"

"Indeed, I was but newly widowed at the time. Yet still my lord and I could not resist each other," Ingvilt said with a little laugh. "But look, here comes my lord—" The door opened and Ingvilt rose and greeted her husband, meeting him at the door with a full mazer of wine.

"And how have you been amusing yourself today, my dear ones?" asked Sir Johann, giving his wife an affectionate kiss, and hugging his son who came running across the room to see his da.

"We went to the gardens. Your squire escorted us. The lad has a lovely singing voice but he was disheartened today."

"Ah, yes. The murder. And you, sir," said her husband as he seated himself on a bench near mine. "What of you?"

"What of me?" I asked, momentarily confused. Perhaps it was the wine.

"Aye. What of your lord's business here with our king?"

"It proceeds apace," I replied diplomatically.

"Muirteach has been asked by the king to assist in finding the slayer of poor Malfrid," interjected Lady Ingvilt. "And he has already found the weapon."

"Oh?" said Sir Johann, taking a long draught of his wine. "Tell me of it."

I told him how I had found Duncan Tawesson's weapon in the alleyway and how Duncan was now held in custody. Sir Johann looked perplexed, his genial face troubled.

"To kill his own daughter—"

"I am not convinced he has done so," I admitted.

The hazel-eyed maid refilled our glasses. I found the warmth the drink left in my throat and belly pleasant and perhaps it led me to continue confiding.

"But who else could have done such a thing!" exclaimed Ingvilt, her eyes wide.

"I am not sure. Someone with a need for vengeance against Tawesson. You heard what happened to his gyrfalcons?"

The lady nodded her head yes. "Indeed," she replied, "but I do not think my noble husband has heard all of the story."

I told them of the attack on the birds.

"But that is terrible!" Sir Johann exclaimed. "They were magnificent! Each one of those birds is worth a king's ransom. What fiend would commit such a crime?"

"Perhaps Duncan cheated someone in the past," suggested Lady Ingvilt.

"Perhaps," I said.

"Has he not traded in this port before? He might have cheated someone with connections here on the mount."

It was an interesting thought, one I had not reflected on before. It might prove of interest to investigate some and see what Duncan's previous business ventures had been. "You are wise, my lady, to suggest it," I replied.

"Aye," said Sir Johann, laughing heartily despite the serious topic. I thought the strong Gascon wine had affected him as well. "My Ingvilt is uncommonly wise for a woman."

CHAPTER 11

I returned to my quarters shortly before the evening meal to find my wife there before me. I watched a moment as she plaited her hair and re-arranged her linen coif around it.

"His Lordship was wanting you." Her voice sounded sharp to my ears.

"Oh?"

"Yes. Where were you?"

"I met the Lady Ingvilt and her husband and shared some wine with them in their lodgings."

"Yes. I can see that you are in your cups," Mariota observed.

Although there was some truth in my wife's words, they stung and I responded angrily. "I asked of Peter Leslie. And in addition they offered cheerful company, while you were too busy with those birds to offer any companionship."

"Muirteach!" I saw my wife's blue eyes filling with tears.

I crossed the room to her. "I'm sorry, *mo chridhe*, I spoke thoughtlessly."

"As I did. Forgive me, Muirteach. Let us not quarrel."

I took my wife in my arms and we kissed, my nostrils filling with her scent. "Mmm—" I felt the warm softness of her body under her clothes and caressed her, reaching for her rounded hips beneath the smooth textured wool.

"Muirteach, stop it! We must go."

"I'm not hungry for food." I gave her buttock a little pinch.

"Ouch! Muirteach! Well, you may not be, but I am—" We disentangled ourselves and straightened our raiment a bit before leaving our room.

"You said His Lordship was seeking me?" I asked as we exited the building.

"Aye," responded Mariota while we walked. "Something to do with transcribing an agreement, I believe."

"I'll see if I can attend upon him after the meal. Did Gudni return from Leith?"

"Yes, or else I would not be here. He returned earlier. The queen is a kind woman. She wishes to know how the wounded falcon gets on, so I then saw her in her bower and told her of it. And Gudni—I offered to take him some bread and cheese. He's stayed to keep watch over the falcons. He feels it's the one thing he can yet keep safe."

"I wonder if I might speak with him?"

"Of course, Muirteach. Come with me after the meal,

when I bring his victuals."

We approached the New Tower that housed the main hall and went in. All was hubbub there, His Lordship already seated at the high table. My wife and I hurriedly found our seats, near to Henry Sinclair who greeted us eagerly.

"Muirteach. And Mistress MacPhee. How have you been, lady?"

"Well enough, I thank you."

"We did not see you at dinner."

"No, after we…" Mariota hesitated, and I guessed she did not want to speak of poor Malfrid's body. "After I helped Muirteach with something I went to the mews and assisted Gudni with the injured falcon."

"Ah, yes. How does the bird get on?" Henry looked at my wife, his hazel eyes full of concern. She smiled a little.

"She makes some progress, I think. Her Majesty has taken an interest in the bird's progress as well."

"And the lad? How does he do?"

Mariota shrugged. "He says little, but I worry for him. After he learned of his father's arrest he went into Leith this afternoon to check on his father's ship. I think it did him good to be away from here for a time."

Henry nodded sympathetically. My wife sighed and wiped her fingers on her napkin.

"Mariota?" I asked. "You are not hungry?"

"I have no appetite tonight, Muirteach," she said, despite her earlier claims to hunger. "Forgive me."

❖   ❖   ❖

After the meal was finished and the folk dispersed I walked with Mariota back towards the mews and the shed beyond where Gudni remained with his two remaining birds. Mariota had saved some bread and cheese and a bit of roasted goose for Gudni, and had somehow procured a small jug of ale. The light was fading and we could see the glow of a lantern coming from the doorway to the shed.

"Gudni?" Mariota called.

Gudni sat on a pile of straw, whittling at something. He looked up and flashed a tentative smile in my wife's direction. Mariota brought out the food and the smile widened into a broad grin. Gudni fell to eating with a good appetite. I smiled. I remembered how it felt to be a lad, always hungry.

While Gudni devoured his meal, Mariota went over and looked at the bird. The wounded gyrfalcon's splinted wing stood out like some kind of strange paddle in the dim light. Her eyes did not look bright—dull and glazed with misery, reflecting off the lantern light in the darkness of the shed.

"How does your patient?" I said, trying to make a jest.

My wife did not seem amused. "Not so well, Muirteach. Look at the eyes. I'm worried that there may be evil humors in the wound."

I nodded. Gudni finished eating and I went to ask him of his trip to Leith. "How did the crew? How did they take the news?"

"Too much drinking," Gudni replied in answer to my first question. "They not know—maybe find another ship," he continued, answering my second.

"Lord Sinclair was wondering about the book your father spoke of. The *Inventio Fortunatae*."

"It is not here," said Gudni.

"Have you seen it?"

"Gone," Gudni replied again. "It is gone."

"But where could it be? Is it on the ship?"

Gudni shrugged without interest. "I searched. It is gone."

"When was it last seen?"

"My father knows. Not I." And Duncan Tawesson, I knew, had other things on his mind tonight than the *Inventio Fortunatae*. I hoped he was well treated in his cell. At least Cruickshanks had not spoken of any methods to encourage a confession.

"Did he bring it here, to the castle?"

Gudni nodded.

"Perhaps someone stole it the night the birds were injured."

Gudni shrugged again. He seemed to have little interest in the lost book, and no doubt thought it of little import, with his foster sister slain, his foster father imprisoned and one of the remaining falcons sorely injured and no doubt worthless. Mariota had by now finished changing the bird's dressings. She gave Gudni some instructions, and a quick little hug. We left him there whittling by lantern light, humming that strange tune to his falcons while he worked.

❖ ❖ ❖

Malfrid's burial mass was held the next day. Mariota and I attended, as, of course, did Gudni. Peter Leslie, I observed sourly to myself, had the decency to show his face at the chapel. Lady Ingvilt and her maids put in an appearance as well. Agnes kept smiling flirtatiously at Peter Leslie when she thought no one was looking at her, but I did not observe Peter smiling back.

Queen Euphemia had kindly paid for the mass and she and her own ladies attended, the queen's long dark face looking sad as the mass continued. King Robert, however, did not attend, and neither did my Lord of the Isles. But I saw Henry Sinclair there, along with a smattering of other curious folk from the castle. So in fact, the small chapel grew quite crowded, although of course Malfrid's own father could not attend. He remained Cruickshanks's prisoner, held in some cramped cell below the guardhouse. As the mass progressed I tried to concentrate on praying for the soul of the poor lass; the continuing guilt I felt at her death added force to my prayers.

The breeze blew cold, with grey clouds rolling in from the Firth of Forth. Mariota, standing next to me, shivered in the damp of the old chapel and at the burial in the graveyard. A damp *dreich* wind cut through our mantles and chilled us to the bone while we watched two manservants shovel dirt atop the shrouded form in the grave. Then, the service over, Gudni, Henry, Mariota and myself repaired to Henry's room at his invitation. We drank a joyless cup of funeral ale and then dispersed.

I left Mariota and Gudni outside Henry's lodgings and walked towards the guardhouse, intending to visit Duncan in his cell. The jailer greeted me and, after I gave him a groat, led me below-stairs and unlocked the cell door to let me in. He locked it behind me and retreated up the hallway towards the stairs, leaving me with a small lantern. In the dim light Duncan did not appear to be too badly treated, despite his black eye and split lip. He sat, abject, in the filthy straw on the floor of the cell, staring at nothing that I could see, but he roused and looked up when I entered.

"You're not looking too badly today," I said, shining the lantern in Duncan's direction.

"I've the devil of a headache," he replied, squinting with his uninjured eye in the lantern's glow.

"From the whisky you were drinking, and not the beating they gave you, I don't doubt," I replied. I told him of his daughter's burial. Duncan listened, his face stoic. I surmised that the drink and his imprisonment had drained all hope, and all emotion, from him. Then I told him of Gudni's visit to Leith.

"Aye, best to let the crew go," Duncan agreed when he heard. "God knows when I'll be free." He did not mention the other possibility, that he would not be freed, and neither did I. "How do the falcons get on?" he asked after a moment.

"My wife is somewhat worried that the female's wounds

may fester. I believe she is set to try some new remedy today—a hot poultice with some herbs—yarrow, I think. The male does well enough."

Duncan nodded. "That's good. But then, they did not injure him."

"The female holds her own," I added, wanting to cheer him on this dreadful day.

"Aye," Duncan said. "She is strong. I'd thought to name her Dancer, for the lights you see sometimes in the night sky. They're common where I found her."

"Why, I wonder, did they only attack the females?" I pondered aloud.

Duncan answered my question with his own mournful one. "Why did they kill my daughter?"

I wished I had thought to bring some *uisge beatha*. I know I could have done with a drink, and thought Duncan would not have refused either. "Duncan?" I finally asked after an uncomfortably long moment.

"Aye?"

"When did you last see your dagger?"

Duncan thought and rubbed at his swollen eye. "I'm thinking it was the night the birds were harmed. I had cut some meat for them, and then I left my knife in the shed before we visited the Lady Ingvilt and her husband. I thought it might be best not to take a weapon to that gathering, so I left it there, with the birds. The next day I did not think of it at first, what with the birds missing and maimed. And then, later in the day, when I remembered it and went to get it, I could not find it."

"So whoever stole the dagger also attacked the birds," I thought out loud. "Who here might have a grudge against you? Enough of a grudge to hurt your gyrfalcons—and Malfrid."

Duncan remained silent. The rotten straw on the floor of the cell smelled of mold and urine.

"Surely there is someone," I continued when he did not speak.

Duncan shrugged his broad shoulders wearily. "I'm not knowing. Do you think I've not asked myself the same question? Over and over again, here in this black cell? No, I've no idea. There's no one."

"What of past connections?" I prodded.

"I've docked in Leith before but never been to the castle," Duncan finally continued. "It wasn't until this trip, with the gyrfalcons and the white bears' furs, and the unicorn's horn, that I thought I'd try to deal directly here. I meant to have made my fortune here, for the children. Instead I've lost all. But I knew no one here at the castle until we arrived."

"At court, no. But what of the port? Leith? Have you enemies there?"

Duncan looked blank, then shook his head obstinately. "I deal fairly with folk. Always have. I pay my crew what's due them for honest work and I have a good reputation; I don't cheat. I have no enemies in Leith."

"What of your crew?"

"No, I treat with men fairly." And Duncan shut his mouth,

mulishly, and refused to say more on the subject.

I needed more than this. "Think, man," I badgered him. "Surely there is someone."

Duncan shook his head again. "It's little enough that I'm in these parts, and few the folk I know here," he protested.

"What of your family in Kintyre?"

Duncan laughed, a sound with no mirth in it. "I've not seen them in years, and know nothing of them." He took a breath. "I don't care if they hang me, Muirteach," he finally continued. "They already took my life from me when they slew my daughter."

"What of Gudni? What of your son and your ship?"

"He's welcome to it. I've no wish to live. They can kill me," Duncan repeated, without bravado. "I care not."

The defeated tone of his voice frightened me. "But what of the real killer? Don't you want vengeance?"

"Will that bring back my Malfrid?"

I could think of no answer to that. After a moment I took the lantern and left him there in the darkness. The heavy wooden door to his cell thumped shut behind me.

CHAPTER 12

Although Duncan insisted he had no enemies in Leith, I thought to journey there myself and make some inquiries. I enlisted Henry Sinclair who professed himself eager to go, bored with the poor weather and lack of physical activity at court. We rode out that afternoon, much like the day a few afternoons earlier when we had set out for Leith on the rumored trail of gyrfalcons and first met Duncan and his children. Despite the seriousness of our quest, I felt like a schoolboy unexpectedly freed from his studies. I had not realized the castle, Malfrid's death, and my own guilt in the matter had oppressed me so until we were on the road to Leith.

The weather did not match my mood. A steady drizzle worked its way through our cloaks as we rode the few miles from Edinburgh to the port. Our horses snorted, their breath showing a misty white in the unseasonably cold air.

We entered the gates of Leith and proceeded through the bustling streets to the docks. A raw cold wind blew in from the sea and cut through our mantles as we walked down the docks to find the *Selkiesdottir*. No one answered our calls when we hailed. Finally an old sailor on a nearby boat heard our shouts and deigned to respond.

"They've gone," he said, shouting at us from the height of his ship, a trading cog from Bristol. "The crew."

"Where?"

"Most took service with other vessels. But Gybb remains, he's gone into town.

"Where to?" I repeated.

"The Sow's Head, most like—down that way." He pointed down a particularly disreputable-looking alleyway. I looked at Henry, who nodded towards the *Selkiesdottir*.

"We'll just be a moment," I said by way of justifying our behavior.

"Matters naught to me," replied the old man and he continued his business.

A rope ladder hung over the side of the *Selkiesdottir*. We left our horses tied at the docks and climbed aboard, the ladder swaying in the breeze and knocking against the ship. The vessel looked to be abandoned, as the man had said. We searched the tent on deck that served as Duncan Tawesson's small cabin, finding a logbook but no sign of any other books.

Certainly not the *Inventio Fortunatae*. Then we entered the hatchway and explored the hold of the small ship. There were a few bales of wadmal, a coil or two of walrus hide rope, and tar, along with some bundles of ratty furs of secondary quality. Surely nothing there explained why anyone would murder Duncan's daughter.

As I shifted a bundle of cloth I heard a creaking sound above us. "Shh—What's that?"

Henry had heard it, too. "Someone above decks," he whispered, one hand reaching for his dagger. We stood silently, listening to the footsteps over our heads.

"It's most likely to be—" hissed Henry. "What did the man say the fellow's name was? Gybb?" I nodded. We waited as we heard the creaking steps cross the deck to the hatchway. Then Gybb, or whoever it was, began to descend the ladder. In the dimness I looked tautly at Henry and we ducked behind the bales of cloth and furs.

Steps crossed the hold. They neared us and the breath stopped in my chest as we heard the unknown visitor shove aside the same bales we had just examined. He came closer and I glanced at Henry, who nodded. We stood upright, revealing ourselves.

I saw a knife glint in the darkness and heard Henry cry, "Watch out!" The knife slashed downward. I felt a sharp pain and warm blood on my arm. I heard Henry curse in the darkness as the assailant struck again. I grabbed the man's wrist. He struggled against my grip and threw a punch at me with his other hand until Henry tackled him, twisting his arm behind his back. We heard a clatter as the knife dropped to the floor. Henry's fist slammed into the man's face and we finally subdued him. He coughed and spat blood onto the floor.

"Now," I said. "You'll answer our questions. Who are you?" Through the light filtering down from the open hatchway, we looked into the face of a grizzled sailor, wrinkled and weather-beaten from years at sea. A face I recognized from our first visit to the *Selkiesdottir*.

"Who be you?" he countered. "You be the ones with no business here. That man from the cog was telling me some strangers had boarded my ship."

Henry and I glanced at one another, dismayed. "We're friends of Duncan Tawesson," Henry finally answered.

"Where be the lad? Gudni? Why ben't he with you?"

"Gudni remains back at the castle mount. He knows not that we're here."

The man snorted, until Henry tightened his grip on his back-bent arm. "But you say you're his friends," he said, grimacing. "Why should I believe you?"

"For Malfrid's sake," I said.

The man's expression changed, from angry suspicion to sorrow. "Let me up and I'll treat with you. There, that be better." He sat up and wiped his bloody nose. "Now, tell me your names."

"I am Muirteach MacPhee and this is Baron Henry Sinclair."

"And I be Gybb. Gybb Saylor. I've crewed with Duncan Tawesson for night onto sixteen years."

"So you can help us," I said. "Duncan is in prison, at the castle mount. They think he killed Malfrid. His knife was found all bloodied, hidden under some stones in an alleyway."

The old man scoffed. "That be fool's talk. Gudni was telling me sommat of it yesterday. Duncan loved that girl. We all did."

"Whoever stole his knife and killed the lass must have known Duncan, and had some reason to hate him sorely," I added. "Can you think of anyone with such a reason?"

Gybb shook his head. "Duncan treats folk well, his crew and those he trades with. There ben't no enemies."

"But he has one. And so did Malfrid."

"Aye, poor lass. I watched the wean grow up." Gybb spat out a glob of blood and looked at us both. "Bastards, they were, what done for her. Aye, I'll help you, and be glad to. Despite this," he added, wiping again at his bloodied nose.

"And despite this—" I said, rubbing at the cut on my own arm, "we'll accept your help, and gladly."

"Come let's repair to a tavern. The Sow's Head? I could do with some ale," put in Henry. "And doubtless we'd all think the better for it."

❖   ❖   ❖

Gybb Saylor proved a garrulous companion. He told us details of Duncan's latest voyage to lands west of Greenland, where Duncan and Gudni had captured the gyrfalcons and traded for furs with the Skraelings there. He told us of Malfrid's mother in the far regions of Greenland, how Duncan had some years ago left her with young Malfrid and Gudni and returned a year later to find the farm in ruins, the two children running wild, and Malfrid's mother dead of a wasting sickness.

"The two weans had done what they could, but were fair starved themselves. Gudni be always a good hunter, even as a young lad, and that is what saved the both of them."

"And that was some years ago?"

"Aye, about four years gone it would be. Since then the children have sailed with us."

"No one in Greenland grudged them anything? Duncan had no enemies there?"

Gybb shook his head and took another swig of ale. "There's few folk live there, on the outskirts of Christian lands. Especially on the west coast. It be close to deserted now. The ice has gotten bad in those regions, too. In the old days the sailing was better. Every year now there be ice, even in summer, and bad storms. But no, Duncan didn't have no enemies there."

"Or anyone with a grudge against Malfrid? Or her mother? Someone who wanted the farmland, perhaps?"

Gybb shook his head again. "I know of no one. Astrid Gunnarsdottir had no family. There be an older daughter, from her first husband, but folk said that girl died, just about the time Astrid bore Malfrid. If anyone wanted that land they could just take it; there be no one there now to guard it. But the land's worth little, the weather be bad there. No one wants it now. Only the Skraelings." And there were no Skraelings at court, none but Gudni.

As the afternoon waned we learned nothing of use and finally left Gybb Saylor to guard the *Selkiesdottir* while we returned to Edinburgh.

When we reached the castle defenses I was glad to see the sun had not yet completely set behind the great hill to the west. Arthur's Seat they called it, Henry informed me. We entered the gates and left the horses at the stables. I bade Henry goodbye and returned to our room where I found Mariota.

"How do the birds do?" I asked her.

"A bit better. Och, Muirteach, what happened to you, *mo chridhe*?" my wife exclaimed as she saw my arm and the makeshift bandage I'd applied. "Here, let me dress that properly for you. What happened?"

I told her while she cleaned and dressed the cut. It was not deep, but felt better as she attended to it.

"Muirteach, this makes no sense," Mariota protested as she washed the cut with some tincture. "All men have enemies. Who are Duncan's?"

I shrugged, wincing as my wife probed a sensitive spot. "Cruickshanks, for one. He's eager to pin the blame on someone. What of Peter Leslie? Have you seen him?"

"No, I spent most of the day with the queen and her ladies, and then went and saw Gudni, and the bird. Poor lad. I worry for him, his sister dead, and his father wrongly accused of the murder."

"His foster sister," I pointed out again.

"Gudni may have admired Malfrid," admitted my wife, as she finished tying the bandage about my arm, "but I refuse to believe he would have harmed her. Not after all they'd survived together, as you've just told me. Perhaps he'd have fought with Peter Leslie if he were jealous. Young lads fight. But I've heard nothing of that."

"Well, perhaps it is past time to seek out Peter Leslie again," I said as we prepared to depart for supper.

❖   ❖   ❖

We cornered Peter as the castle folk dispersed after the meal. Tonight the lad wore an unfortunate cotehardie of blue cut short above the arse, with ridiculously long daggotted sleeves. No doubt he thought he cut a fine figure.

"Peter! Peter Leslie!" I called.

The lad turned and gave a hesitant smile. "Muirteach MacPhee. Have you learned anything new?"

I shook my head. "No, but I would speak with you."

"Lead on," said Peter without hesitation.

We left the hall and walked across the court, near to the old chapel where Malfrid lay buried.

"How can I help?" Peter asked artlessly.

I scowled. He did not act like a guilty man. "Where were you the evening Malfrid was killed?"

"As I've told you. Serving in the hall. First, readying the tables. Then serving. Then cleaning after."

"And you did not leave during that time?"

Peter shook his head no, then stopped. "Well, just once."

This was news. "For what?"

Peter glanced at my wife, who had remained silent. "I needed to relieve myself. I went to the jakes."

"By yourself?"

"Sir, I don't shit with my friends," said Peter with an air of offended dignity. I almost laughed but just nodded. I'd check his story with the other squires; perhaps they would remember something of it.

"What of the other squire? The one you fought with some time ago. What was that about?"

Peter hesitated. "It was a matter of honor, as I've said."

"Well, you had best tell us more of the story. Who did you fight with? Or we'll speak to him and see what he says of the affair."

"He is no longer here. The boor was squire to a French knight, who came to court for a time. He's left since."

"And? What did you fight about?"

Peter flushed, and then slowly answered. "He said I was a catamite. And he made fun of my clothing. So we fought, and I took out a front tooth for him." Peter smiled a satisfied smile, his own teeth looking like those of a wolf for just an instant. "He'll not be so handsome now, back in France."

Mariota spoke. "Peter, perhaps you can help us. That afternoon, when we all strolled in the gardens, did Malfrid speak of any enemies? Either of hers or her father's?"

Peter shook his head. "No, my lady. You were there, you saw us. She spoke of nothing of the sort. She told me of her life on the ship and in Greenland. But she said nothing of any enemies."

"And the ring? You did not give it to her on that day?"

"Indeed not! I lost that ring days before, as I've told your husband."

"Then how did she get it?"

"I've no idea. It is strange."

But if Peter Leslie did not know Malfrid possessed his ring, then he could have killed her, and not taken the ring since he did not know she had it.

And where had Malfrid gotten Peter's ring? There seemed to be all too many lost items these days—lost daggers, lost rings, lost books. What tied them all together? We spoke a bit more with Peter, then bade him farewell. I cursed and my wife looked at me oddly as we proceeded towards our lodgings.

"What is it, Muirteach?"

"Too many lost things. Someone is behind it all."

"I'm not doubting that for an instant. Who could it be? Who has access to everything?"

"What of Agnes? You've seen her flirting with Peter. Perhaps she was jealous enough of Malfrid—"

Mariota laughed. "To kill her? Over that lad? I do not think so. Although it might well be worth speaking more with her."

"Well then, who? Duncan had access to the book and the

dagger, as did Gudni."

"Aye, but not the ring," my wife pointed out.

"No, not the ring."

"When did Peter last see it?" Mariota asked.

"He swears he lost it two days before Malfrid was killed, the day Gudni and Malfrid performed for everyone."

"Was it a ring he wore often?"

"He claims it was," I answered. "He claims to have removed it when washing up, after practicing with staffs with the other squires. That was in the morning. Although he believes he put it back on; he does not remember exactly but thinks perhaps he lost it when we watched the falcons fly." I shrugged. "But, as he does not remember, he could well have lost it earlier. When they were practicing."

"And where was that?"

"I believe they practice at staffs out past the mews, between there and the stables? There is an open area used for such things."

"So Gudni could well have found it, if it was dropped there," my wife said. "Or anyone might have found it. Even Agnes. But then why plant it on Malfrid's body?"

"Perhaps Gudni gave it to her as a token. Perhaps he found the ring by chance, and thought his sister would like it. Perhaps it was just luck that the ring was Peter's." I scowled. "That's too many chances for my liking."

"Aye, Muirteach," my wife agreed as we entered our

lodging. "It's too many chances for my liking also."

I did not point out to my wife that many of those chances led to Gudni. No doubt she herself was well aware of that.

CHAPTER 13

The next morning I woke up early, to see the dawn just lighting our quarters. Mariota had left the bed before me and was not in the room. I rolled over into the hollow her body had left on the mattress. My wife entered the room a moment later.

"What is it, *mo chridhe*?" I asked sleepily. "Is all well with you? You look pale."

"Everything is fine, Muirteach," my wife replied a little tartly. "I woke up early, that is all."

I grunted, rolled over, and shut my eyes again, wanting to sleep a few moments more. I became aware of someone watching me and opened one eye to see my wife gazing at me.

"What is it?"

"I'm going to check on Gudni and the falcon. Her dressings

will need changing, and I must reapply the poultice. I shall see you when we break our fast."

I muttered something under my breath and went back to sleep as my wife left the room.

I stole a few more moments of slumber until the growing light and clatter of folk going about their morning routines aroused me again. I rose finally, a shameful slugabed, washed and dressed and made my way toward the Great Hall where some folk had gathered to break their fast. I saw Mariota in the yard as I approached the tower, and joined her.

Mariota smiled at me, her nose wrinkling a little in that way I loved. "Wonder of wonders. You're awake."

"Aye. How are your charges?"

"I fear for one of them. But she still survives. I'm not used to doctoring birds, *mo chridhe*."

I smiled at my wife. "You're a fine physician. No bird will dare die while you are physicking it."

A shadow crossed Mariota's face. I guessed she remembered patients she had seen to who had not lived, and I sought to change the topic. "Shall I fetch you some bread and small ale?"

Mariota nodded as we found our seats and she sat while I went for our viands. There was a crush about the table where the bread and ale were set out informally in the mornings. I grabbed a pitcher and a loaf and was about to return to my wife when I heard a familiar voice. I looked across the aisle to see Lady Ingvilt and pert Agnes smiling at me in tandem, with young Magnus in tow. Lady Ingvilt motioned to me and I approached her, feeling suddenly all too aware of my limp and my humble clothing.

"My lady. Can I be of some assistance?" I asked, making a clumsy little bow.

"Good morn to you, Muirteach," Ingvilt replied with a smile.

"And to you, my lady. How are you and your son this morning?" I smiled at Magnus but he did not smile back, intent on smearing honey on his breakfast bread.

"How do things progress with your investigation?" Ingvilt asked me while her son continued eating.

"Many things are lost, but little found so far."

Ingvilt gave a little laugh. "Now that is cryptic, Master Muirteach. Just what we would expect from His Lordship's Keeper of the Records." I returned her smile and she continued speaking. "And what of Duncan Tawesson?"

"He remains in custody until the Royal Assizes are called."

"Think you he is guilty? It is hard to believe a man would kill his own child."

I glanced at Magnus, wondering that she would speak of such things before her son. The lad kept eating and Agnes was speaking to him of something as she got him another slice of bread and helped him spread the honey upon it. I shrugged. "It was Duncan's knife I found. Yet I doubt he killed his daughter."

Ingvilt arched a shapely eyebrow. "Then who do you think could have done so? You must find the killer—everyone here could be in danger." The curve of the lady's lips did not indicate much fear, despite her words.

"I do not know who could have killed the poor lass," I replied, oddly bothered by the conversation. "Now, my lady, if you'll excuse me. My wife awaits me."

"Of course." Lady Ingvilt picked up a bit of manchet bread and brought it to her lips. "I am thoughtless. Forgive me." I watched her take a bite.

"No pardon is necessary," I said. "But I must go for now." I left the lady and her maid and son, and found my wife again, sitting in front of an empty place at table.

"Here, sweeting." I put the pitcher and the bread on the table.

"And so you finally remembered me." My wife's tone reminded me of the sour ale I'd drunk at The Sow's Head.

"What is the matter, Mariota? I was just speaking with the lady; that is all of it. She asked of the investigation."

"Nothing, Muirteach," snapped my wife. "Nothing at all is the matter." She picked at the fresh bread I had brought her.

"Are you not hungry?" I asked, annoyed.

"No, Muirteach. No. I have no appetite."

"Well then, let us leave. But give me a moment yet. I am still hungry, even if you are not."

Mariota waited, toying with her food, whilst I finished filling my stomach. Then we left the hall, my wife walking stiffly beside me.

"Mariota, what is the matter?" I hissed at my wife as we crossed the court between the hall and the old chapel.

"Nothing is the matter, Muirteach. Why should you think so?"

"Mariota, you have hardly touched your food these past days. You are acting strangely and your voice would curdle milk this morning. Yet you insist nothing is amiss. You are my wife, *mo chridhe*. Tell me what troubles you."

"Nothing troubles me, Muirteach, and it's fine I know I am your wife!" Mariota's poor humor found voice as she vented her choler. "If there is something I need to tell you, rest assured that I shall. Did not His Lordship want you to attend upon him this morning? It grows late; he will be expecting you. And I must leave you, I must see to the birds again. I promised Gudni I would bring him some bread."

We had reached our lodgings. My wife broke away from me and stalked rapidly towards the mews. Cursing, I turned away and went to seek out His Lordship.

❖   ❖   ❖

Later that morning as we prepared to leave the royal presence, His Lordship having concluded his business with His Majesty, I pleaded with the king not to call the assizes immediately.

"So," King Robert said while a servant poured him some wine, "Cruickshanks has Duncan Tawesson under guard."

"Yes, my lord."

"And it was his dagger that you found, secreted in the alleyway."

"Yes. But I do not believe him to be guilty. He claims someone stole his knife from their lodgings, the night the gyrfalcons were attacked."

"Indeed?"

"And we found Peter Leslie's ring on the girl's body, yet he denies he gave it to her."

"Strange." The king blinked, and I remembered Mariota's father mentioning he suffered from some choler in the eye.

"And one more thing is missing—a book of Duncan's about the northern regions. A record of a journey he made there with an English friar some years ago."

"That may also be peculiar, yet it solves no slayings," King Robert replied, taking a sip of wine from the silver goblet that sat on the table in front of him.

"If you could just give me some more time, sire. I feel sure Duncan did not murder his own daughter. What motive could he possibly have?"

The king took another sip, considering, then set down the goblet and rubbed again at his red eyes. "Yes. We will wait on this," he finally agreed. "But the man stays in custody."

After His Lordship dismissed me I went to seek Cruickshanks at the guardhouse. I found him gambling with some of his men. The bone dice clattered cheerily on the wooden table. Apparently it was a slow day.

I told Robert Cruickshanks what the king had said. He nodded his head, but his expression was doubtful.

"Who do you think did do it then, Muirteach? If it was not

Duncan Tawesson."

"Peter Leslie or Gudni. Or even the maid Agnes. She was jealous of Peter's attentions to Malfrid, but Gudni had the most opportunity to steal the knife."

"We could bring the lad in for questioning," Cruickshanks said while another man at the table took a throw and rolled a nine. "You're out, Tam," Cruickshanks told him. "Go see to oiling that chainmail." Tam swore and stomped away from the table. "Do you think it's warranted?" Cruickshanks continued to me.

"I'm hopeful we'll find more evidence. As of now there's nothing substantive to tie anyone to the killing."

Cruickshanks shrugged and reached for the dice. "We could still bring Gudni in."

"And what of the squire? And the maid? Let us wait on it a bit," I said. Disgusted, I abandoned him and the others to their game, and went to see Duncan in his cell below. A narrow shaft of light from the torch in the hall illuminated the dungeon and the figure of Duncan, sitting in the straw. He did not look as though he'd moved from when I'd left him there the night before.

"Duncan!" I called.

He stirred. "Och, Muirteach."

"I've spoken with Gybb Saylor. Yesterday. All's well with your ship. He says he'll stand watch for you."

"Gybb's a good man." After a moment he asked, "How fare the two falcons?"

"The female still lives. My wife says she is mending."

"And my son?"

"He cares for them constantly, helped by my wife."

"That's good, then." Duncan did not ask if I'd found his daughter's killer and I had nothing to tell him of this.

"Do you need anything? Are you well treated?"

"Well enough."

"Enough meat and drink?"

"Some bread." Duncan laughed mirthlessly. "No meat, and naught to drink but water."

"I'll see what can be done. The king himself has taken an interest in your case."

"Taken an interest in my falcons, more like."

I was glad to see Duncan still had the spirit to be skeptical. His next comment brought me less joy. "But who killed my daughter?"

"We do not know yet. Are you sure there is no one here who bears you a grudge?"

"No one, as I've told you."

I hesitated a moment. "What of your son?"

"Gudni?"

"Aye. He had opportunity to steal your knife. And he could have maimed the birds."

"Gudni would never do such a thing! And he'd do anything for Malfrid."

"You don't think he could have been jealous of Peter's attentions to her, and slain her in a fit of rage?"

Duncan shook his head slowly, like a stubborn ox. "The boy would not hurt her. I'd swear to it."

"You may have to," I observed darkly and left him in his cell.

CHAPTER 14

I t still lacked some hours to midday when I departed from the guardhouse. At least Duncan was not being mistreated but I had no optimism. Unless I could find the real killer, Gudni or Duncan would die. That thought did little to lighten my mind, which was as leaden as the skies above. As I walked across the castle courtyard the skies opened up and a few drops of rain splattered on the dirt at my feet. I muttered a curse and pulled my *brat* more closely about me. So far the September weather had been fairly mild, but that looked to be changing, what with the chill yesterday and the increasing rain. I continued plodding back towards my lodgings; there were some contracts His Lordship had dictated that morning that needed to be recopied and I thought to use this miserable day to do it.

With my hood pulled up over my head and my eyes on the muddy ground, with my mind on my bleak thoughts and not on where I was walking, I nearly bumped into Peter Leslie who strode towards me.

"Oh, Master MacPhee. I am sorry."

"I was not minding my direction. Where are you going?"

"The day is too miserable for the tilt yard," Peter said, flashing a smile. "Sir Johann has sent me to attend upon the Lady Ingvilt. I have a pleasant singing voice, and the lady delights in song," he added disingenuously. "You are welcome to come along. The lady enjoys your company."

I did not quite see why the Lady Ingvilt would enjoy my company. I am but a poor island man, not some polished courtier. Yet despite those facts, and the fact that I was a happily married man, I found Ingvilt's undeniable charm intriguing, and Peter's comment pleased me on this wet day. Not to mention that the prospect of mulled wine, a fire, and music had more appeal than re-copying dry old charters. I promised myself I would finish the charters after dinner. And besides, this would give me the opportunity to speak more with Peter and with Agnes. Perhaps one of them might let something slip. So I followed Peter to Lady Ingvilt's chambers. Some braziers there put forth a cheerful warmth, and all was as pleasant inside as it was dreary outside. In fact, I found it difficult to believe it was the same day.

Lady Ingvilt greeted me and Morag, the dark-haired maid, quickly brought me a mazer of warm mulled hippocras.

In the corner Magnus played with his wooden horses, while Ingvilt chatted with her ladies as she embroidered patterns of flowers on a piece of linen. Agnes, however, was not to be seen. When I mentioned it Morag said another lady of the court had requested her help that day with some mending of fine cloth, as Agnes was a skilled seamstress.

"Of course I consented," Ingvilt said. "I could scarce deny Lady Isobel, she is a dear friend. But how fortuitous it is that you met up with Peter." Ingvilt motioned me to sit on one of the padded benches. "You will enliven this dreary sad day."

The time passed sweetly enough as we played at riddles and, after Peter had sung a ballad or two, we progressed to livelier games. Magnus grew restless and to placate him Ingvilt suggested we play blind man's bluff. After several mazers had been drunk it fell to me to be the blind man and I sought the laughing voices around me, my eyes covered, listening to the rustle of the women's gowns, Magnus's giggling, and the low chuckles of Peter as he nimbly eluded my flailing grasp. Then my hands touched something soft and yielding, the silky feel of brocade, and that alluring scent reached me—Lady Ingvilt's perfume.

"I am well and truly caught," Ingvilt murmured in my ear as she reached up and removed my blindfold.

I blinked owlishly as the light struck my eyes, my heart pounding pleasantly at her touch. "Nay, my lady. I fear I am the one captured."

Ingvilt moved away with a smile and announced that it

was close to time for dinner. We straightened our disheveled attire and left that merry place.

❖　❖　❖

Outside the drizzle had turned to a steady downpour. The ladies held their skirts up away from the wet dirt as they tottered down the path on their high wooden pattens. Morag kept a tight hold on Magnus, who wanted to stomp in every puddle. It seemed he stomped in most of them, and I saw the maid's green skirt splashed with muddy water. I pulled my own wrap around me against the chill and followed the jovial group towards the Great Hall, Ingvilt holding lightly onto my arm for balance in the slick mud.

"Muirteach—oh."

I heard the voice of my wife and turned, my face flushing.

Mariota stood a few feet away, taking in the group around me. I watched my wife swallow, and then master her expression. "Forgive me, husband. I did not realize you were so occupied."

"It's of no matter, Mariota," I said, feeling the truest churl.

"Yes, please join us, mistress," put in Peter Leslie.

Ingvilt did not relinquish my arm as Mariota came closer. "I trust you spent a pleasant morning?" my wife said.

"Indeed. We were telling riddles and passing the time jesting in my chambers," said Ingvilt. "It is a pity you were not there to join us."

"Yes, where were you, Mariota?"

"With Gudni for a time, seeing to the birds. Then I waited on you in our chambers until I thought to come searching for you."

"And how do those poor birds?" asked Ingvilt. "What a senseless thing."

"Indeed, it is a tragedy," answered Mariota, her expression serious. "But the wounded one slowly heals and gains strength each day."

"And the lad. What is his name? Gudby?"

"Gudni, my lady. He is desolate but strives to master himself." My wife did not add, *as we all do*, but I could see her struggle to remain calm in the tense set of her lips as we progressed towards the hall.

A group of nobles approached from one of the council halls. "But look, here is my husband with Henry Sinclair," exclaimed Ingvilt brightly, dropping my arm as the men approached. "My lord," she said, curtseying despite the muddy ground.

"How did you spend this bleak morning, my sweet?" said Sir Johann. "And Magnus—what sport did you find, my son? Come, let us not tarry outside in this downpour. You'll spoil your gown, Ingvilt."

Ingvilt took her husband's arm and we followed them into the Great Hall.

The richly painted ceiling and walls echoed with the clamor as folk found their seats. Sir Johann and his lady went to their places at the *rewarde*, the table to the right of the high table, while my wife and I found our own more humble seats down the side table on the left.

"Mariota," I began awkwardly.

"What is it, Muirteach?" my wife answered crisply as the food began to be served.

"I'm sorry, I did not mean—"

"Sorry for what, Muirteach? Surely you've no need to regret anything. You but spent a pleasant morning."

"I thought to find out more from Peter Leslie."

"And did you?"

"No, I did not. We had not the chance to speak privately. The lady and her maidservants were there, full of chatter. And the little lad."

"I can quite imagine." Mariota smiled brightly at the dark-haired maid who had found a seat a few places down, across from us at the table. "And what is her name?"

"Morag, I believe. She is a good-hearted girl."

"I am sure," replied my wife. We ate in silence for a time.

Our meal completed, we left the hall, still not speaking until we reached our rooms.

"*Mo chridhe*," I started to say, as the door shut behind us.

"Muirteach, don't say anything!"

"But why are you angry?" I asked, although I knew why my wife should be angry with me. The smell of Ingvilt's perfume still lingered in my nostrils and the excitement I'd felt at her touch likewise lingered in my mind, despite my many efforts throughout the meal we had just eaten to push those thoughts away from me.

"I am not angry," my wife snapped. "Nor am I humiliated that my husband spends his time in another lady's bower."

Now I grew angry at this accusation, for all that there was some truth in it. "Well, at least that lady and her friends are pleasant companions!" I yelled. "And willing to spend some time in friendly conversation, unlike others I could name!" With that I threw my mantle back on and stalked from our room, slamming the door behind me.

In the passageway outside I had the misfortune to see my liege lord, the Lord of the Isles.

"Ah, Muirteach," he observed dryly. "How does it go this afternoon?"

I wondered how much he had heard of our argument. "I am just about to begin on those copies, Your Lordship," I said.

"Excellent," he said. "And Muirteach…"

"Yes, my lord?"

"Go warily. There are deep waters here."

"Yes, my lord," I repeated, not knowing precisely what he referred to. "The copies will be accurate."

"I was not in any doubt of that," replied His Lordship. "And your inquiries? How do they proceed?"

At least I knew something of this to tell him, I thought with some relief. "Tawesson insists he knows no one in Edinburgh who might have a grudge against him. I begin to suspect the foster son, or perhaps that red-haired maid of Lady Ingvilt's, who was jealous over the matter. And there is Peter Leslie. His ring was found on the girl's body, yet he denies having given it to her."

"And so he would, would he not?" answered His Lordship enigmatically, and proceeded on his way out of the building.

Meanwhile, I realized that for all my fine talk, I did not have the charters with me. They were back in my room, in my satchel. Cursing, I turned around and stalked down the hallway to our quarters.

My wife still sat on the bed. She wiped her face with her hand when she saw me enter the room, but I could see her cheeks were wet.

"I've forgotten my satchel. That is all," I said, still angry—whether with her or with myself I did not know.

"It is on the chest where you were leaving it this morning," replied my wife.

I took it up and left the room again, disregarding the choked sobs I heard behind me as the door closed.

❖   ❖   ❖

I thought to take the charters to one of the council rooms where some south-facing windows let in the sullen light from the overcast afternoon. As I walked in that direction I saw Henry Sinclair. He crossed the yard to join me.

"Muirteach," he greeted me heartily, "how do you fare today?"

I little wanted to tell him of the harsh words I'd just exchanged with my wife, so instead I muttered something about needing to finish some scriving for His Lordship. Henry nodded sympathetically.

"Well, it is a dreary afternoon. One might as well spend it in labor. There is good light in my rooms. Do you care to copy your charters there? I have some ale and we could talk while you are working."

Easily persuaded, I accepted Henry's invitation and we repaired to his room, which also boasted a south-facing window. A table faced the light, as if made for the work of a scribe, although a few books and papers belonging to Sinclair sat piled haphazardly upon the fine wood surface. Pleased, I retrieved my papers from the satchel while Henry cleared the table. I commenced copying while Henry poured us both some mazers of ale from the pitcher on the sideboard.

"I thank you for accepting my invitation," Henry said, after we had both taken a drink.

"The work will go faster with your company," I replied.

"Well enough," said Henry, taking another swig of his ale. "Truthfully, though, I wished to have a chance to speak privately."

"Oh?"

"About Ingvilt."

"What of her?" I said, hoping I sounded nonchalant. Although I feared I flushed at his words.

"She is a beautiful woman."

"And married," I observed.

"As you are yourself."

"I've done nothing," I protested, feeling the heat rise in my cheeks, condemning me despite my words. "Why do you speak of her?"

Henry swallowed more ale. "She is well aware of her loveliness. And she will use it when it suits her. I have known her for years, since I first visited the Norwegian court."

"Well, she has not used her loveliness on me, Henry. She is a married lady, with a noble husband."

Henry laughed. "It's little enough you know of life at court, Muirteach."

I thought of Ingvilt's beauty and charm, of her perfume and the soft touch of her hand on my arm, and swallowed, my throat dry like some thirsty hound's. "How did you first meet her?" I asked. "Ingvilt?"

"As I said, we met in Bergen. One of the first times I visited there. Ingvilt was newly arrived at court, from Greenland, a protégée of Ivar Bardsson's. She sailed along with King Haakon—Prince Haakon he was then—when he returned from his venture to the western lands."

"Oh?"

"Yes, and she caught the eye of young Haakon on the voyage back to Bergen. But shortly thereafter she married Earl Olav."

"And when was that?"

"Close to fifteen years ago now. I was but a lad, and almost married to a royal princess."

"Indeed?" I had already heard that story from Henry. Still I feigned interest, took a gulp of ale, and concentrated on finishing a sentence neatly on the charter.

"Yes, the wee sister of Prince Haakon," my host continued. "But the *puir* lassie died, as did Ingvilt's husband. She married Sir Johann and later I married my Jennet. I lost my chance to be a king. But I'll have the earldom of Orkney yet. It should be mine by right, not my cousin's."

I dipped my pen back in the ink and continued with my copies.

"That is why I want the *Inventio*," continued Henry as he refilled my beaker.

"What?" I asked, momentarily confused. I had still been thinking of Ingvilt.

"Haakon went west; there are old trade networks there. And rich lands as well. I want to see them."

"Further west than Greenland?"

"Aye, so they say."

It mattered little to me, as I'd never yet had the chance to sail the ocean. But those mysterious lands sounded curious and enticing. Or perhaps I longed simply to leave the situation I found myself in here far, far behind me. "I thought Greenland to be the ends of the earth," I commented.

"No, no," Henry replied earnestly. "The Norse have sailed even further west, and found lands rich in timber and grapes. You've heard Duncan speak of it. But the weather has worsened the past few years, and fewer ships make the voyage to Markland. Few even travel to Greenland now, I've heard."

"Just Duncan Tawesson."

"Aye. Duncan." We drank, and I attended to my copying for a time, my pen scratching at the paper, until Henry broke the silence.

"I would still tread warily, Muirteach. Your wife is a fine woman, and lovely as well."

"Indeed she is," I said innocuously. I briefly wondered if Henry had overheard our argument, but finally decided his acute hazel eyes simply missed little of what transpired, even in so vast a place as the Great Hall. We dropped that topic and sipped our ale whilst I continued working on the charters.

"Have you spoken again with Peter Leslie?" Henry asked, after a time.

"Briefly. He insists he lost his ring several days before Malfrid was slain. His previous fight, with that French squire, was over the cut of his ridiculous garb. I doubt the lad has the wits to commit a murder. He certainly does not have the wits to dress sensibly," I added, out of sorts with our conversation.

Henry left that comment unanswered, and wisely changed the subject. "And Gudni?"

"His father does not think the lad could have done it. He feels the boy is too gentle a soul to commit such a mortal sin."

"Hmm," said Henry. "Perhaps that is true. Yet Gybb Saylor claimed the lad was a fine hunter."

"There's a difference between hunting and murder!" I exclaimed. "Although perhaps it was Gudni. For I am sure Duncan did not slay Malfrid."

"Well then," returned Henry equably, "who did?"

CHAPTER 15

That afternoon, the charters copied and Henry's store of ale exhausted, I returned to my lodgings, thinking to steal a nap. However, when I entered the room, the sight of my wife already lying on the bed startled me.

"Mariota! Are you unwell?" My wife rarely lay down during the daylight hours, while I myself was usually eager to steal a nap. Sloth is a grievous sin, I know, but not the least of mine, as I was coming uncomfortably to realize. This dreary afternoon a nap had seemed far preferable to my incessant thoughts of perfumed court beauties.

"Muirteach," Mariota said sleepily in welcome, sitting up.

"Why are you not with the falcons?" I asked, a little disconcerted to find her there. "Or with the queen and her ladies?"

"The falcons do a bit better. And the queen wished for quiet this day."

"And you?"

"My head aches and I thought to rest awhile."

I saw dark shadows under my wife's eyes. "And is your headache any better the now?"

Mariota smiled. "A little." For a moment we were in harmony, our quarrel forgotten. "And you, Muirteach?"

"I completed His Lordship's charters," I answered, "and spent time with Lord Sinclair."

"Oh. And have you learned anything else that might clear Duncan?"

"And Gudni? No."

Mariota's face fell. "What's going to happen, Muirteach? Duncan must be innocent—"

I scowled. "And there are no signs of anyone else being involved. But come, *mo chridhe*, it will soon be suppertime. The sun has finally shown her face and the afternoon is fair enough. Wash your face and let us walk in the garden a short time before we go to the hall."

Mariota managed another smile and shortly thereafter we left our lodgings. The late afternoon sun was pleasantly warm as we walked the short way to the walled garden. The noise of other voices we heard from outside the walls let us know we would not be alone there.

"Och well," I said as Mariota wrinkled her nose at the sound, "if we wanted privacy we should have stayed in our room."

She tried to laugh and gave a tight nod. "Aye, perhaps we should have, Muirteach," she replied, giving my hand a little squeeze.

I looked at my wife, smiled, and pushed open the gate.

Inside the gardens were several lords and ladies, attended by their maids and a few squires, Peter Leslie among them. I scanned the crowds and saw Lady Ingvilt, richly attired in a blue brocade gown with a red houppelande. Magnus ran wildly in circles nearby while the dark-haired maid, Morag, tried vainly to catch him. Peter sang and strummed at his lute while Ingvilt's red-haired maid, Agnes, now returned to her mistress, sang harmony. She had a pleasing voice.

The song finished, Ingvilt clapped a little, then looked up and saw us.

"Oh, Master MacPhee," she said. "And Mistress MacPhee," she added more slowly.

"We do not mean to intrude," I said, smiling despite my efforts not to. "We but thought to walk in the gardens for a time before the supper gathering, as did these other folk." I gestured towards the others wandering the grounds.

"Oh, it is no intrusion." Ingvilt smiled. "Come and join us."

I could feel Mariota stiffen next to me but I paid that little heed as we joined the party. Peter struck up another tune and began to sing a merry folksong.

"Will you not join in?" Ingvilt urged me. "You have a fine voice."

"Indeed he does," said Mariota, letting go of my arm. She wandered over to a bed of herbs and began to intently examine the angelica and foxglove while I stood next to Peter and Agnes and joined in on the chorus of the ballad—a simple "Fa-la-la-la" and not too hard to learn.

As the song broke up folk clapped and began to chatter, and I thought to take the chance to speak a little more with Peter Leslie, but he, surprisingly, forestalled me by raising the subject first.

"Muirteach, have you learned aught of how poor Malfrid came to have my ring?" Peter asked with all the curious innocence he could muster. The man was either a simpleton or very clever, and as yet I could not be sure which.

I shook my head. "No, I've heard nothing else."

Agnes, who had been standing close by within hearing distance, chimed in, "But, Peter, what ring was this?"

"A gold ring with a chalcedony stone. I lost it some while ago."

"But did not Lady Ingvilt find a ring a few days ago?" Agnes said. "After the party, the night you all came along with the ship's captain—that *puir* lass's father—and that strange dark boy. I mind she found it amongst some cushions. But I did not see it—doubtless she still has it secreted away and will give it to you if you but ask her."

I wondered at that and wandered over with Peter, who insisted he would ask the lady of it this instant, redeem his ring, and clear his own name. Mariota still scrutinized the herbs nearby, with uncommonly focused attention. In the distance I could hear Magnus shriek with glee as Morag tried vainly to catch him.

But Ingvilt looked quite confused when we asked her of the matter, with a blank expression in her green eyes. They cleared after a moment and she smiled. "No, Peter, I am sorry, it was this ring that I found." She extended a white hand to show a little gold ring with a ruby and a pattern of entwined wreaths. "It had slipped off my finger and I found it at last between two cushions in my chamber. And I was heartily glad I did find it, as it is one my dear lord gave me and I value it as much for that as for its beauty."

Peter was no doubt disappointed, yet I felt relief. We returned to Agnes who shrugged her shoulders when Peter told her what Ingvilt had said.

"I'm certain she wore the gold ring all that evening," she said, her nose wrinkling in perplexity for an instant. "Och well, perhaps she did lose it, then. I'm not really knowing for sure. Nor caring," she added, with a pointed glance at Peter. To my mind the girl acted like a jilted lover, but not a murderess.

Mariota meanwhile had rejoined us and listened to this explanation without speaking. It began to grow late. Morag and Magnus stopped their game of tag, Morag looking winded and young Magnus not at all. After one more ballad our merry party left the lovely gardens and entered the hall for supper.

❖   ❖   ❖

That evening as we readied ourselves for bed I fancied my wife looked troubled. I wondered if she still carried a grievance from our earlier quarrel, but was hesitant to raise the subject. She had seemed in good enough spirits at supper. So I said nothing and instead gave her a quick kiss before I closed my eyes.

The next morning Mariota left early, as had become her habit, to visit the birds and see how they fared. I rose and dressed, alone in our rooms, when a loud banging on the door reverberated through the chamber.

"Who knocks?" I cried, hastily finishing the last of my toilette and fastening my *brat* around me with a silver pin.

"Master MacPhee, my mistress has sent me to find your wife." I opened the door and saw Peter Leslie, his handsome blonde face looking overwrought.

"She is with Gudni in his quarters, seeing to the injured bird. But tell me, Peter, what is it?"

"One of the maidservants. Agnes. She fell sick in the night—she does very ill indeed. My lady thought of your wife's skill at healing and sent me to ask for her."

"Well," I repeated, "she is with Gudni. Here, I will go with you to fetch her." I stepped out, closing the door behind me.

The sun, barely risen, had not yet begun to burn through the mist, and the air felt cool. I wrapped my mantle more tightly about me. We walked the short distance to the shed beyond the mews through a muzzy fog while Peter told me what had happened.

"'Tis a bloody flux she has, or so my mistress says. The *puir* lass grew ill in the night, or perhaps it was early morn when she took sick. I am not knowing precisely. But she's very ill."

"Most likely it is nothing serious, just something she ate that disagreed with her. And my wife does have some skill in these matters. Don't fash yourself over it, Peter, no doubt she'll give the girl a posset to settle her stomach and all will be well."

We had reached the shed. I saw Gudni's brow furrow as he greeted us, and wondered if the expression came from concern over his falcons or dislike of Peter Leslie. The squire seemed oblivious to this, and admired the magnificent birds, especially the white female with her still-splinted wing. Despite Gudni's expression I fancied the injured falcon's eyes seemed brighter today. She attempted to flap her wing and screeched as we entered. The uninjured tercel joined in.

Gudni made his soft noises, attempting to quiet the birds. My wife, who'd been intent on re-bandaging one wing despite the gyrfalcon's efforts to confound her in this task, looked up and saw us. Her own face mirrored her confusion as she spoke. Apparently she had not expected to see me.

"Och, Muirteach. And Peter? Whatever is it, then?"

Peter delivered his message. My wife quickly finished the falcon's bandage, tying the linen in a knot, and began gathering her things together.

"Poor lass," I said, "no doubt she's eaten some food that disagreed with her. Too much flummery, no doubt, or marchpane."

"I hope that is all," murmured my wife as we left Gudni with the gyrfalcons and started walking rapidly towards Lady Ingvilt's quarters.

When we arrived we found Lady Ingvilt looking most distraught, her blonde hair falling out of her plaits and across her face. She wore a green houppelande hastily thrown over a fine linen shift.

"I am so glad you are here, Mistress MacPhee," babbled Ingvilt. "I have done everything I could to make the poor girl comfortable."

"Let me see her," my wife said gently.

"Yes, of course. Yes, she is in here," repeated Ingvilt, leading us to an antechamber outside her own bedchamber. A few pallets lay there on the floor, serving as bedding for the maids. On one of them lay Agnes, her body contorted. Sweat beaded her brow, and she looked near as pale as the white linen sheet that lay about her, disarranged by her tossing. Mariota knelt next to the pallet and felt the lass's forehead, took her pulse, examined her eyes and tongue. Agnes stirred and retched violently into a bowl, the bile frothy and green, the stink of it bitter and warm.

I felt my own gorge rise as I watched and forced myself to swallow. "How does she do?" I asked.

"She's very ill, Muirteach. Can someone fetch some hot

water?"

Ingvilt ushered Peter and myself towards the open doorway that led to the outer room of her apartments. "We'd do better out there. Let your wife tend to her, Muirteach, we are just in the way."

Mariota nodded tersely at these words and the three of us left her in the room with Agnes. Peter went to fetch the water while Ingvilt and I stood aimlessly in the outer chamber, trying not to listen to the muted groaning noises we heard through the closed door.

"Where is Magnus?" I asked.

"I feared for him, and had Morag take him out to see the horses," Ingvilt replied. "I could not bear it should the lad pick up some contagion from the lass."

"What did the poor girl eat last night?" I asked. "None of us are sick."

"We had some broth here and poor Agnes suffered a chill later in the evening. I urged her to take some of the broth to warm herself. I hope it had not gone bad. The girl was already shivering, though, so perhaps it was not the broth. She may already have been ill."

"I've heard of no sickness in the castle," Peter commented, after he returned and delivered the pitcher of hot water to Mariota.

"This time of the year the evil humors accumulate with the changing weather," I replied. "At least that is my wife's belief. It is easy to fall sick in the autumn."

Ingvilt brought some wine and we supped it for a time. The morning sun climbed higher, burning slowly through the fog outside and eventually finding its way through the mullioned glass windows into the room. We did not speak much and after some time we realized the noise in the antechamber had ceased. A bit later Mariota emerged from the room, her own face nearly as pale as her patient's had been.

"How does she do? How fares my sweet Agnes?" inquired Ingvilt.

"Somewhat better, I think," Mariota replied. "She sleeps. I gave her some valerian to calm her and stop the spasms, and some tormentil root to stop the flux. I am hopeful the worst of it has passed. What did she eat last night?"

"Just dinner, the same as all of us. Although the lass does have such a taste for sweets! She ate a great deal of the marchpane, I believe. At least she mentioned how tasty it was. But later, once we returned, she had that chill. I gave her some broth we had here, as I just told your husband. Perhaps that is what made her ill. And yet, she was shivering beforehand, so she may already have been sick."

"Perhaps so," Mariota said. "I will leave her to rest for a time. Who here can tend her?"

"I will watch her," Ingvilt said.

"You have no maid to see to her? Are you not tired, milady?" asked Mariota.

"Well, in truth I am fatigued." Ingvilt considered. "Perhaps Morag could keep watch when she returns. I can send Magnus someplace where he shall not be harmed by evil humors. Lady Margery has a son here at court, close to Magnus's age. Magnus could go there until poor Agnes is well recovered. I will take him there myself, Lady Margery will not refuse me."

Just then there was a noise at the door, and Morag returned with Magnus in tow. We heard voices as she admonished her excited charge to be quiet. Eventually, Magnus calmed some and Morag could speak with her mistress. Ingvilt told her of her plans for Magnus and Morag readily agreed to watch over Agnes. She seemed biddable enough, and eager to help her friend.

My wife nodded as the arrangements were completed. "I will leave, then, for a time. If she wakes, give her some more of this tincture in some hot water." She handed a small pottery vial to Morag. "I shall return in a few hours to see how she does."

"I thank you, mistress," Ingvilt said, as she gathered together an extra shift for her son and some of Magnus's toys, "for your kind care of Agnes. I care for all my maids as though they were my own dear daughters."

"No thanks are needed, my lady," my wife replied. "I am pleased she does somewhat better."

"Indeed," said Ingvilt, "as am I." She took a small purse from a casket that sat on a sideboard and handed it to Mariota.

"That is not necessary, my lady," protested my wife.

"No, you must take it. I'll not hear otherwise. I am so very grateful for your care of her."

At length Mariota reluctantly pocketed the money and we left Ingvilt's chambers, descending the narrow staircase to the street.

"What ailed Agnes?" I asked as we walked towards the Great Hall.

"I am not altogether sure, Muirteach," my wife replied. "The poor girl was very ill. I mislike leaving her there."

"You must eat something, *mo chridhe*," I said. "You can see how she does a bit later."

"Yes, and the Lady Ingvilt will also be coming to dine," Mariota said in a quiet voice. "As will the squire. She'll do well enough for now."

The entire vast hall seemed quiet despite the large numbers of folk partaking of the main meal. Perhaps word had gotten round of Agnes's illness and folk were worried of it. We ate quickly and left the hall directly after the meal ended.

Mariota stopped by Ingvilt's to check on Agnes. I was pleased to see her emerge from the lodgings a few moments later with a satisfied smile.

"She still rests easily," my wife said to me. "I hope the worst has passed." A worried frown crossed her face, like a little cloud obscuring the sun. "Yet I believe I shall spend the afternoon with her. I am not altogether comfortable about her. Perhaps we should nurse her in our rooms."

"Why?" I demanded. Our lodging here was small and cramped.

Mariota looked around, as if fearing she might be overheard, and when she spoke her voice was quiet. "Muirteach, I fear the lass was poisoned."

"That's ridiculous!" I scoffed.

"Not so ridiculous. And perhaps Lady Ingvilt might have cause to do so. Or even Peter Leslie."

"What are you saying, Mariota?" I demanded. "You talk like an *amadain*."

My wife flushed angrily at my words. She bit her lip a moment, then continued calmly, as if explaining something to a child. "I am saying, Muirteach, that if Ingvilt, in fact, had taken Peter's ring after he lost it at the gathering, as Agnes thought, then Ingvilt would be the person who gave the ring to Malfrid."

"But the lady denied doing so"

Mariota looked at me as though I were a simpleton. "Anyone can lie, Muirteach."

I refused to believe it. "What of Peter himself? If there is poison involved, why not look to him? And even if Ingvilt did give the ring to Malfrid, that still proves nothing. She might have found it and thought it just a bonny token to give a pretty young maid."

"Or perhaps she murdered Malfrid," suggested my wife. "Or perhaps Peter did, and then poisoned Agnes, afraid she would give him away somehow out of spite and jealousy."

"Mariota, you have gone mad! The Lady Ingvilt is a kind woman!" Mariota said nothing in answer and I continued after a tense moment. "And she has no reason—what possible cause could she have to murder the lass? Peter Leslie could well have wished the lass out of the way. But badly enough to poison her?"

"Aye, Muirteach, it makes no sense does it? What reason would either of them have to murder the girl?" My wife answered my question with more questions.

"And Malfrid was not poisoned," I pointed out.

"No. But do you think a woman cannot use a knife?"

CHAPTER 16

My wife's words disturbed me for all that I thought them foolish. Lady Ingvilt could not have killed Malfrid. She had no reason to. I thought of the lady's concern for Agnes and weighed that against Mariota's suspicions, and I came to the conclusion that my wife was fanciful, overwrought, and overtaken by ill and evil humors, such as were known to often bother women. But Peter Leslie might well be guilty, as there seemed to be bad blood enough between the squire and poor Agnes. I renewed my resolve to watch him closely.

I spoke with the lady herself later that afternoon. I had accompanied Mariota back to see to her patient. Agnes continued to rest comfortably although she slept deeply without waking. In part that may have been due to the sedative and healing draughts my wife continued to give her. Ingvilt had returned to her rooms after seeing Magnus safely ensconced with the Lady Margery.

"The poor girl," Ingvilt repeated to me while Mariota examined Agnes in the next room. "I am so relieved she does better this afternoon."

"It must have been a fright for you," I said, worried at how pale the lady looked.

"Indeed. She was so ill last night that her cries woke me from a sound sleep." Ingvilt rubbed at her eyes. Her hair, now elaborately coiffed and plaited, glistened like white gold in the afternoon sun, although the light did little to disguise the shadows under her lovely green eyes.

"You must be very tired, my lady. You have been sorely tried today."

"Not as sorely tried as my poor maid," Ingvilt replied with a little laugh. "I feel responsible for the lass; she is the daughter of my husband's niece. I swore to her mother I'd take good care of her. She worried so about sending Agnes to court."

"No one could fault your care of the girl, my lady," I replied.

"I hope not," Ingvilt said with a tremor in her voice. "Well, we must leave it to the Blessed Virgin. And to your wife, to see how she recovers."

At this point my wife emerged from the chamber where the sick girl lay.

"How does she, Mistress MacPhee?"

Mariota looked at Ingvilt. I could not help but contrast

their appearance. Lady Ingvilt indeed looked an angel, or like the Blessed Virgin herself. Her fine clothes accentuated the soft curves of her figure. My wife's white coif was mussed and wrinkled, her blue eyes darkly shadowed by worry and fatigue. There was a stain on her overtunic; I did not want to think of what it was.

"She breathes more evenly, my lady," Mariota replied. "She sleeps still. I have hopes she will recover well, but I will remain and watch over her tonight."

"There is no need—" Ingvilt started to say, but my wife quickly dissuaded her.

"I do fear she might take a turn for the worse, and you, my lady, are exhausted, I am sure. Please let me watch over the lass tonight."

At length Ingvilt consented and ordered Morag to make up a pallet for my wife in the anteroom where Agnes lay ill. I knew, from past experience, that it was better not to argue with my wife about such matters and remained silent while this agreement was reached.

"There, *mo chridhe*, you see," I said, unable to resist chiding my wife a bit, "there is no need for any worry. The Lady Ingvilt takes every care for the girl."

At this comment I fancied Ingvilt looked oddly at my wife but the moment quickly passed. As it was but a short time to the evening meal I went back to our room to gather up a few things my wife had requested.

After nearly two years of marriage to one of the medical

Beatons I had gained some skill in telling one herb and tincture from another. I selected the tinctures and herbs Mariota had requested, opium poppy, tormentil, and valerian, all carefully labeled in her clear, somewhat rounded hand, as well as a few other items my wife had requested: her comb, clean shift and such things, and then I went back to Ingvilt's rooms.

Sir Johann had returned from the day's hunt and Ingvilt had already offered him a mazer of hot, spiced hippocras. The drink proved welcome, as the day had continued chill. She offered me one as well and our fingers touched briefly as she handed me the goblet, flashing a quicksilver smile. Magnus remained with Lady Margery and the room seemed pleasantly calm without his prattle, despite the sick lass in the room next to us. Peter Leslie and the dark-haired Morag were also present and we listened to Sir Johann describe the day's sport at length until the time came to leave my wife with her charge and proceed to the Great Hall for supper. Peter himself said little, as befitted a servant, while Sir Johann rambled on, and I learned nothing from the squire's silence that might help me.

Once arrived at the hall, I chanced upon Henry Sinclair, and sat near him. He asked me of my wife. I told him of the maid's illness and my wife's decision to stay with her the night.

"No doubt that is wise," Henry said, his hazel eyes narrowing a bit.

"Aye, she is devoted to her work," I replied. "In that, she takes after her father. Were you knowing that when we spent time in Oxford the foolish woman dressed as a man and tried to attend medical lectures there at the schools?"

"Really!" Henry was clearly astounded. "And what came of that?"

"Nothing good," I said darkly, reaching for some fish in sauce.

After the meal ended I accompanied Lady Ingvilt and Sir Johann back to their lodgings, and stopped by briefly to speak with Mariota. Ingvilt's chambers had not their usual liveliness that night; the lady herself pleaded exhaustion and retired to her curtained bed in the inner chamber early, along with her lord. So I too retired to my own room and bed, in our lodgings across the way, although images of the fair Ingvilt locked in the embrace of her elderly husband prevented me from sleeping for some time. I took myself to task, told myself sternly that I was a married man, and that surely I loved my wife despite her stubborn nature. Yet still, thoughts of Ingvilt's soft white limbs entwined with those of her lord inflamed my lust, and I confess I did but little to fight them. I tossed and turned, and found myself awake when the crow of the cock heralded the coming of morning.

❖   ❖   ❖

I must have eventually fallen back asleep after that, there being no one else in my bed to disturb me, and I woke again somewhat later. A grey cold morning light filled the room and I heard the drumming of falling rain outside. I felt curiously ill at ease; the last remnants of some unpleasant dream fell away from me as I rubbed the grit of sleep from my eyes, washed my face and hands, and dressed.

My Lord of the Isles had hunted along with the king and his nobles the day before but this morning the rain fell from thick leaden skies and I suspected he would be wanting me to wait upon him. I proved not disappointed in this; he hailed me as I left my room and ordered me to attend upon him after breaking my fast. He had heard, from Sir Johann most likely, of the maid's illness and appeared unsurprised to hear my wife nursed the lass.

"She is skillful, your wife. And intelligent as well, for a woman. Although she is headstrong. She minds me of her father at times."

"I fear her father is more biddable, sire," I said. His Lordship laughed and preceded me out of our lodgings and through the driving rain to the Great Hall.

It had grown late and I felt famished, so I did not check on my wife and her patient. I thought to ask Peter Leslie when I saw him in the hall. I found him busy filling the basins for folk to wash their hands after eating.

"I know not, Muirteach," he said. "I sleep with the other squires, not in my lord's chambers, and I did not attend on my lord this morning."

Just then I saw the lord and his lady enter the hall, her hand resting lightly on his arm, her bright red houppelande flowing gracefully, a vivid and pleasant spot of color on this dreary day. Ingvilt saw me and flashed a smile; I fancied, however, that the smile looked taut and strained. They proceeded to their seats at the high table and I found my own place at the lower table.

Immediately after breaking my fast His Lordship beckoned to me, and so it was not until much later in the morning that I was free to seek out my wife and the Lady Ingvilt. However, when I reached her chambers the lady herself was not there and it seemed unnaturally quiet. No one answered my knock, but the heavy door was unlocked and it pushed open at my touch.

"Mariota?" I called.

The door to the inner chamber opened and my wife emerged, her face white.

"Mariota, what is it?" I asked, shaken at the sight of her face.

"Agnes is dead, Muirteach," my wife replied. "She died this morning, while the others were at the hall breaking their fast."

"And the Lady Ingvilt?"

Something, it could have been annoyance, flashed across my wife's face before she spoke. "She waits upon the queen this morning. She and her husband have spoken of returning to his own properties, in the north, and leaving court soon. I think they fear contagion."

"And you, *mo chridhe*?" I asked belatedly. "How are you?" I crossed the space between us and took my wife in my arms. But Mariota remained stiff and did not relax, and, after a moment, I let her go. "How do you do?" I repeated.

"You know I do not like to lose patients, Muirteach," my

wife replied tartly. "And I am exhausted. How do you think I am?"

"Can you not rest now?"

"They are to come and remove the body to the chapel," Mariota replied. "I think it will be soon. It was terrible, Muirteach," she continued after a moment. "I thought she was improving, all the signs pointed to it. And I fell asleep for a time but then, before dawn, I awoke and the poor lass was retching again, doubled up with cramps. I did what I could but it was not enough. And Muirteach—"

"What, *mo chridhe*?"

Mariota looked at me a moment. Then her lips tightened. "Och, it is nothing."

"Let me see the body," I said, and I followed my wife into the chamber where Agnes's corpse lay still on a pallet.

Although my wife had cleaned and neatened the body, I could see a bit of frothy liquid still visible, drying on the girl's lips. A basin of cloudy water sat on the floor near the pallet, with a rag in it that Mariota had doubtless used to wash the poor lass. Agnes's face looked greyish pale in death and even her brilliant hair seemed not to shine so brightly. Mariota had closed the girl's eyes and, although Agnes did not look entirely peaceful, at least I found some comfort in the thought that her soul no longer suffered great pain.

A vial stood on a chest next to a clay cup. I recognized it as the one Mariota had given to Morag the day before. Some of Mariota's other tinctures and her medical satchel also lay on the chest. Mariota looked at the corpse and her eyes filled with tears. "I couldn't save her, Muirteach. Such a young lass, and I couldn't save her."

"No," I said. "I'm so sorry, dear heart." Sadly I closed the door and Mariota and I returned to the outer room.

"Leave me, Muirteach. I will return to our rooms and rest later, after they—" Mariota swallowed a moment before she continued, "after they come and collect the corpse."

So at length, I left my wife there alone and went to check on Gudni.

❖   ❖   ❖

Duncan Tawesson still rotted in the dungeon below the guard tower and as yet I knew of nothing that might release him. I could not face him, but had promised my wife I would check on the falcons. I dragged myself, all unwilling, to the shed past the mews where I recognized, with some surprise, Gybb Saylor sitting along with Gudni.

"Muirteach," Gybb greeted me. "Gudni is thinking of taking the remainder of the stores back to the ship. The birds are well enough to travel, he says. And his father still rots in prison here for the murder of his foster sister."

"Fine I know that," I replied churlishly, feeling renewed guilt that I had not yet proved Duncan's innocence.

"No, now, Muirteach," Gybb said placatingly when he saw my expression. "I did not mean to fash you."

"But all you said was true," I admitted miserably. "I've

failed to find Malfrid's killer. And your father will most likely hang for my failure." Gudni said nothing and at first I wasn't sure if he'd understood. "He'll die."

Gudni nodded. He had heard me, and understood. Gybb also nodded. "He understands you, fine enough. Whoever did this is a wily enemy and we must stalk them with cunning. But for now Gudni wants to return to his ship. He commands the *Selkiesdottir* now."

Gudni spoke up suddenly. "I want to be on the sea. It too close here, too closed up."

I nodded. Perhaps the key to Malfrid's murder was not to be found here at all. Perhaps it lay to the north, or in the mysterious lands to the west Henry and Duncan had spoken of. And perhaps Gudni would find it, sailing that mysterious sea.

My stomach growled, putting a stop to my ponderings. "Have you eaten?" I asked. Both men shook their heads no. "It will be time to dine in an hour or so, and I doubt they'll mind an extra mouth or two. We can wait here until then."

We passed the rest of the time playing knucklebones. Gybb played well and Gudni possessed an ability to bluff that served him in good stead. They won every penny I had on me. Gybb produced a flask of *uisge beatha* and the hour passed in a warm haze.

When the time came to eat Gybb and I left Gudni crooning to his birds with the promise to bring him some victuals. He had refused to leave them and did not seem to miss the crowds in the hall. He preferred the solitude of the shed and the company of his birds. I stopped by our room and found Mariota sleeping soundly, her hair tousled about her face and the blanket bunched up about her. She did not wake, and neither did I wake her. I returned to Gybb, who waited outside, and we continued our somewhat unsteady procession to the Great Hall.

"Muirteach," Gybb said suddenly, "where is the wee lass buried? I'd like to see Malfrid's grave."

"Aye, and with all my money you've won you can afford to pay for some masses for her soul," I observed darkly.

Gybb laughed but he stopped laughing when we halted by the grave outside the chapel.

"Poor lassie. She was like a ray of bright sunshine on that old ship. Always smiling and kind, she be."

The mounded grave still looked fresh. Someone, my wife, or perhaps Gudni, had placed a few Michaelmas daisies on the dirt, their wilted violet petals pale against the dark loam.

After a few moments in silence we continued to the hall. Henry Sinclair hailed us, and we told him of Gudni's decision to go back to sea. He nodded. "There's naught for him here."

"And what of his father?" I inquired, belligerent.

"Most likely Duncan cares not if he lives or dies now," Henry replied. This accorded with what Duncan himself had told me, so I did not argue the point and guiltily berated myself again, both for Malfrid's murder and for not having yet found the clue that would free her father. Lady Ingvilt saw me and flashed a smile, and I forced myself to smile back at her as we made our way to our places at the lower table to the left of the dais. In such a throng one more person was not unduly noted; I explained that Gybb was one of Gudni's men and that satisfied the steward. We washed our hands, sat, and began to eat once the servants brought food to the table.

Gybb ate with single-minded intensity. The unfamiliar setting did not disrupt his appetite for the pottage of leek and chicken, the stewed eels and the cold venison, a leftover from the main meal at noon. At length the king and queen rose to leave the hall, the signal the feast had ended. We rose to leave as well.

As we left the hall I caught the Lady Ingvilt's eye and smiled at her. She smiled back and I felt desire for her swell within me as I remembered her sweet touch during the game of blind man's bluff. Mariota had said that Ingvilt and Sir Johann would soon leave court. The lady looked pale and I hoped Agnes's illness would not spread to her mistress.

I had thought our glances went unobserved, but I am not a courtier, skilled in deceit. And Gybb Saylor was an observant man.

"Who be that fine lady you were smiling at?" he asked as we walked back to the shed with some manchet bread and roast venison for Gudni.

"That was the Lady Ingvilt, the one who has been so kind to us while we've been here. The lady herself was once at the Norwegian court."

"Was she indeed?" Gybb looked thoughtful.

"Aye."

"She minds me of someone," Gybb muttered. "I can't think of who."

"She is originally from Greenland, I believe, but left when she was young. Perhaps she has the look of the folk there." Most Norse I knew seemed to have blonde hair and looked similar to each other.

"That must be the way of it," Gybb agreed as we reached the shed beyond the mews.

As soon as we handed him his dinner Gudni fell to eating eagerly. We spoke of playing another round of dice when we heard voices and saw shadows at the door. I looked up, surprised, as the door opened. "It is the Lady Ingvilt. And Peter Leslie," I said.

"Hello, Muirteach," the lady greeted me, her eyes lingering on my face until I felt a warm flush rise up my cheeks.

"My lady," I replied. "And Peter. Welcome," I continued, ignoring the glare Gudni briefly flashed in Peter's direction. Perhaps the squire had not noticed it. I went forward and kissed the lady's hand, feeling it soft and yielding beneath my own.

"I thought to come and see how the injured bird is faring," Ingvilt murmured. "Such magnificent creatures they are."

"She improves, my lady," I replied. "Is that not so, Gudni?" The lad muttered assent. He was shy, I realized suddenly. "I am grieved to learn of your maid," I continued.

"We are all grieved, are we not, Peter? Perhaps I sought some diversion by coming here," Ingvilt added, looking frankly at me. Again I noticed those golden flecks glimmering in the cool green of her irises. "My chambers are not the same without sweet Agnes. They seem gloomy and cold." Ingvilt smiled briefly. "And I thank your goodwife, Master MacPhee."

"She is desolate she could not save Agnes. My wife mislikes losing patients."

"Where is your wife?"

"She rests now in our chamber."

"I brought a little gift for her, Muirteach. A perfume I thought she would enjoy." The lady pulled a small vial from the bag that hung from her girdle and handed it to me.

"I will insure she receives it, my lady."

"And give her my thanks as well. It is a shame she had not the skill to save poor Agnes. But perhaps no one could have done so. Now, how do the birds get on?"

Ingvilt and Gudni examined the birds. I watched the boy come out of his shell a bit as he showed his charges to her, Ingvilt charming him with her interest in the raptors.

"And who is this?" asked Ingvilt after she had looked at the falcons.

I introduced Gybb Saylor. "My lady," the old man said, greeting her courteously enough.

"Gybb has sailed with Gudni's father for many years."

"Indeed? But then, Duncan Tawesson is not truly the boy's father. Did he not say he found the lad? But even so,"

Ingvilt said, flashing a smile in Gybb's direction, "you know the northlands."

"Aye, my lady. I sailed with Duncan on his early trips to Greenland. I was there when he met Malfrid's mother. In Saemundsfiord, that was."

"A great many years ago, that would have been. Was it not?"

Gybb nodded. "The lass, Malfrid, was close to fifteen, so it is nigh onto sixteen years it must be now."

"Well, we must hope the true killer is found and your master released with all speed," Ingvilt said. "Come, Peter, we must go. It grows late and my lord awaits me. Will you accompany us, Muirteach?"

CHAPTER 17

Flattered, I departed with Ingvilt and Peter, leaving Gudni and Gybb playing knucklebones by lantern light.

Outside it had grown dark. Peter carried a lantern. Ingvilt took my arm and I found the lingering touch of her fingers on my sleeve sent little thrills down my spine.

"So, my lady, you are to leave the court, I hear?"

"Aye. My husband fears contagion." Ingvilt gave a little shiver as she spoke.

"Your poor maid. I will pray for her soul's repose."

"She was a pleasant, lively girl. I shall miss her sorely."

"When will you leave?"

"My lord has some business to conclude, so we shall most likely leave a day hence."

"And where are his estates?" I asked.

"To the north and west. Near Aberdeen. A lonely place. And my lord is often occupied while we are there." She sighed a little sigh. "But I must go where my lord bids me."

"I am sure you also are busy while you are there."

"Yes, there is much to manage." Ingvilt laughed, and ran a pink tongue over her lips. "I prefer life at court, to be truthful."

I swallowed, my throat suddenly dry. "I have little experience with court life." I gazed into her eyes, losing myself for a moment in the vast green of them, like the cool waters of the northern sea. "Although I have enjoyed my days here, my lady. Court life is most diverting."

Ingvilt's laugh tinkled again through the darkness of the night. "Indeed, it can be, Muirteach. It can be most diverting."

We reached the lodgings and I bade the lady goodnight, taking her hand and pressing it once again to my lips; savoring her scent, the soft feel of her flesh beneath her gloves. The moment seemed to last for a lifetime. Then the door of Ingvilt's lodging clanged shut, like the gates of heaven closing against the damned, and I turned forlornly and went across the street to my own lodgings and my own wife.

❖   ❖   ❖

Mariota stirred sleepily as I entered the room and clumsily knocked into an empty chamber pot with a clatter.

"It's you," she murmured.

"Did you get some rest?" I asked as I took off my mantle.

"I slept for a long while. It was dark when I awoke for a

time, but then I drifted off again. And you?"

"I stopped by before the evening meal, dear heart, but you were sleeping sound and I did not wish to wake you."

"Yes, I feel better." My wife's face darkened. "Unlike poor Agnes."

"A sad thing," I observed.

"Muirteach," my wife said abruptly, "there is something about the girl's death that troubles me. She was improving, I know she was. Then suddenly her condition worsened."

"Cannot that happen, *mo chridhe*?"

"Her symptoms were strange. I fear she was poisoned."

That again. Irritated, I answered without care. "How ridiculous! You spoke of this before, *mo chridhe*. But who could wish to poison Agnes? And who could have done so? I doubt Peter Leslie had the opportunity. You yourself kept watch over the lass."

"Muirteach, you are an *amadan*!" My wife sat up in bed, wide awake now. "You do not see it, do you?"

Being called a fool has never improved my temper. "What do you think happened, then?" I said shortly, biting the words out.

"I have already as good as told you. Och, never mind, Muirteach. You must be tired, and I am as well. We'll speak of it in the morning." With that, Mariota, rolled over, her face to the wall, and closed her eyes. Whether she slept or not, I do not know. I only know that I myself did not sleep, not for a long time, but lay there in the darkness, thinking not of my wife, but guiltily of someone else's golden hair, throaty voice, and musky scent.

❖   ❖   ❖

The next morning when I awoke I found Mariota already up and dressed.

"I believe Gudni intends to move things back to the *Selkiesdottir* today," I said, "despite the king's request that he remain here."

"That was before Malfrid's death," my wife pointed out. "Ah well, then, I shall go and speak with him, and see how my patient fares before she is taken away," she added, with a tight laugh. Then she left, closing the door behind her.

I rose and dressed as well, finding in my bag the gift Ingvilt had given me for Mariota. I set it out on the table, thinking it would please Mariota to find it, all unexpected, when she returned.

My morning ablutions completed, I left our lodgings and headed out into the bustle of the castle mount. I spied Gudni and Gybb Saylor loading a cart near the shed and went to greet them.

"Peter Leslie just left here," said Gudni. "He brought gift." He gestured towards Gybb. "Whisky. From the lady."

"Aye," Gybb said, wiping at his mouth after taking a sip. "That lady still minds me of someone. Perhaps Malfrid's mother, that might be it. Perhaps they were kin, in Greenland." He took another draught from the flask. "But I asked her, when we spoke last night. She said her folk were not from Saemundsfiord. She is a kind lady, and lovely. Very thoughtful." Gybb drank again. "Are you wanting some, Muirteach?"

It was still early in the day, the sun just cresting the roofs of the many buildings on the castle mount.

I laughed. "Nay, Gybb. It is still early yet. But I thank you."

Gudni made a face. "The lad hasn't the taste for *uisge beatha*," Gybb joked. "He prefers good ale, do you not?"

Gudni made a face again, then nodded. "Don't like whisky," he said. "In Greenland, no whisky. Not even ale. Just goat milk."

Gybb chortled, then coughed and spat some phlegm out on the ground. He winced.

"Are you unwell?" I asked.

"'Tis naught, a gas pain most like." He belched. "There. Now come and help me, Gudni. We'd best get this cart loaded before the sun rises much higher."

"So you're returning to the *Selkiesdottir*?" I asked Gudni. "What of your father?"

Gudni's shoulders slumped and his face darkened. "Too sad here," he said.

"We'll remain in port until all is decided," Gybb interjected.

"Until my father is released," Gudni added, staring at me in a way that made me feel very guilty. For neither Robert Cruickshanks nor I had anything new to report. Guiltily I realized that indeed, in the past days I had spent much more time thinking on the charms of Lady Ingvilt than on who could have slain poor Malfrid.

And was Gudni truly free of suspicion? There was no convincing proof, and even if Gudni had killed Malfrid, Duncan seemed little inclined to turn against his own foster son. Still, did not Gudni's desire to leave now, with his own foster father still imprisoned, put the lad under a cloud?

"Was my wife here earlier?" I finally asked.

Gudni smiled.

"Indeed," replied Gybb. "She came by to see to the birds, and then bid us a pretty fare-thee-well. She is a fine woman." Gybb coughed again and spat.

I needed no one to sing my wife's praises to me on this morning and may have scowled a bit. "I fear you grow ill, Gybb."

"It's naught, as I've told you," Gybb insisted, shoving a bale of dark brown pelts onto the cart. "We'll get a good price for these, Gudni, in Saint Andrews. Or perhaps in Aberdeen."

"Did the queen buy all the white fox pelts?" I asked, thinking idly that two of those pelts would make a fine gift. For my wife, or perhaps for Ingvilt before she left the court.

"They are sold," Gudni replied. "To the queen herself. Just bearskin left, and these western pelts." He gestured to the brown pelts, with thicker shaggy fur on portions of them.

"What animal is that?" I asked. I'd never seen anything like them.

Gudni shrugged. "Like a bear, or a cow. A big animal. From far to the west. We traded for them with the Skraelings."

They looked to be warm pelts, but they were soon obscured by another parcel of what looked like walrus tusks and another bale of wadmal. Nearby, the cages with the two remaining gyrfalcons sat, waiting to be loaded onto the cart. "Well, I shall leave you to get on with it," I said. "I must go and find my wife."

"Aye," replied Gybb. "Farewell then, Muirteach."

Gudni just waved as I turned and left them. I walked back to our lodgings where I found my wife organizing the supplies in her medical bag.

"What is this, Muirteach?" she asked, holding up the vial I had left on the table.

"A perfume. A gift—"

Mariota's face lightened and she opened the vial and sniffed. "Och, Muirteach, it smells so lovely!" she said before I could finish my sentence. "Thank you!"

I had been about to say that Lady Ingvilt had given it to me for her, but my wife's delight in the gift, thinking it was from me, was so great that I selfishly let it go.

Mariota embraced me with none of the restraint she had shown over the past few days. She smelled the perfume again and smiled. "It is a lovely scent, Muirteach. Where did you ever find it?" Without waiting for me to answer she dabbed some of it on her neck and a flowery scent filled the air, roses and something more unusual that I could not place. "Thank you again, *mo chridhe*. Shall we go to break our fast?"

A few moments later we entered the Great Hall, and found Henry Sinclair finishing his breakfast.

"My lady," said Henry, kissing Mariota's hand. My wife blushed a little, but smiled. "What is this new perfume?" he asked.

"A gift," Mariota murmured. "From my husband."

"Delightful," Henry said. "I must kiss your hand again just to smell it one more time." He did so, and Mariota reddened again, smiling. "I will have to find some for my Jennet. And when do you depart?" Henry asked us.

"I believe my lordship's business with the king grows close to conclusion. Perhaps in a few days, I am not knowing for sure."

Henry nodded. "And Sir Johann and his lady depart soon as well?" Mariota made a little grimace that I elected not to notice.

"I believe the death of her maidservant has distressed her sorely. As it did my wife," I added, seeing Mariota's wounded expression. "She tended the lass."

Henry looked serious. "It is indeed sad. What illness did the girl die from, mistress?"

Mariota bit her lip. "She had a flux. I thought she improved; indeed she *had* improved, but that last night she grew worse again. And I could not save her." She looked as though she wanted to say more, but then stopped. My wife's merry mood of a few moments earlier had vanished like the sun obscured by a dark cloud.

"I am sorry, mistress," Henry said quickly. "It was not my intent to distress you."

Mariota shrugged sadly. "The poor lass will be buried today. I shall attend the mass. Muirteach, will you accompany me?"

"Of course," I offered gallantly, although I fear I thought less of Agnes's soul or how a poisoner could have contrived her murder, and more of the possibility that Lady Ingvilt would attend her maid's burial mass as well.

"And what of Duncan Tawesson?" asked Henry, evidently all too eager to bring up another unpleasant topic. "He remains in custody?"

"Aye, and Gudni and Gybb Saylor plan to leave today and return to the *Selkiesdottir*. Which I find to be a curious thing," I answered.

"You cannot fault Gudni, Muirteach," put in my wife hotly. "It is melancholy indeed for him here, with his poor sister dead and his own father rotting unjustly in the dungeons for the murder."

I winced, finding my wife's words unduly sharp, and they stung me to the quick. "Don't act the shrew, Mariota," I responded harshly, before I thought better of it. I winced again as I saw her complexion pale, then flush red, and her eyes fill with tears. "Forgive me, *mo chridhe*. I did not mean it," I hastened to say. "I am sorry."

Mariota nodded, her face taut, but our previous harmony had vanished completely. We finished our bread and cheese, bade Henry farewell, and walked out of the hall, together, yet leagues apart.

CHAPTER 18

s we returned to our lodgings in strained silence I saw Gudni's hired cart still standing half-loaded, and wondered at that, as I had thought Gybb and Gudni would have been well on their way by now. And my surprise increased when we reached the entry to our chamber and I saw Gudni squatting in front of the door, his face solemn.

"Mistress, you must come," he said to Mariota.

"What is it, Gudni?"

"Gybb. He ill. Very sick."

I thought of the cough I had heard earlier. "He sounded as though he was catching a chill this morning."

Mariota glared at me but did not reply, busy gathering her supplies together. "I shall see you later, Muirteach," she finally said as she completed her task. "If you are not here I shall look for you in Lady Ingvilt's chambers." And with that parting shot she followed Gudni out the door and down the stairs.

I hoped Gybb had not succumbed to whatever illness had killed Agnes. However, there was little I could do about that. As the day was chill and His Lordship had no need of me I found myself somewhat at loose ends. Obviously, my wife did not want my help; she had made that clear enough. So I wandered out of our lodgings and somehow my path led me across the street to Ingvilt's rooms. I told myself the lady simply enjoyed my company and my conversation, and that my wife had little understanding of the niceties of life here at the king's court, despite her time with the queen and her ladies.

I climbed the stairs and knocked on the door. The noise reverberated through the landing but I heard no answer. Feeling oddly disconsolate I turned to leave and was just about to descend the staircase when the door opened behind me. I spun around.

Ingvilt stood in the open doorway. Her hair, unplaited, fell about her shoulders like a shower of white gold. The long blue cotehardie she wore had a few buttons undone at the top, showing the creamy flesh of her neck and a bit of her delicate linen shift.

"Muirteach—" She stood aside to let me in.

"My lady," I said, kissing her wrist, hoping I acted like the most experienced of courtiers. "I did not think to find you here."

"Indeed I am, although so busy. We are packing furiously.

I have just sent Peter Leslie and Morag for extra trunks, and Magnus begged to go along. The trunks are stored in one of the back buildings. They will be gone some time, I imagine."

"And Sir Johann?" I asked.

"He is with the king. He also will be gone some time."

"Oh." Close together as we were in the doorway, I could smell her perfume.

"But I forget myself, Muirteach," murmured Ingvilt. Her voice was so soft, nearly a whisper. I had to bend my head close to hers to catch her words. "You must come in."

The door shut behind us. I stared at her like some drowning man for a moment, and then, suddenly, Ingvilt filled my arms. My hands gripped her hair, and our lips met. She nipped at my lips like a fox; I tasted blood. The salty taste fueled the fire of my ardor and I thought of nothing else.

❖   ❖   ❖

I could not say how much later it was that Ingvilt pulled away from my caress.

"What is it, my love?" I mumbled.

"Muirteach, you must straighten your clothing. They will be returning."

The full realization of what I had just nearly done hit me like a blow to my guts. "My lady, I—"

"Ssh," Ingvilt said, putting a soft white finger on my lips. "Don't say anything. But you must leave. My lord returns and he can be jealous—although we've done nothing wrong."

"Nothing wrong?"

"We've but caressed each other, and kissed a bit," Ingvilt replied in a disturbingly matter-of-fact manner. "We've not lain together."

Guilt gnawed at me. I thought of my own father, whose lust had ruined so many lives. And I thought of my wife. Hurriedly I straightened my clothing and bade Ingvilt goodbye. Our final kiss lingered on my lips like the taste of her fine Rhenish wine but, like too much wine, left a sour feeling in my gut.

❖ ❖ ❖

I returned to our room, my steps leaden. I felt an ache in the pit of my belly as I pushed open the door, and saw our chamber empty. Mariota was not there.

Shamed, I let out a sigh of relief. I did not yet have to face my wife. But where had she gone?

Perhaps she still tended to Gybb Saylor with Gudni, although the old man doubtless had just a touch of some evil humor. Their cart still sat in the street near the shed, abandoned despite the furs and goods stacked on it. I resolved to go and find out the news, in spite of the gnawing discomfort I felt at the thought of seeing my wife.

As I neared the shed I heard loud groaning, and the sounds of someone retching. Gybb Saylor did not seem to be recovering quickly. I entered and found Mariota kneeling next to a straw pallet on which Gybb lay, nearly bent double with the force of his convulsions. Gudni sat near the gyrfalcon's cage, his face solemn, crooning again to his birds who seemed agitated by the patient in their midst.

"Mariota," I called. My wife, intent on sponging Gybb's pallid face, had not heard me enter. At the sound of my voice she looked up and shook her head.

"He's dying, Muirteach. I fear he is dying." Her blue eyes were filled with tears and remorse washed over me like ocean waves breaking on a rocky coast. How had I come to betray my sweet wife?

Gybb writhed and moaned, gone far beyond hearing our words.

"*Mo chridhe*, tell me what to do."

"Bring me some more water from that pitcher there; fill the basin. Perhaps if I sponge him off—I've given him emetic herbs, he seemed better for a time, then he worsened. I fear he is poisoned."

And if he was indeed poisoned, where might that have come from? Like shards of broken pottery I began to piece together a picture and it was not a pretty one. For Peter Leslie had brought the old man the flask of whisky. He might have had cause to murder Agnes. But what reason would he have to murder a sailor?

I filled the basin and brought it to my wife. Gybb's eyes remained closed, his breath shallow, his heartbeat rapid. She poured a little vinegar in the water and continued sponging Gybb's limbs. His teeth chattered, yet he still sweated copiously. His eyes opened, then rolled back in his head and I could see little except the whites, with broken blood vessels spotting them as he strained.

At length Gybb quieted. His breathing grew shallow, as faint as a swallow's wing. Gudni watched wild-eyed. I looked at the lad and tried to smile. He just gazed back at me, biting his lips.

Mariota glanced up at me for a second, her face grim. I could see droplets of sweat on her forehead from her efforts, her face flushed and her eyes intent as she turned her attention back to her patient. She saw me watching and shook her head again. Gudni observed silently; the falcons also sat quiet now, watching with wide and feral eyes.

Gybb gave one last breath, a little breath, like the last grain of sand falling from an hourglass. Then he was gone.

Mariota felt for his pulse, and held a small mirror up to his nose. Gybb's face was pale and still, all animation gone. His soul had left his body. I fancied I heard the rustle of wings as it escaped to heaven—or hell, perhaps, for it was little enough I knew of the state of Gybb Saylor's soul. But I knew a bit of mine, this afternoon, and I shuddered at the knowledge.

Mariota wiped the tears from her cheeks and took a faltering breath. Then she sighed deeply and, after a moment, closed Gybb's sightless eyes. She straightened his limbs and began to wash the body while Gudni looked on. Gudni also had tears in his eyes.

"I am all alone. There is no one," he said.

The thought of his foster father in the dungeons did not

ease my mind. I too had once been a lonely boy, at loose ends once I left my place in the monastery, sensible only of my isolation. But I had had a place with my uncle Gillespic.

"You'll come to Islay with us," Mariota said briskly to Gudni after a moment. "You'd be welcome, would he not, Muirteach?"

I nodded.

"But perhaps your father will yet be freed," my wife continued, "for I am thinking that neither Gybb nor Agnes died from a simple flux. No one else here has been taken ill."

I shook my head, outwardly calm, although my heart began racing like some cornered wild thing. I tried to swallow my panic away, not wanting to entertain my own growing suspicions, let alone those of my wife. "Mariota, you just do not like to lose patients, that is all of it. There was no poison here."

"If you are truly believing that, Muirteach, then take a drink of the whisky left in the flask that Peter gave to Gybb this morning," returned my wife, her voice like cold iron.

Coward that I am, and painfully aware of my failings, I found I could not do it. I held the flask in my hand and shook my head.

"No, Mariota. I cannot."

Gudni had watched this exchange in silence. He rose and went outside, still without speaking a word. Which left Mariota and myself opposite each other, on either side of Gybb's corpse.

"You are thinking that both Agnes and Gybb died of poison, are you not?"

My wife nodded.

"And Peter brought Gybb the flask of whisky."

"He claimed it was a gift from Ingvilt," Mariota replied.

"He could have lied, and brought it himself. But what reason would Peter to do such a thing?" I asked obstinately.

"Muirteach," my wife replied in a cold, tired voice, "I do not believe it was Peter. Was not Agnes saying the lady had found a ring? Perhaps it was Peter's ring she found."

"Which would mean Ingvilt gave it to Malfrid."

"Or planted it on her after she was already dead," my wife began.

"Ridiculous," I retorted weakly. "Lady Ingvilt could not have knifed Malfrid."

"Why not, Muirteach?" my wife cried. "Because of her lovely face? Her alluring scent? You think those white hands could not use a knife—or break a falcon's neck?"

I watched the cracks in my gilded castle, like some *sotelty* at a great feast, begin to widen and the pieces fall and crumble at my feet. But I was still too stubborn to admit as much to my wife.

"I do not believe you," I repeated mulishly. "I am convinced it must be the squire. He brought the drink himself, and lied about the lady's involvement. To hide his own guilt. What reason would the lady have to knife Malfrid, a lass she'd never even seen before a week ago?"

"Perhaps it is Duncan she meant to hurt," my wife replied, a little calmer now.

"But why?" I persisted.

"Is she not from Greenland? And this poor man said she minded him of someone he once met, did he not? The answer lies there, Muirteach. The answer lies to the north."

Loath as I was to admit it, my wife's words had some truth to them. But I refused to tell her this, or perhaps I could not quite give up my gilded dreams.

"I will ask her, then. I will go and see the lady and ask her. For I do not believe you, Mariota."

"Well, you can no longer ask Agnes, can you, Muirteach? Her innocence is proved by her death. Or this poor old man? He'll be answering no questions now."

"Someone will have to notify the guards. He'll need to be buried. I will go and tell them of the death, and leave you to tend the corpse," I said, my own voice cold now, and I left my wife alone with the dead man in the mews.

❖　❖　❖

Mariota's words, like some corrosive poison, worked their way into my mind, widening the cracks in the glittering surface of my desire. I felt her suspicions seep through my thoughts as I walked towards the guardhouse.

It could not be possible. Ingvilt had no reason to poison Gybb. She did not even know the man. And to poison her own maidservant—it was preposterous. And yet—

If the answer lay to the north, we would not find it. It had died along with Gybb Saylor.

By this time I had reached the guardhouse. Robert Cruickshanks and a few of his men sat inside, drinking some ale and playing at knucklebones again.

"Muirteach, what brings you here? Have you found that one piece of evidence yet that will free Duncan Tawesson?" Cruickshanks's tone was almost jovial as he greeted me. For myself, I did not feel in a jovial mood and with effort suppressed my urge to belt him in the face.

"No," I answered shortly. "There's been another death. My wife suspects poison, although I think it more likely to be the same flux that killed the maidservant. But whatever killed the man, the body needs burying."

Cruickshanks turned his head laconically to one of his men. "You, Tam, get the shovel. And you, Uisdean," he continued, looking at my slight frame and crippled leg. "Take the body to the chapel and inform the priest. Dig the grave. It's late already and the burial can take place tomorrow if that suits Father Benneit."

Tam and Uisdean put down the dice and departed on their errand. "You said your wife suspects poison?" Cruickshanks asked after they left.

"Yes."

"Who does she suspect?"

"Perhaps foolishly, she suspects the Lady Ingvilt. The dead woman served as Lady Ingvilt's maid. But I suspect the squire, Peter Leslie. He brought Gybb Saylor, the old man who died today, a flask of *uisge beatha* the morning he died. Peter claimed it was a gift from the lady, but it could just as easily have come from him."

Cruickshanks's eyes narrowed. "Who is that man? Gybb Saylor? I've not heard his name. And why should either of those two give him whisky?"

I shrugged, uncomfortable with the conversation. I explained who Gybb was and why he'd been at the castle mount. And then I told Cruickshanks how Peter claimed the Lady Ingvilt had sent the man the flask of whisky. "I think she said it was for old times' sake, as they both had spent time in Greenland." I shifted my weight, wishing to be gone from this place. Now I had not only betrayed my wife, in thought if not totally in deed, I was about to betray Ingvilt as well. "But Peter could have poisoned the drink, even if it did come from Ingvilt. Or perhaps both the maid and the sailor died of the flux," I put in hopefully.

Cruickshanks looked grim. "No one else has been ill that I know of. Yet the Lady Ingvilt—what reason would she possibly have to poison her maid, and an old sailor man? And Peter Leslie would have no reason to poison a sailor, although perhaps he wished to be rid of that saucy maid."

"I have no idea. That is why I am inclined to think it was only mischance. Yet Sir Johann intends to leave the court and go to his own lands, fearing contagion, after the death of the maid."

"And there is nothing to prove the lady has done this," Cruickshanks said, echoing my own thoughts. "Although we could have what's left in the flask tested."

"Aye. But that will not tell us who put the poison in the flask. And if they both leave with Sir Johann there'll be no way to learn if either one is responsible, or not."

"You are friendly with the lady, are you not, Muirteach?"

How had Cruickshanks known of that? But I nodded, a sinking feeling in my gut.

"See what you can discover. Perhaps if you speak with her the lady will let something slip. For we could not hold her without some proof, despite your wife's suspicions. Where is the flask of whisky?"

"My wife must still have it, I suppose." I should have thought to bring it with me.

"Get it from her, "Cruickshanks ordered. "We'll feed it to a cat and see if it dies."

I left and went to our rooms where I found my wife awake and putting a few things away. Tam and Uisdean had already taken Gybb's corpse to the chapel. I told Mariota what Cruickshanks wanted while she washed her face and smoothed her hair.

"Of course, I have it here. I shall take it to him," Mariota said, reaching for her linen coif and rearranging it about her head.

"No need, dear heart. I can take it to him. You get some rest."

My wife looked at me skeptically. "I shall take it, Muirteach. I am not all that tired."

"You do not believe I'll give it to him." The realization stunned me. I stared at my wife as though she were a stranger, a slim woman standing stiff with anger and determination, blonde hair neatly pulled back in a plait under a white coif, blue eyes sparking with irritation as she glared at me.

"Indeed, and I do not. For you are so besotted with that Norse witch you cannot conceive of her doing any evil deed. You have said as much yourself."

I said nothing for a moment. The distrust hung in the air between us like some thick fog.

"Take it to him yourself, then," I said after a long moment. I turned on my heels and left the room.

CHAPTER 19

I walked the walls of the castle, but I could not outpace my thoughts. My wife did not trust me. And, God help me, I still lusted after a woman who could well be a poisoner. That had brought me no closer to knowing who had slain Malfrid, while Duncan still rotted in a castle cell. It was not my most pleasant afternoon. In addition it began raining again, at first a misty penetrating mizzle that quickly changed to a downpour that soaked its way through my mantle and turned the ground beneath me to a thick and viscous mud, a muck that squelched and sucked at my wet shoes with every step I took.

Finally, feeling like some bedraggled rat, I returned to our room hoping to speak again with my wife. But I did not find Mariota there.

❖   ❖   ❖

Cruickshanks had charged me with questioning Ingvilt, and as the afternoon light dimmed I thought to go and speak with her. She often spent time in her chambers at this hour, and the driving rain precluded any garden excursions, so I thought to find her in her rooms.

I climbed the dark wooden steps to her chambers and knocked on the door. Ingvilt herself opened it. The light from the windows behind her shone on her golden plaits, while her face remained in shadow.

"Muirteach," she said with a smile, and drew me inside to the solar. "An unexpected joy to see you this dreary afternoon." The door shut behind us and Ingvilt drew me into an embrace. Her breath smelled faintly of spices—cloves and cinnamon. And, God help me, I responded, feeling the excitement between us grow as we kissed.

She nipped at my lips and then drew back a moment. "But Muirteach, you are soaked through. Here, take off that wet cloak and sit by the brazier while I get you some wine."

"Where is Morag?" I finally thought to ask. "And young Magnus and Peter?"

"Peter assists my lord and Morag is busy fetching some things from the laundress in preparation for our departure. I sent Magnus with her. We are quite alone." Ingvilt's smile flashed for a moment.

I took the drink she offered me and sipped at the hot wine,

feeling the welcome warmth spread down my throat and into my stomach. "I thank you for this, my lady. It tastes well on such a *dreich* day."

"Do not be so formal, Muirteach," Ingvilt said, sitting down and then moving closer to me on the bench. She reached up to touch my hair, which had curled somewhat with the wet weather. "We are all in disarray here," she continued, "as tomorrow we plan to leave court. There is a great deal to do."

"I should leave. I prevent you from your duties."

"No." Ingvilt placed a hand on my chest and pushed me back against the wall, just a little. I could feel the warmth of her fingers through the sodden linen of my shirt. She took the glass from my hands and set it on the table to the side, then kissed me again, a longer kiss, soft and smooth like velvet or some rich wine. "No," she repeated, after a moment. "No, Muirteach, do not leave. I do not wish it."

"God help me, I do not wish it either," I moaned, digging my fingers into her golden plaits, bringing them down about her shoulders like a shower of brass, and kissing her roughly as I tried to submerge my guilt in a tide of passion.

After some moments I pushed away like a drowning man gasping for air. Ingvilt's hair had pulled out of its bindings and fell about her face; her green eyes shone wide and unfocused as she gazed at me.

"My lady—"

"Ingvilt," she said. "You must call me Ingvilt."

"Ingvilt, we must stop. We shall be damned."

Ingvilt's smile flashed again and her eyes narrowed a bit. "We've all sinned in our lives, Muirteach." She smiled again, more slowly, and ran her tongue over her lips. "And this is such pleasant sin."

"We are both pledged to others; we are married."

"That is what confession is for, Muirteach. It is the blessing of our Lord Christ who provides forgiveness for our sins. We are but flesh," she continued, running her fingers along my arm. My own nerves tingled in response. "And the flesh is weak."

"We have not sinned in the flesh," I protested, without much heart.

"Yet," murmured Ingvilt, caressing my cheek again.

"Ingvilt, you are leaving tomorrow to go with your husband."

"Then should we waste what moments we can steal today?"

With effort I gently removed her hands from my cheek and stood up. "No now, we must not continue." I kissed her gently on the lips; they tasted bitter as wormwood, not sweet, as a few more walls of my gilded fantasy crashed about me.

I watched her green eyes turn colder and she settled herself on the bench a bit apart from me. I took a sip of wine to steady myself and then drained the cup. She made no move to pour me another glass, so at length I reached for the jug and served myself. "Tell me of Greenland," I asked, in part to break the strange new discomfort between us. "It sounds mysterious."

Ingvilt made a pouting face, like a little girl denied a sweet.

"I was but young, and it was all I knew. It was a desolate place, and barren, and cold. We worked hard there, and still starved, and I found myself glad to leave it behind me."

"And how did you come to leave?"

"I was young," she repeated. "A friar came, a priest. I begged for succor and he helped me, protected me and took me to Bergen with him."

"But what of your family? Did they not want you to stay?"

"My father had died some years before. He journeyed to the western lands one summer and did not return. My mother remarried. There remained nothing for me, no reason to stay. So I left."

"There are few Christian folk in Greenland, are there not? Did you know Malfrid or her mother? Tawesson said they lived in a place called Saemundsfiord."

Ingvilt shook her head, and began to replait her hair. "On no, that is in the Western Settlement. I lived in the Eastern Settlement, many days' sail away. That is where I met Ivar Bardsson, who took me with him to Bergen."

"Tell me of the Skraelings. Did you ever meet any?" In part I wanted to learn more of Gudni's folk. In part I just longed to keep speaking with Ingvilt, despite our estrangement.

"I never dealt with them. They would flee from us. Although once, when we were starving, a man brought us some seal meat." An unpleasant expression flitted across her face and I felt pained to have brought bad memories to her mind.

I thought to change the subject. "Do you recall the book Henry mentioned? The *Inventio Fortunatae*?"

"What book was that?" Ingvilt looked blankly at me.

"One Tawesson claimed to possess. A book recounting tales of a voyage he made to the far northern lands many years ago."

Ingvilt laughed and took a sip of wine. "Tawesson does not strike me as a scholar, nor a writer of books."

"No," I agreed. "He claimed a monk wrote down the story of the voyage, a man named Nicholas of Lynne."

"And why should I know of that?" asked Ingvilt, running her tongue over her lips for a moment. I found myself distracted, despite all my noble intentions to put my cravings for her aside.

"Duncan claimed they set sail from Greenland. I thought you might have known of it."

"No, I never met Nicholas of Lynne, nor Duncan Tawesson for that matter, until I met him here this past week. And certainly I never heard of such a journey. But we lived deep in a fiord, not near the coast. So perhaps news of the voyage did not reach us, if indeed the tale is true. You know how sailors tell tales."

"And this Ivar Bardsson you spoke of? Who was he?"

"The king's agent, and a priest. He took me under his protection when I had to leave. I owe him much, that man. He was kind, a true man of God." Ingvilt shoved a pin into her braids and began to rearrange her headdress. "But those days are long gone. Why should we speak of them now?"

"I am curious, that is all," I replied. "I have not travelled as you have."

Ingvilt smiled again, and adjusted her veil. "Yes, I have travelled far in my life." She refilled my glass and we drank a bit longer.

"My wife fears your maid was poisoned," I said after a time. Perhaps, I hoped, Ingvilt could offer some simple explanation.

"Really? How distressing! Who could wish to poison Agnes? She was a dear girl, although careless at times. It makes no sense whatever! And how does your wife think this could have happened?"

I shrugged my shoulders. Ingvilt refilled my glass again. The wine and warmth of the room befuddled me a bit. "Perhaps Peter felt the lass was in his way. There was some jealousy, was there not?"

"Oh, Agnes was quite jealous of Peter," Ingvilt replied.

"She was careless?" I asked.

"Aye, and talkative. Jealous as well, I fear. And you say your wife thinks Agnes was poisoned? By Peter? I cannot believe the lad would have done such a thing. It is shocking!" Ingvilt stretched like a cat and reached for me but then a noise at the door stopped her. "That will no doubt be Morag, and Magnus, back with the laundry," Ingvilt said, giving her clothing a final adjustment.

"I shall leave you then, my lady," I said. I picked up my cloak and hastily made my farewells, then departed as Morag and Magnus entered the room, feeling like some rabbit caught in a poacher's snare.

❖   ❖   ❖

I made my way back to our room, reeking of wine, and found Mariota there. I noticed she had applied more of her new perfume. I saw her nostrils flare and her lips tighten as she looked at me, and I felt the lowliest worm.

"And how are you, *mo chridhe*," I asked her, trying to sound as if all was well between us.

"Well enough." The tone of my wife's voice did not make me feel all was well between us. "But I took the flask to Cruickshanks."

"And?"

"They fed the dregs to a stray dog."

"And?"

"The dog lies dead in the guardhouse. And his death throes resembled those of poor Gybb, and those of Agnes."

So someone had indeed poisoned Gybb Saylor. Either Peter, or Ingvilt, unless Gudni had poisoned Gybb's drink, and that made no sense whatsoever. "Have they gone to fetch them?" I asked. "Will they arrest them?"

"Indeed, Cruickshanks was loath to admit it could be either the lady or the squire, but I think he is now convinced. That it is one or the other of them."

"But they plan to leave court on the morrow."

"So I believe he will make his move tonight," my wife

replied. From outside our small window we heard a clamor and my wife pushed open the shutters, which had been closed against the day's earlier rain. We both looked outside to see a company of guards approach the building opposite. "They are here," Mariota said.

I raced down the stairs, leaving the door open, and arrived on the street in time to see some guards exit the building, with Lady Ingvilt held firmly by both arms. Two other guards came out the door with Peter. They hustled the both of them down the mount towards the guardhouse. The armor of the guards and the lady's red houppelande glowed like jewels in the last shafts of light from the setting sun, which had finally found its way through the dark and lowering clouds.

"I must go and see Cruickshanks," I said shortly to my wife, who had also come down to the street, and I turned to follow the party towards the guardhouse.

"I shall go also," my wife insisted, easily keeping pace with me.

We arrived at the guardhouse in time to see the Lady Ingvilt, seated regally on a stool, protesting her innocence. Peter Leslie stood nearby, with castle guards on either side. I saw an ugly bruise swelling purple on his handsome face.

"Now, whatever reason would I have to poison an old man I have never met?" Ingvilt demanded.

Cruickshanks stood, facing Ingvilt and scowling. He obviously had not wanted to bring the lady in and he oozed obsequiousness as he replied. "You must forgive me, my lady, but we did give the dog the remainder of the whisky in the flask you sent the man, and—well, you can see for yourself." He gestured to the still corpse of a mangy dog that lay on the table between them.

"But I did not poison the drink! Why would you suspect me? I sent the flask with Peter, he could have done it." She turned and looked at Peter. "He must be mad."

Peter started to protest, but the guards grabbed him roughly and he fell silent.

"Beg pardon, my lady," Cruickshanks went on, "but the woman healer thought the man's death suspicious and gave us the flask."

Ingvilt glared at him. "Well then, perhaps she put the poison in the flask, wanting to incriminate me herself, for now I do misdoubt my husband's squire would have done so." She flashed Peter a smile. "He is but a lad, and a good one, and would have no reason to harm an old sailor. Perhaps that boy—what is his name? Gubni?—wished to rid himself of the old sot. He did not fall sick, did he?"

"No, my lady, not to my knowledge."

"Well then, look to that foreign lad. He will be your killer. If indeed the slayer is not that island woman, the healer. She knows much of herbs, does she not?" Ingvilt sought out Mariota's face and locked eyes with her for a moment. "And she might wish to do me ill," Ingvilt added enigmatically, then brushed at her skirts. "Have I your leave to go?"

"My lady, I'm afraid we must keep you here for now. And

the squire as well."

"That is ridiculous! Where is my husband?"

Torches had been lit in sconces set against the stone walls. They gave off a flickering light and filled the air with the resinous scent of burning pine. A brazier burned in the center of the room, giving off still more warmth. In fact, despite the cold day outside, the air in the crowded room grew close. I felt an urge to vomit, and swallowed down bile, tasting a whisper of warm acid in my mouth. Or perhaps my stomach roiled at Ingvilt's attempts to implicate my wife. Thankfully, Cruickshanks did not seem to be taken in by those. After all, Mariota had brought him the flask herself.

"Where is Sir Johann?" Ingvilt repeated, her voice shriller, more insistent, cutting through the stuffy atmosphere like a razor. "Where is my dear husband?"

At this moment the door to the outside burst open again, bringing another gust of cold, wet air that caused the torches to flare momentarily. Sir Johann himself entered, followed by his groom.

"What's all this?" demanded the old knight. His voice sounded harsh, his features ruddy and incensed. "What do you do here with my lady? And my squire?"

Ingvilt began to cry a little, tears trickling down her cheeks. She opened her mouth to speak again but Cruickshanks forestalled her. "Sir, your wife and squire have been accused of causing the death of one Gybb Saylor."

"Who is that? Gybb Saylor? By the teeth of Christ! I've

never heard of the man. What trumped-up lies are these?"

"She sent the man a flask of whisky, entrusted it to your squire here, and the man died later this same day. And this dog," Cruickshanks gestured to the emaciated corpse on the table, "drank the remnants in the flask and died thereafter."

"That proves nothing." Sir Johann, concerned, looked at his wife. "Sweeting, they have not injured you—"

"No, my lord," replied Ingvilt more evenly, wiping a few tears from her cheeks. "The man but seeks to discharge his duty. Though he is sadly mistaken, indeed."

Sir Johann glared at Cruickshanks. "Who brought these charges against her?"

"The wife of the scribe brought the flask to me, thinking the man's death was suspicious."

"But that does not prove my wife poisoned the drink. Nor my squire. Anyone could have done so."

"Perhaps," ceded Cruickshanks. From the look in his eyes I judged him to be somewhat relieved, although he stood his ground. "If they had access to the flask. And those folk are your wife, your squire, and Duncan Tawesson's foster son."

Sir Johann roughly pulled his wife up by her arm from her seat on the stool. "God's teeth," he swore again. "Come, Ingvilt; we'll plead your case before the king himself. Such foolishness. This man has his arse where his brains should be."

"Sire, your lady wife must remain here." I found I had to give Cruickshanks at least a little credit for standing up to Sir Johann.

"Not one instant longer, by the eyeballs of Christ. And I'll not remain at this court any longer. We'll both be gone and to Hell with the lot of you."

Sir Johann strode from the hall, dragging Ingvilt along with him. The guards by the door looked to block his way and started to draw their own swords but after a terse nod from Cruickshanks they let the couple go. The heavy door slammed shut, sending another gust through the room and the torches guttered again.

"That went well," observed Cruickshanks as his men sheathed their swords. He gave orders for Peter Leslie to be taken to a cell, then crossed the room to where I stood with my wife. "What next, Muirteach? What do you advise?"

CHAPTER 20

I had nothing to advise, as Cruickshanks well knew. Still, the suspicious death of Gybb Saylor did help clear Duncan's name.

"Not that I'm willing to release him yet. It was his knife you found, after all."

I nodded. Mariota stood beside me and I felt her shift anxiously from one foot to another. After all, Ingvilt had just accused her of the poisoning. But Cruickshanks turned towards her and smiled.

"Dinna fash yourself," he said to Mariota. "If you had poisoned the man, why would you have come to me with the flask? But it's just possible that the lad added poison to the old man's drink, and that it was neither Sir Johann's lady, nor his squire. Duncan's son and the old man served together on that ship, did they not? Perhaps he bore him a grudge. And if he's done that," he continued, as my wife started to open her mouth, "then there is no telling what else he may have done. The boy is swarthy, a black man, after all—the devil's own color. You said he did not drink when you saw them together, did you not, mistress? He could well have known it to be poisoned."

Mariota shook her head. "No, no. It is only that the lad does not like whisky. I am sure he is innocent."

"When would he have had the chance to add the poison?" I asked, feeling the need to speak up for my wife.

Cruickshanks shrugged his broad shoulders. "When the old man went to take a piss? Who knows."

"No, I'll not believe it of him," Mariota protested. "Gybb Saylor was his friend!" I thought I heard her mutter, "Are all men such fools?" under her breath but I could not be sure I caught that aright, and decided to not ask her. Cruickshanks, however, refused to be swayed from what he saw as his duty.

Mariota and I reluctantly accompanied Cruickshanks back to the mews, accompanied by a few others of his men, where we found Gudni slicing up some meat for the two remaining birds by the weak light of a rush candle.

"They want you to come to the guardhouse," I said.

Gudni looked up at my voice; a furtive, feral look in his eyes. He did not speak, but turned slightly, the late twilight from outside the open door of the mews barely illuminating him in the shadows. But the rushlight showed the fear in his face.

"No." He shook his head. "No."

"You'll come with us," Cruickshanks said firmly, frightening the injured gyrfalcon, who flapped her wings and squawked.

"No," Gudni repeated and turned round, holding the small knife he'd been using to cut the meat out in front of him.

"Now, lad, don't make this worse," said Cruickshanks, reaching for the boy's wrist. Gudni's knife flashed out.

"By the balls of Saint Peter," Cruickshanks swore, grasping at his wrist, where a scarlet stain was spreading beneath his fingers.

"Gudni, no!" Mariota cried, but two of the guards went for him and I heard a clatter as the little knife hit the floor. Then a sickening thud as one of the guards punched the lad in the face a time or two while the other held Gudni's hands behind his back. Meanwhile I held Mariota back as she struggled to go to his aid.

"Muirteach, leave me be," she cried, but I did not let go.

Gudni made no sound but his eye began to swell and his nose to bleed.

"Take him to the guardhouse," ordered Cruickshanks.

"But he's done nothing! Please let me see to him," Mariota begged.

"Nothing!" ranted Cruickshanks, and I thought he was going after us next. "The lad's attacked me and he could well be a poisoner."

Gudni understood this last and started to struggle in his

captors' arms. "No, no, no poison!" he yelled, until the guard hit him again and knocked the breath out of the lad. I felt Mariota wince beside me, and I may have winced myself.

Cruickshanks spat at Gudni and signaled. The guards started towards the door, dragging Gudni with them. Mariota and I followed at their heels, sick at heart.

"My birds," Gudni called to Mariota as they pulled him out of the mews.

"I'll see to them," Mariota called back over the scuffle. "Don't worry for them." With this, Gudni seemed satisfied, or perhaps it was a final cuff from the burlier of the two guards that quieted him.

Mariota turned towards me. "I'll stay here for now. I've no wish to go back to that place. Perhaps Cruickshanks will let me tend the lad a little later. And see to his own cut," she added with a tight smile. "Perhaps some of his bad humors will bleed out of him the while."

I left her in the shed then, with the gyrfalcons, and followed Gudni and his captors, trailing after them like some mangy hound.

By now it had grown full dark and I wondered if Sir Johann had taken Ingvilt to the king to plead her innocence in the Great Hall in the midst of supper. That would set tongues wagging indeed.

The guards bundled Gudni down the narrow stairs to a cell near his father's. I wondered what the two would have to say to each other, there in the dank blackness under the guardhouse.

I left the guardhouse then and walked through the darkness of the castle yard to the hall. Torches glowed near the doorway, lighting the entrance. Inside folk still sat at table and some musicians played a lute, some pipes and a crumhorn in front of the high table, where King Robert and Queen Euphemia still sat in state. I saw no sign of Sir Johann or Lady Ingvilt but I did spy Henry Sinclair. A few folk had departed early and the seat next to him was empty. I stepped over the bench and sat down.

"Henry."

"Hello, Muirteach."

"Did Sir Johann appear here with Lady Ingvilt?" I asked abruptly.

Henry stopped chewing his eel pie a moment and shook his head. "No. What is it, Muirteach? Someone said the lady was dragged to the guardhouse, that Cruickshanks had arrested her."

I reached for some fish from the platter in front of Henry. "Are you eating this?"

"Go ahead. You did not dine, did you?" I shook my head. "Well, what happened?"

"Gybb Saylor lies dead in the chapel."

"That's a bad thing indeed," Henry said. "How did the old man die?"

"My wife suspects poison." I told Henry of the day's events, although I did not tell him of my time spent with Ingvilt. I ended with Sir Johann's vow to take his wife before the king.

"They've not been here?" I asked as I finished my tale.

Henry shook his head no. "Sir Johann must be planning to speak with King Robert privately. He'd not want all the court to know his wife's an accused poisoner. Folk might start to speak of witchcraft."

I nodded. "In truth, I cannot believe it of her."

Henry gave me a sidewise glance. "There was some talk in Bergen."

"What?"

"Ingvilt caught the eye of King Haakon, yet she had no connections."

"She is very beautiful."

"Yes, and Haakon a young and lusty prince, so perhaps the attraction was not surprising."

"He made her his leman?"

Henry took a sip of ale and then passed me the beaker. While I drank he continued. "He set her up at court and made her his favorite for a time. Then she made a match with Earl Olav. King Haakon helped to set that up for her; he had tired of her, I believe. But Olav died suddenly after she met Sir Johann. I had accompanied him to Norway, on some business of the king. The earl was an old man. They said he died of some flux." Henry bit off some bread and chewed thoughtfully a moment.

I looked at him sharply. "Agnes had a flux. And so did Gybb Saylor."

Henry's eyes narrowed in unpleasant speculation. "Nothing could ever be proven. At any rate, she married Sir

Johann and sailed for Scotland soon after." He paused. I passed him the beaker again, and Henry took another drink. "Sir Johann loves her," he said.

"She is a beautiful woman," I said, not for the first time.

Henry sighed. "I tried to tell you, Muirteach." He reached for some stew. "Your wife is also lovely. Where is she tonight?"

"I left her with Gudni's falcon, after they took him prisoner. But she is exhausted after caring for Gybb. And I should leave. She no doubt expects me and I should go to her now."

Henry shuddered. "What a waste. Such fine birds. And such a lovely young girl." I surmised he did not mean Lady Ingvilt. The musicians finished and the king rose, followed by all the others seated at the high table. We also stood to leave.

"I must see to my wife," I said as we walked from the hall. "And the falcon."

Henry nodded. "I will let you know what I hear. But watch yourself, Muirteach. And your wife—she suspected the poison first, did she not?"

I nodded.

"Tread warily, my friend," Henry said, grasping me by the shoulders in a quick embrace, which surprised me. "And guard your wife."

Henry's words made me uneasy, and I hurried back to our lodgings and climbed the creaking wooden stairs to our room. A candle burned and Mariota sat on the bed, brushing out her hair. I watched her a moment. I have always loved my wife's hair; it minds me of some shining waterfall. The scent of her new perfume hung in the air as she turned to me.

"Ah, Muirteach."

"Did you rest?" I asked her.

"I did. After I made sure the bird was fed I came back here and slept like the dead." She laughed a little, but I heard no humor in the sound. "A bad choice of words. But I am feeling much better now," Mariota continued. "What of Ingvilt? Did they appeal to the king in the Great Hall, before everyone?"

"Not yet, but the lady still insists on her innocence. So it must have been Peter, and if so, they'll get it out of him. Or if neither poisoned the *uisge beatha*, well, Gudni had access to the flask and he did not drink any of the whisky."

Mariota whirled about to face me. "If they did not— Muirteach! Are you indeed bewitched?"

I fancied I felt icy guilt run through my veins instead of blood. Perhaps I had truly been ensorcelled. Or tempted by the Devil in the form of Eve. I did not know how to answer my wife and simply shrugged my shoulders.

"How does the bird get on?" I finally asked instead.

"I should go check on her. And go to the guardhouse, and see if Cruickshanks will let me see to Gudni." My wife's tone made it clear she would rather be in the mews, or even the dungeons of the guardhouse, anywhere, rather than here with me. She finished re-plaiting her hair and reached for her mantle.

"I'll go with you," I said.

My wife's lips tightened and I expected her to say that

there was no need. I waited, my heart thudding in my chest for her response. But three people were dead, and my wife is a practical woman. So she nodded at length, a terse, short movement. "Well enough, then, Muirteach," she said, "let us go." She picked up the candle and lit the lantern from it, then blew out the candle and we left the room.

The flickering light of the lantern guided our steps. There was no moon shining that night and the blackness of the cloudy sky felt absolute, although the night noises of the castle surrounded us like a blanket. From a ways off came the sounds of some drunken courtiers returning to their quarters, the soft whickering of the horses in the royal stables, some barking from the kennels out beyond the mews. Near the mews the loaded cart still sat, a solid darker lump in the black night. We passed it by and entered the shed. The birds sat quietly in the darkened room but roused when we entered. I think they expected Gudni.

Mariota found Gudni's knife lying on the floor and picked it up with a grimace. She went to the table, found the meat scraps where they had been left in a bowl, and began to cut them up for her charge. I fancied she looked pale, or perhaps it was just the dim light. She chopped without speaking to me. I felt awkward, unused to this disharmony with my wife.

"Mariota—" I began.

"What? What is it, Muirteach?" Her voice cut as sharp as the knife she wielded,

I swallowed, hesitating. I was not even sure what I wished

to say to her—perhaps I longed to beg Mariota's forgiveness. But despite my guilt, despite the fact that Ingvilt could well be both a witch and a poisoner, I realized with some horror that the Norse woman still stirred me. Perhaps she had indeed ensorcelled and bewitched me. But even realizing that, how could I truly beg my wife's forgiveness? I had proved myself no better than my own dead father, lecherous and deceitful.

"*Mo chridhe*," I finally began again, but my wife turned and faced me, holding the knife in her hands. Her stance mirrored that of Gudni's earlier today as he faced Cruickshanks and his men.

"What?" Mariota repeated. Her annoyance finally found voice and she let loose a torrent of words. "Muirteach, you are an *amadan*! Do you really believe Gudni would poison Gybb Saylor? He's but a lad, Gybb his only friend. And yet you let them take him, Muirteach, you let them take him! How could you be such a vile serpent!"

I let her words wash over me, like a river in full spate carrying everything in its wake.

"My heart, I am sorry—"

"Sorry! Muirteach, he's but a lad! He's in a dungeon! And he is innocent! Sorry—you are sorry. Is that all you can say?" My wife swayed a moment as if dizzy, then turned again and resumed her chopping.

I knew not what to say. Mariota did not know the half of it. She did not know of my unfaithfulness, although no doubt she had guessed. My wife is far from a fool. True, Ingvilt and

I had only kissed and caressed. But not through any want of desire on my part.

"What is it, *mo chridhe*?" I asked as my wife paused in her work for a moment.

"It is naught, Muirteach. My hand must be tired, that is all." She dropped the knife and I heard it clatter on the table. Mariota picked it up again. "My fingers feel numb and I am clumsy. I must have slept on my arm strangely."

She returned to her work and I waited, staring into the dark corners of the shed. I wondered how Gudni fared in his cell. And his father. No need to ask how Gybb and Agnes fared, for they were both cold corpses now. I thought of Peter, with his fancy clothing and artless manner. And of Ingvilt, of her flashing smile that never quite reached her eyes. The knowledge that she could well have poisoned both her maid and Gybb oozed through me like some cold, dark poison itself. But would Ingvilt truly have killed Malfrid? And why murder Gybb? What reason would she have to do such evil acts? Perhaps the answers, as my wife had suggested, indeed lay to the north.

Mariota finished her cutting and took the pottery dish of chopped meat to the falcons. They stirred in their cages at the scent of the meat.

She opened the cage to feed the tercel. He made a jab at her hands.

"Be careful, *mo chridhe*," I said, "he'll claw you."

"Why, Muirteach? Does it matter to you? Why should you

care if he tears my hands? Why should I care? Have you not already ripped the heart out of my chest?"

Her words struck me like the stab of cold iron. I crossed the room, meaning to take her in my arms and beg her forgiveness, but Mariota turned towards me first.

"Do not touch me, Muirteach. Do not even think it!"

Her words stung more than if she had cut me with her blade. I stepped back and dropped my hands to my side. In the dim light I could see the glitter of her tears, little streams flowing down my wife's face.

"No, now..." I stepped back, leaving my wife to feed the bird. "I'll just sit and wait for you here. You are overwrought," I added injudiciously.

"Overwrought! That is what men always say when a woman speaks with passion! Overwrought! And why should I not be, knowing that my husband ruts with a poisoner!"

"I did not—"

"No, for sure you did not. You were just coming home with the stench of her perfume covering you, with her love marks on your neck—Muirteach, what am I to think? What am I to do?"

"I did not swive her," I said stubbornly. I held to my only defense, a meager one, as more gilded walls crumbled to bits. "It, it just happened."

"She has played you, Muirteach, and you are a bigger fool than ever I thought you could be to have been so ensnared. Now we are both well and truly trapped."

"*Mo chridhe*, forgive me—I shall never see her again—"

"No, for she will leave with her husband on the morrow and you'll not have the opportunity. But not for want of desire!"

The birds squawked loudly and Mariota turned her back to feed them again. I did not know what to say; there was truth in my wife's words although I hated to admit it.

"Forgive me," I started again.

"Muirteach, I am your sworn wife." She spoke without facing me, looking at the birds. "But to forgive you—I cannot. Muirteach, you have betrayed me. You have betrayed us. You have betrayed our love." She turned away from me.

I started once again to beg her forgiveness, but before I could utter any more words Mariota swayed, dropping the bowl and knife as she tried to reach for the table. I heard a crash as the thick pottery bowl broke into pieces, and watched in shock as my wife fell to the floor.

CHAPTER 21

For just an instant I could not move; I stood paralyzed in the darkness of the shed. Finally I came to myself and dashed over to Mariota. I lifted her body and cradled her head gently, holding her in my arms to see her face. Her eyes flickered open and I exhaled the breath that I had not realized I held within me in a relieved rush. Her face gleamed ghostly white in the dim light. Fine drops of sweat beaded her brow.

"Mariota," I cried. "What is it? Are you taken ill?" I drew another grateful breath when my wife spoke, although her voice sounded weak and faint.

"The birds—"

The tercel's cage stood open and he seemed to be well aware of that fact, eyeing the scene before him—my wife, collapsed on the floor, myself kneeling before her—with curiosity. No doubt he'd want to escape his prison.

"Close the cages, Muirteach," my wife commanded faintly.

I rose and did so quickly, then returned to where Mariota lay. Mariota's breath came shallowly, like the fluttering of some small, weak fledgling. I felt her pulse, rapid and erratic. "Mariota, what ails you? Can you tell me?"

"I feel numb," my wife managed to say.

"Can you walk? Let us get you back to our room."

Mariota attempted to sit up and then stand, but faltered. At length I took her up in my arms, and despite my bad leg I carried her all the way back to our chamber. I could feel her heart beating faintly against my chest as I bore her through the dark streets, and I fancied she already grew cold, that death itself crept up her body as we made our slow way towards our lodgings.

I felt another stab of fear in my guts as I stumbled up the stairs with her and into our chamber, and laid her down upon our bed. The scent of her new perfume lingered in my nostrils as I tried to cover her with the rough woolen blanket.

"My heart, are you better? What must I do?"

"My medical bag, Muirteach. And water—my throat burns."

I gave my wife water and she vomited it up. Then I gave her the emetic herbs she asked for; she vomited again and again. The candle burned lower and she shivered with cold, although she kept sweating. I covered her with more blankets, yet still she shivered as though it were the coldest night of winter.

"What is it?" I asked her at one point as I set the basin down and wiped her brow. Perhaps she was just ill. Perhaps Agnes and Gybb actually had had the flux and she had been exposed to the contagion as she nursed them.

"Muirteach, I swear I am poisoned. But I've neither eaten nor drunk anything from that witch." She retched again and moaned.

"What is it, *mo chridhe*?"

"A cramp," Mariota replied, wincing. "Oh, no—" She doubled over, and I smelled hot bile as she vomited green froth into the basin. Then she writhed and grabbed at her abdomen, throwing off the blankets. I looked and saw a scarlet gush from between my wife's legs, staining the sheets and her shift with bright red blood.

"Mariota, you are bleeding—" I said, like some simpleton.

"Yes, Muirteach. I am losing our child."

❖   ❖   ❖

"You did not tell me you were with child," I finally said, stunned, after I had removed the bloody linen, wiped my wife's face and cleaned her legs. The flow of blood diminished somewhat, although the coppery scent of it still lingered in my nostrils. Mariota lay back against the bolster on the bed, nearly pale as the linen that covered the pillow.

"How could I, I have only just known—and you yourself were so entranced by that damned sorceress! How could I have told you? Oh, I am going to be sick again—" Mariota heaved, but nothing came out, just a bit of froth. "I am poisoned," she said faintly after a moment. "But how?"

I thought I knew and the thought froze my marrow. "Mariota, I think I know. I know now, but I did not, I swear—" Mariota looked at me. "The perfume," I continued. "The perfume I gave you. It was from Ingvilt. She asked me to give it to you, she said you would like it—"

"That witch," said my wife.

"And you thought it was from me, and were so pleased, and then—I let you think, I did not tell you—for I was so pleased you were happy. You must forgive me, *mo chridhe*—"

"We have both been foolish," my wife said weakly. "But now I know what to do. Get me loosestrife, and cornflower. And valerian. It's in a flask, a tincture." Her voice faded a bit as another cramp seized her.

I fumbled in my wife's medical bag, looking for the herbs she asked for. Eventually I found them and managed to brew some of them in hot water, add the tincture, and get some of the mixture down Mariota's throat. I cared for my wife through that long night. But at length the vomiting stopped, and finally the bleeding ceased as well, and as morning light finally lit the room Mariota slept, breathing regularly with slightly better color. I shuddered; the realization of her narrow escape from death sank deep into my soul and my own heart grew icy with the terror that I would lose her.

And if she had died—who would have believed me? I

would have been the poisoner, the agent of killing my own heart's greatest treasure.

Dawn broke. My lustful fantasies lay in crumbled shatters around me, as I sat by my wife's bedside. I resolved then to gain vengeance on that witch and see justice done. My previous desire for her had burned out, but the dregs and guilt of it lay thick and heavy in my gut, as cold as burned-out ash. And as dead as the tiny child, no bigger than my fist, that my wife and I might have had together. I only prayed now that my wife would live, and that our love might grow again.

❖   ❖   ❖

I saw the daylight grew stronger through the cracks in the shutters, closed tight against the night air, and folk began to stir. I heard noises from the room next to ours and guessed the Lord of the Isles was awake. I glanced at my wife; she slept quietly, breathing evenly, and so I left her for a moment to knock upon my lord's chamber door.

"What is it, Muirteach?" The Lord of the Isles had just about finished dressing, his plaid wool mantle pinned at his chest with a large good brooch sporting a bloodstone. The saffron of his linen *lèine* showed under the mantle and his hair glinted where silver hairs mingled with the dark ones.

I described what had happened the night before. The Lord of the Isles listened intently, his grey eyes narrowing.

"I will send a servant with some hot broth. I shall also send word to the queen; she's taken an interest in your wife, has she not? Perhaps Her Majesty would like to send someone to tend her." His Lordship thought a moment. "And I'll send a messenger for her father."

My wife's father, Fearchar Baton, was the lord's own personal physician and a noted healer. I swallowed, my throat dry with anxiety. "Thank you, my lord. That might be wise. Although I'm thinking she does better this morning."

"Well, you've yet another crime to lay at that Norse witch's feet," commented His Lordship. "For it is doubtful that the squire or Duncan's son are guilty. Although Cruickshanks might well accuse you of poisoning your wife yourself. It's no secret you've been lusting after that Norsewoman. Folk have noticed and you might indeed be suspected. Perhaps it's best you not mention her at this time."

My face flamed. "And what then? Let her escape with her lord this very day?"

"I'm not saying that, Muirteach, but proof is needed before any accusations would stand. And you could be the man to get it."

"There's a dead dog in the guardhouse, if people want proof."

"Aye. But now, if you were to find aconite in her quarters, or some other poison, that might indeed be proof that the lad Gudni had not added the poison to that old man's flask. Or that you had not put it in your wife's perfume yourself." With these cheering words, His Lordship left me once more with my wife, promising again to see that some broth was sent to our room.

Pleased to see Mariota still slept quietly, with somewhat better color, I took the vial of perfume from the table. Another test might ascertain if it was indeed poisoned, but Ingvilt then would neatly have incriminated me as well. A knock sounded on the door. I opened it to find His Lordship's manservant with the promised broth. He agreed to remain with my wife, after I promised him a silver groat, and I set out to find Henry Sinclair. I needed an ally and felt he was my only hope.

I found Henry heading towards the stables and walked along with him. He said he intended to ride that morning to his castle in Rosslyn, but stopped and listened, his face grave, when I told him what had happened to Mariota. "Aye, indeed, I'll be glad to help you, Muirteach. And should you want Mariota in a safer place to recover, we can send her to Rosslyn. My Jennet would be glad enough of another woman's company and she would do fine enough there."

It seemed wise to let Mariota rest for now. I hoped she would be well enough to travel in a few days and we agreed to speak of such things later on. Henry arranged for one of his own servants to relieve His Lordship's man and stay with my wife. We walked with the servant to my chamber and after seeing my wife settled, for she still slept, and giving instructions to the servant, we spoke of what we might do.

"I spoke with Sir Johann this morning when we broke our fast," Henry told me. "They plan to remain here one more day and then depart early tomorrow, leaving Peter to rot in the dungeon, I suppose. Sir Johann hopes to appeal to King Robert today; that is the reason for their delay. However, the lord is out of favor with His Majesty it seems, and Queen Euphemia attempts to intercede on his behalf. Sir Johann has ties with her family."

Henry looked at my sleeping wife. His servant sat on a stool next to the bed. "Do not fash yourself, Muirteach. Malcolm has been with me for years. You can trust your wife's care to him while we do what we must. So you, at any rate, had best search their chambers for the poison today. You could do it while folk are dining at noon. And I'm thinking that King Robert would hear their story somewhat before that, so you would have a good while to look. Their servants would also be at luncheon. And I shall distract Ingvilt, and make sure they do not return too quickly."

"She'll not suspect you?"

"She may, and she should, but I know the lady well. Leave her and Sir Johann to me for the time."

So as the noontide approached and folk made their way to the Great Hall I left my wife's bedside and instead made my way into Ingvilt's lodgings. I watched the dark-haired Morag leave with young Master Magnus, and turn towards the Great Hall. I waited a bit longer until most folk had gone. Then I entered the main door and climbed the stairs to Ingvilt's chambers. The door had been locked but I forced the lock open with my *sgian dubh*, and entered the rooms.

The main room looked just as always, the cushioned

benches set against the walls, although some open chests spoke to the packing that continued. I did not spend much time there and passed through the small antechamber, the pallets where Agnes had died, and went into the main bedchamber. Although the room had no fireplace a brazier warmed the space, the coals still glowing. A small casket, made of intricately carved walrus ivory, sat on a table, locked. I looked for a key, found none, and eventually I just pried it open. I heard the clasp crack with satisfaction, caring not that I'd broken such a lovely thing. Inside, gold and silver rings and pins glinted in the light from the window, but I saw no vials of aconite, no henbane.

A large painted wooden chest stood at the foot of the bed, I rummaged through it, strewing colorful woman's garments about like flower petals. Here also there were no vials, but hidden deep within the chest I found a red cloak, stiff with blood. Wrapped within it was a dried bird's wing, its white feathers stained with more blood. And under the whole lay a book—the *Inventio*. Well enough, I thought, as I tucked the book into my *lèine* and re-folded the cloak about the falcon's wing. Malfrid's murderess had worn this thing, and had also killed the gyrfalcon. But where had she hidden the poison?

Several other, smaller chests were piled up in a corner of the room, already waiting for the planned departure. A search of the first yielded nothing, just his lordship's tunics, cotehardies and hose, neatly folded and packed. A smaller trunk held Magnus's clothing neatly packed away, along with a carved wooden horse and knight.

I scanned the room. Where could it be? Perhaps the witch had dumped it down the garderobe, once she was finished with it. Yet I thought not. She might wish to kill again and would want to hold onto it.

A sound disturbed me and I turned to see the door to the bedchamber creak open. Magnus stood there, his eyes large in his thin face and a truculent set to his chin.

"Master MacPhee," the lad said politely. Then he took in the mess I'd made of the chamber. "What do you do here?"

I swallowed. Now I'd be lying to a child. "I am searching for something. Something your mother asked for. A little vial. Where might she keep such a thing, do you know? It's kind of a game."

"Where is my toy horse?" Magnus demanded.

"I think it is packed away, is it not? You are traveling to your father's lands soon, aren't you?"

Magnus nodded. "But I want my horse. They say I must travel in the cart with Morag. If I have to do that, I want my horse."

I took the small trunk in which I'd seen the child's clothing and passed it to the boy. "Here, you look for it."

Magnus found his plaything at once, a carved and painted destrier made of wood. "Good. Now I shall have my horse. But I still do not want to ride in the cart with Morag."

"Where is Morag?" I asked. "Is she not worried for you?"

"I ran away." That meant she'd soon be coming here to look

for her charge. I had but little time left, and nothing except the cloak, the bird's wing, and the book to show for it. Although perhaps that would be enough to damn the witch.

"Magnus, where would your mother hide something precious? Something she did not want anyone to find. Does she have a secret hiding place?"

"Well, if she does not want anyone to find it, why should I be showing it to you?"

I thought frantically. "It is a kind of game we are playing. Like find the kerchief. She thinks I shall not find this but I am determined. Will you help me?"

"What will you give me?"

"Another horse?" Magnus stared at me, his protuberant blue eyes hard. "A troop of horses? Say five?"

The lad blinked, then nodded, satisfied. He made his way to the table that stood across from the large curtained bed. Atop the table stood a little folding shrine with a statue of the Virgin and Child carved from ivory. "Look in there," he said. "It's mother's secret hidey-hole. She thinks I don't know of it, but I do. Not even Father knows of it."

I went to the shrine and looked but saw nothing untoward. "Look," Magnus instructed. "Pick up the mother."

I picked up the statue of Our Lady. On the surface it seemed nothing remarkable. It was made of walrus ivory, carved from a single tusk, finished sweetly and painted. The Virgin's robe was blue, her hair golden. Some gilded trim adorned it. I turned the piece upside down, and saw a seam around the bottom of the Virgin's robe. I twisted it, like a stopper, and revealed a hollow space. And within that lay the small pottery vial I sought.

"I thank you, Master Magnus," I said, putting the vial in my pouch. I replaced the false bottom and quickly setting the carving back in its place in the shrine. "I have won the game."

CHAPTER 22

"When do I get my horses?" demanded the child.

"I will get them for you. But for now let this be our secret. I will get you six horses, not five," I added hastily as Magnus opened his mouth mutinously. We heard footsteps on the staircase. "Will that not be Morag?"

It was not Morag but Ingvilt who opened the door. She wore a filmy gown of some gauzy and no doubt costly silken fabric from Cathay, and a brocade houppelande atop that.

"Master MacPhee! Muirteach!" Ingvilt said, flashing a confused smile that hardened quickly as she glanced about the room. "What are you doing here? And here's my little runaway," she said, looking at her son.

"I was helping Master MacPhee. With a game he was

playing," said Magnus complacently.

"Indeed? And what game could that have been?" Ingvilt asked, her eyes like ice as she gazed about us. "You have made a great mess with your playing, the both of you. We shall have to have Morag replace everything."

Just then Morag appeared, breathless from running up the stairs. Her face was flushed and her eyes worried. "Lady, I've looked everywhere for him—oh, there you are, you imp. You are a wicked boy to run away like that."

Magnus grinned defiantly back at his nurse. "Yes, Morag, he is here indeed," Ingvilt said, catching hold of Magnus by one arm as he squirmed. She tightened her grip. "I wonder you did not look here for him first. But take him now and go—to the stables, perhaps. Magnus, would you like to see the horses?" Her son nodded.

"Yes, my lady," Morag answered. "But what has happened here? Those trunks were all packed."

"We were playing a game—" Magnus put in.

"You are lucky not to be whipped," Ingvilt said sharply, glaring at her son, who dropped his gaze to the floor.

"But we were playing—" he said in a quieter voice.

"Indeed. And I must speak with Master MacPhee, so you are spared. For now. Get along, before my humor changes."

"But I want to see who wins," Magnus howled, before Morag dragged him out of the room. We heard them tromp down the stairs, and after they left the room was quiet for a moment.

"So, Muirteach," Ingvilt finally said, "what brought you here? Did you find what you sought?"

"Perhaps some of what I sought, my lady. Did you plead your case before His Majesty?"

Ingvilt nodded.

"And what did the king say?"

"He gave us leave to depart," Ingvilt responded, watching me with steely eyes. "He thought Gybb's death due to the flux. As was that of Agnes." She paused and walked over to the table where a pitcher and some glasses sat. "Will you have some wine?"

"No thank you, my lady." I thought of Gybb's death throes. I had done drinking with Ingvilt. "And so the king believes you innocent?" I continued.

She smiled, came close to me. I willed myself not to move away. Ingvilt raised her hand and caressed my cheek, but I felt a sharp scratch. I pulled away quickly and rubbed at my cheek. Ingvilt smiled again. "Muirteach, that's just a remembrance for you." She kissed me on the lips but I remained cold to it, like a dead man. "What, do you not find me pleasing?"

My cheek tingled oddly where her ring had scratched it and my tongue felt clumsy as I strove to answer. "You know I do—I did." My heart pounded erratically as she gave my cheek another caress, her perfume filling my nostrils.

"It will do," she said.

"It is a curious thing," I said after a moment. "My wife has been ill."

"I am sorry to hear of it, Muirteach. Are you?"

I nodded. "Of course I am sorry. But she does better. I believe she will live." I fancied I saw a shadow cross Ingvilt's face.

"Well, that is good news indeed," she replied.

"It was a near thing, though. She was with child, and lost it."

""I am sorry indeed, to hear it. I did not know she was breeding."

"No. Neither did I. Tell me, Ingvilt. Why slay Malfrid?"

"Muirteach, what are you speaking of? Are you mad?"

"No. I found the bloody cloak. In your trunk. And the falcon's wing."

"And so you snuck in here, and used my own son against me—" The lady's eyes held me, as frigid as the northern sea.

"Ingvilt, I have the cloak. I've seen you wearing it. And it is covered in blood. Why kill an innocent girl?"

"I killed her to save her."

"To save her? Save her from what?"

"Save her from mortal sin."

I laughed. "You do not seem so afeard of mortal sin, my lady. And certainly not if you've slain the girl. For murder is a mortal sin, is it not?"

Ingvilt just smiled, a smile that chilled my blood. "I did it to save her," she repeated.

"And Agnes? And Gybb Saylor? We know they were poisoned, Ingvilt. Why? And now, why try to poison my wife?"

"But the perfume was your gift, was it not, Muirteach? So you yourself are the poisoner." She looked like the serpent in Paradise, smiling a little as she granted me the gift of knowledge. "Your wife is an intelligent woman, Muirteach. She will never trust you again."

"Perhaps," I said, with a sick feeling in my bowels. That was all too possible. "And I may no longer deserve her trust, as you well know, my lady. But then, tell me, what of Malfrid?"

"I had nothing to do with the lass's death."

"Really?" The woman had just confessed to Malfrid's murder. She must indeed be crazed to now deny it. I produced the cloak. "And what of this, then?"

"So you really do have it. Where did you find that?" Ingvilt bared her teeth as she saw the wing.

"At the bottom of your trunk, well hidden. Why did you not burn it?"

Ingvilt shrugged. "There is no fireplace."

"So why kill the lass? She was surely an innocent."

"She may have been innocent, but her father was not. It was he who made me what I am."

I stared at her, utterly confounded.

"Duncan Tawesson," she continued, "came to my mother's farm in Greenland one summer when I had but fourteen years. He was a dashing sailor and I but a young maid."

"You fell in love with him." I rubbed at my cheek, which still throbbed where Ingvilt's ring had scratched it.

"Yes, but he had eyes only for my mother. He had no

interest in me. For that he'll pay."

"Go on."

"He stayed much of that summer, then left towards the autumn, with his boat and his sailors. It was a harsh winter that year. Bitter and cold. The ice grew thick, the fiords all choked with it. You could walk across them. We ran out of food and feared we would starve. A Skraeling man saw me on the fiord, when I tried to fish through a hole I'd hacked in the ice. The man brought us seal meat, but he took something from me in return. And he came back, over and over again, all that winter. And left something with me at the end of the winter when he sailed away in his funny little skin boat. Something I carried with me for nine long months."

I began to see a little more, a glimmer of understanding. "So Gudni—"

"Is my own son. And Malfrid my half-sister. I hid the pregnancy. I tried to lose the child, but the stubborn babe refused to die. I gave birth alone, in the hills, shortly after my own mother birthed Duncan's child, a baby girl. But I did not want my son. I put the bastard out on the rocks to drown and I left the fiord. Indeed, I thought to walk all the way to the open sea and drown myself in it, although hunger made me faint and weak. I yearned for death, for absolution from my shame. But as I neared the coast I saw a vessel. They saw me there on that barren coast, and took me up, and gave me succor. The ship held Ivar Bardsson and his party, men from the Eastern Settlement. They took me away, and believed me when I said

I was the last person alive on that fiord. They did not seek further. I departed with them and never returned."

"And you left your own mother to starve there, with her baby girl."

Ingvilt nodded. "She deserved it. She had betrayed me with Duncan. He should have been mine. But he came back," she mused. "I thought them all dead for the past fifteen years, until I saw him here."

"But why kill your own sister?" My tongue felt unaccountably numb, the words difficult to shape.

"Had Duncan favored me, I'd not have been defiled by that Skraeling. And then I saw the way that Gudni looked at Malfrid, that day after they had performed for us. He lusted after the girl and she was his own aunt. I killed her to save her from that shame."

"And to punish Duncan."

"Perhaps." Ingvilt smiled. I watched while she ran her tongue over her white teeth.

"And the falcon?"

"I needed blood. In Greenland the men would bury walrus jaws in the churchyard to insure good hunting. I wanted a successful hunt." Ingvilt smiled again, and I fancied I saw blood on her lips, like a wolf after a kill. "And of course, Duncan loved the birds."

I shuddered. "And that is when you stole his dagger."

Ingvilt nodded.

"And the book, the *Inventio*. Why steal that?"

Ingvilt shrugged her shoulders. "Duncan valued it. It meant little to me, but he valued it. So I took it from him."

"As you took his falcons, and his daughter."

Ingvilt nodded.

"Then Gybb Saylor came and saw you, and he remembered you."

"Perhaps. More importantly, I remembered him and could not take the chance. It is a shame Gudni does not drink whisky. I thought he would."

"You would kill your own son?"

"I have another."

"And Agnes?"

"She recognized Peter's ring. If the foolish maid had held her tongue she'd still be alive today."

"But now you've told all of it to me."

"But you'll not live to tell anyone else, Muirteach."

My surprise must have shown as I faced her. "It won't take long," Ingvilt continued. "Folk will think it the same flux that killed the others." She laughed as she saw my confusion. "That scratch on your cheek, Muirteach. That ring held poison."

I did not want to believe her. "My wife still lives," I countered. Ingvilt's eyes narrowed. "You have not won that throw."

"And she will believe you wanted her dead. She'll not mourn for you, Muirteach." The venom in her words struck me like a cold knife deep in my bowels.

"Not if I have proof it was you."

"You do not understand, do you, Muirteach? You are dying. You will die here, and no one will know what you found."

It was true my hands felt numb, and my cheek tingled, but I would not believe her. "What of you and I, my lady? What was that?"

Ingvilt laughed, a brittle sound like splintering ice. "Nothing, Muirteach. A diversion. A distraction. And you did not suspect me, did you? You suspected my husband's poor squire. As if that fop could kill anyone. He'll never make a knight."

I had indeed been a fool, as my wife had told me. "You'll not succeed." I managed to form the words, although it was growing harder to speak.

"But what proof could you have?" she continued. "There is nothing to connect me with the deaths of Agnes or that old man."

"Look to your shrine, lady. You may find something missing."

Ingvilt's eyes flicked to the table where her shrine stood, I noted with satisfaction, but she did not examine it. "Why, Muirteach? Do you think I need to pray?"

"You may. For murder is a mortal sin." I started walking towards the door, the cloak and bird's wing in my arms and the vial in my pocket. "Goodbye, Ingvilt," I said.

"You'll not get far, Muirteach."

She spoke true. I felt numbness in my legs now, and grew dizzy as well, but the fumes from the brazier had made the room stuffy. I coughed as I made my way to the door, but Ingvilt reached the doorway before me, blocking my way. I pushed against her and we knocked into the brazier, turning it over and sending the hot coals flying across the room, but I barely noticed as Ingvilt and I struggled at the threshold, until the thickening scent of smoke filled my nostrils.

The hot coals smoldered on the silken clothing that still lay strewn across the floor, and burst into little tongues of flame that caught at the linen shifts, brocade and woolen over-garments. I smelled the harsh odor of burning fabric. I pushed Ingvilt away and tried to stamp out the flames, but my legs felt strangely wooden. The fire gained strength, feeding hungrily on the clothing, then caught at the straw of the nearest pallet. Despite my efforts the room began filling with acrid smoke.

Choking, I reached the window and tried to open the shutters, but my arms felt like lead. With a final effort I got the shutters loose. The rush of air from the window only made the flames burn higher. "Ingvilt, we must escape!"

"I will go, but you'll not live to leave this room."

I retched and coughed as the smoke swirled around us. Through it I saw Ingvilt's pale face smiling like some demon as I sank to the floor.

"You have indeed poisoned me," I gasped, believing it at last, as the strange tingling numbness spread through my limbs.

"You shall not stop me, Muirteach," the lady said. She swept past me, moving towards the anteroom. I gathered my will and all my strength, lunged after her, and grabbed hold of her foot, tripping her. We wrestled amongst the licking tongues of flame, she trying to rise and I struggling to hold on to her. The air proved a little better closer to the floor, and my strength increased as I fought with her. I saw the hungry flames attack the bed hangings and begin to devour them. Then Ingvilt clawed at my face. "You'll die here," she gasped.

"Then you will as well," I retorted. "Just as poor Malfrid, and your maid, all of them died—"

"No, no. I'll not die!" Ingvilt shrieked. "They'd burn me three times, like the witch in the sagas. But I'll not die. I'll not!" As she said those words, I saw fire lick at the filmy gauze of her veil. The flames caught on the flimsy fabric and then spread to the long sleeves of her houppelande, closely buttoned about her.

Ingvilt screamed like a devil from Hell. She beat at the flames, trying to put them out, forgetting to fight me as she fought the fire. Behind her, the large posts of the great bed groaned as the fire consumed the hangings and caught on the wooden beams.

I rose, intending to drag Ingvilt out of the room, and tried to help her beat out the fire burning her clothes. The nauseating stench of burning hair, wool and silk dizzied me. The linen of my shirt scorched as I threw myself on her, trying to smother the flames with my own body.

"Ingvilt, come, we can escape this—" I said, rolling towards the doorway and trying to pull her with me.

"And live so that I might be hanged? Or burned again?" Ingvilt gasped. "No now, I'll not do that. But I'm not wanting to journey to Hell alone. You'll come with me." She held me fast as I attempted to crawl towards the doorway, fighting against the coldness of my limbs, which felt numb despite the heat of the fire.

With another groan and a crash one of the bedposts came down, pinning Ingvilt to the floor. I struggled to move it, but the heavy post would not budge. Tiny imps of flame licked at the thick wood. It seemed to me the two of us both dwelled in Hell already.

The flames intensified, the scent of burning cloth and hair grew stronger. Desperate, I gave one final shove and the post rolled away from Ingvilt's body. She lay insensate on the floor, among the charred remains of her clothing and veil.

The fire by now had spread to the table against the wall. I saw the statue of the Virgin as the wooden doors of the shrine caught. Then I smelled the scent of burning ivory and the Virgin burst into flames. I glimpsed a halo of fire around the sweetly carved face before it disappeared, consumed.

Gasping and choking, I tried to reach the window where the air was better, striving to pull Ingvilt's unconscious body with me. I heard voices, and pulled myself up to the sill. Smoke poured from the window and I glimpsed folk milling around below, some staring and pointing while others started a bucket chain. I saw Morag among the crowd, her hands over

Magnus's eyes to block his view of the fire. Behind me the flames crackled. I heard a roar and another crash as more of the bed collapsed.

It was three stories down to the ground and it did not look to be a soft landing. A cart full of dung and muck from the stables blocked the road, positioned close underneath the window. I watched an instant as some men tried to move it away from the burning lodging, but the cart proved heavy and without horses it did not go well. Perhaps it could break our fall.

"Ingvilt, come, I cannot leave you here—" I tugged at her. She remained senseless. Her brocade gown and golden hair still smoldered where I'd beaten out the flames. I dragged and pulled, and finally raised her body to the sill. Although a confessed murderess, and a poisoner, I could not leave the woman to burn to death in this inferno. God knew she would burn in Hell soon enough.

Balancing on the sill, I peered out the window. The folk below shouted and pointed, jostling to see while others ran with buckets of water. I glimpsed the castle guards amid the crowd, and thought I saw Cruickshanks among them.

The room burst into full flame behind me, a roaring inferno. When I do go to Hell for my misdeeds, it will not seem strange to me, for surely it must be like the raging blaze of that cursed chamber. I had no more time to consider. I grasped the witch tight to me and rolled over the sill.

❖   ❖   ❖

Folk said later that fiery demons flew from the windows of the Old Queen's Lodgings before the entire building burst into flames. The Lady Ingvilt and I fell through the sky like Hellish imps, her hair in flames about her, and crashed to earth like the veriest fallen angels, thrice damned.

CHAPTER 23

I awoke. My eyes gradually focused in the hazy light, as if some animal emerged from a burrow into the day. My lips, face, and limbs felt cold and numb, although my heart raced, hammering in my chest, and cold sweat ran down me. My skin felt as though it had been flayed from my body and every muscle ached.

Henry's face appeared, and around me I heard a great clamor of cries and excited speech. "Muirteach, can you hear me?" Henry asked.

I nodded, my throat burning and dry. "Am I dead?" I croaked.

Henry gave a short laugh. "No, but you might as well have been."

"I still may be; the witch has poisoned me," I managed to

say, before I lapsed again into the blackness.

The next time my eyes opened I felt a little stronger and my heart beat more normally, although my bad leg hurt horribly. I heard a voice I did not expect.

"Ah, Muirteach, you are awake." Fearchar Beaton's blue eyes, so like those of my wife, looked at me gravely. I felt a sudden shamed urge to pull the blankets up over me and hide from that penetrating gaze.

"How does my wife?" I managed at length to ask. Fearchar did not answer at first. He brought a pottery cup to my lips and I drank some foul-tasting liquid. A few moments later I was violently ill.

"Your wife does better," Fearchar told me, after I finished retching. "Although she remains weak."

"How did you get here?" I asked, after my stomach stopped heaving.

"His Lordship sent for me, some days ago. The day you fell, it was. And when I arrived here I found not one patient, but two."

"You saved my life."

"And a sorry state you were in, all bruised and scorched and poisoned. It was well you did not get more of that. We found the vial in your pouch and thus knew what it was."

"She gave it to me through her ring."

"So you were done drinking with her, then," said Fearchar and I wondered how much Mariota had told him. "Aye, I saw the scratch there," he continued thoughtfully after another moment. "You'll have a scar on your cheek from it, I'm thinking."

I nodded.

"And other scars as well, perhaps," my father-in-law added. I nodded again. If he wondered how Ingvilt had come to be touching my cheek, my father-in-law was compassionate enough not to call me to account for it.

"She poisoned some perfume and had me give it to Mariota," I tried to explain to Fearchar. "I did not know, and then Mariota thought it was a gift from me—" My voice trailed away into an uncomfortable silence. It seemed to me that ever since I had met Fearchar's daughter, I had done nothing but cause her trouble. "So once more, I am to blame—"

"She recovers," Fearchar finally answered my unspoken question. "Queen Euphemia has been most kind to her, and brought her to her own bower to be cared for, and the Lady Isobel has been most attentive and cossets her continually. Baron Sinclair even sent for his wife from Rosslyn to keep Mariota company."

I swallowed, my throat sore, looked down and saw a splint tied on my bad leg with bandages under that. That explained the pain I felt there. Fearchar saw my glance. "You broke your leg in the fall. It's good you landed on the dung cart, or it might have been worse. Although it was not a clean break. I am not sure yet how it will mend."

"Where is Mariota now?" I asked.

"She remains in the queen's bower, resting. She lost a great deal of blood and is weakened by that."

"And the baby," I said. "She lost our baby."

Fearchar nodded in reply. He looked sad and I realized with a sudden awareness that the lost child would have been his own grandchild. "So that is one more life to lay at Ingvilt's feet," he finally said.

I did not speak for a moment. "What happened to her?" I asked at length, reluctant to hear the answer. "Ingvilt. Where is she?"

"Her flesh was badly burned, her face as well, her hair nearly scorched away. She survived the fall but died shortly thereafter from her burns."

So Ingvilt had not survived, despite my efforts to save her from the flames. I thought with some gratitude that now perhaps I could be free of her. Although that would depend on what happened with Mariota. I asked for water and Fearchar handed me a cup. I sipped at the liquid, which soothed my harsh, dry throat. "And what of the rest?" I asked after another long moment, handing the cup back to him.

"The flames took that entire building but the fire did not spread any further, from what I understand. And no other lives were lost. No one else was even injured."

"Ah," I said, feeling at least some relief. "When can I see Mariota?" I finally dared to inquire.

"When she wakes I'll send her to you, if she wishes to come to you. But drink this now." Fearchar handed me some more liquid in the same pottery cup. I smelled the thick scent of valerian, and the darker smell of poppy as I brought it to my lips, but I complied dutifully with my father-in-law's instructions and soon after fell into another deep slumber.

❖   ❖   ❖

I dreamed I heard a voice calling me, "Muirteach, Muirteach." I struggled out of sleep, opened my eyes, and saw my wife sitting in a chair by my bed. "Mariota," I said. I heard the door close as Fearchar retreated from the room.

"How do you fare, Muirteach?" my wife asked. She looked thinner, pale, with hollows in her cheeks and dark shadows under her blue eyes. I wanted to reach out and grasp her hands, but my wife kept her hands by her side and made no effort to touch me as I lay in the bed.

"I am alive, but beyond that I could not say," I replied. "But what of you, *mo chridhe*?"

"I do well enough," replied Mariota tersely. I saw no softness in her face as she heard my endearment. "And you lived. As did I."

I nodded. I was not in Hell, although this could well be Purgatory.

Mariota bit her lip and tears welled in her eyes. I started to speak but did not know what to say, and an uncomfortable silence fell between us. After a moment Mariota controlled herself. I watched her throat as she swallowed, and then she spoke, as though she wished to sound matter-of-fact. "There is another to see you here." My wife got up and opened the chamber door, gesturing someone inside.

Henry Sinclair entered the room and smiled, his eyes cheerful. "So you remain with us, Muirteach! And it's glad I am to see you. Are you well enough to speak with us?"

I nodded. Henry settled Mariota in a chair and then he pulled up his chair to my bedside. "Then let us hear your story. What happened there, in Ingvilt's rooms?"

I was glad to see Henry, but disappointed, I confess, not to have more time alone with my wife, reluctant though she seemed to spend time alone with me. But I told them of my search of Ingvilt's chambers, of finding the vial, the book, the severed falcon's wing, and the bloodstained cloak. I spoke of Ingvilt's confession and how the fire had started in the main bedchamber, and spread, although I could not convey the horror of those moments in the flames. Nothing could convey that.

Midway through I stopped, and asked for something to drink. Mariota fetched some type of infusion in a pottery cup, but she gave it to Henry to hand to me. Although the cup felt rough in my hands, the drink soothed my throat and at length I continued the story.

"So Gudni and Magnus are half-brothers," Henry murmured as I completed my tale.

"As Gudni and Malfrid were aunt and nephew," added Mariota. "What a sad horror. What a waste."

I could hardly bear to look at my wife's face for the sadness I saw there. "Where are Duncan and Gudni now?

And Peter?" I asked after a moment, both because I wanted to know the answer and because I wished to turn the topic of the conversation to something else.

"They remain imprisoned, but when your story is known there's no doubt they'll be set free," Henry assured me. "I imagine Cruickshanks will be wanting to talk to you soon, now that you are somewhat recovered. But what was Ingvilt's reasoning? Why slay Malfrid? And the falcons?"

"She hoped to punish Duncan for rejecting her as a young girl, and favoring her mother. She blamed the man for many things."

"None of them his fault," put in Mariota sharply, sounding more herself. But her face remained pinched and to my eyes she looked even paler than before.

"You should rest, *mo chridhe*," I told her.

"Yes," she agreed. "No doubt you should sleep as well. We will leave you then, Muirteach," my wife added, and she left the room, leaning heavily on the arm of Henry Sinclair.

The next day I felt well enough to sit up. My bad leg had been splinted and swathed in bandages, my blistered hands where I had hit at the flames also bandaged. At least I still breathed, I told myself, though my throat and lungs ached somewhat from the smoke of the fire. I wondered if my wife would forgive me for my idiocy. If not, I might as well count myself among the dead.

The door opened and Fearchar entered with some sops in broth. "Here, eat this. You'll need strength to mend."

"I'll need strength to face my wife," I said ruefully.

"You were a fool, Muirteach."

"Fine I know it." I did not excuse myself to Fearchar. It was his daughter's life I'd endangered, her heart I had toyed with. "How can I face her?"

Fearchar looked serious, his blue eyes sad. "You must puzzle that out between you."

"It was a sorry bargain she made when she married me."

Fearchar's expression inclined me to believe he agreed with me, but his next words surprised me. "Any man can be a fool and from what I've heard the Norse woman played you well. You've not been at court before."

"And hope to never be again."

Fearchar nodded. "Perhaps you'll leave it a wiser man. Now eat," he said, and left me alone to lick at my wounds like some injured hound, struggling to bring the spoon to my mouth.

❖   ❖   ❖

The next morning I heard a bustle outside and a maidservant came in. She quickly started tidying up, removing the dirty bowl and cup, putting an embroidered cloth on the table and sweeping the floor, all with an air of great industry. She hurriedly helped me to wash my face and put on a clean *lèine*, then smoothed the covers of the bed and plumped up the bolster.

"What is it?" I asked her.

"The king himself is coming."

"Here?"

"He wants to speak with you. Now I must be quick," she said, taking the chamber pot outside to empty it.

A few moments later I heard voices from the landing and a short while after that, the door opened. King Robert himself entered, along with Queen Euphemia, the Lord of the Isles, Robert Cruickshanks, and Henry Sinclair. My wife and her father were also of the party, as was Ingvilt's husband, with Peter Leslie, not so finely dressed today, behind him. At the end of the procession I spied Duncan Tawesson and Gudni. Both looked the worse for their days spent in the dungeons, although I saw with relief that they also had washed and been given some clean clothes to appear in before the king.

Mariota stood close to her father. I gazed at her, filling my eyes and my heart with the sweet sight of her, drinking it in like a man thirsting for pure water. Her blue eyes did not look at me, but focused on the floor as though the oak planks were the most fascinating things she had yet seen at court. Chairs were brought for King Robert and the queen, while the rest of the party crowded into the chamber, filling the small room. I tried to rise, despite my leg, but the king himself stopped me.

"No, Muirteach, do not rise. The Beaton tells us that it will be some time yet before you can stand on that leg."

"Your Highness," I muttered, trying to make some kind of

obeisance from my bed and failing utterly. "I am honored—"

"I want to find out what happened," the king cut in, "on that day. And you are the only one who knows. His Lordship of the Isles, my noble son-in-law, has assured me that you will be truthful."

"Yes, sire," I said, chastened and somewhat shamed. I told him and the entire company what had passed that day in Ingvilt's chambers, showed them the vial of poison, Ingvilt's bloody cloak, the falcon's wing, and told them what Ingvilt had said regarding Malfrid, Gudni, and Duncan Tawesson.

"What say you to this?" the king asked Duncan.

"When I first visited Saemundsfiord, sire," answered Duncan, "it is true that my Astrid had a daughter. And the lass's name was indeed Ingvilt. She vanished at the end of a hard winter. I was voyaging, and when I returned Astrid told me of her daughter's disappearance. We believed her drowned. I did not know she had been with child, nor did my wife, I believe. And I did not recognize her in this woman—would that I had done so. My Malfrid might still live."

"It would perhaps have saved much sorrow," agreed the queen in a low voice.

"Sire, her story does follow," Henry Sinclair offered. "Ingvilt first appeared in the Norwegian court close to fifteen years ago, when Ivar Bardsson returned to Bergen. He told the tale of finding her near the Western Settlement. She claimed her family had died from starvation; he took her story for truth, believed the settlement deserted, and did not seek any further inland."

"And in her twisted fashion she thought to save her half-sister shame by killing her instead?" asked the queen.

"Aye, Your Majesty, that is what she declared. Yet I believe she slew the girl more to gain vengeance on Tawesson, whom she saw as the cause of her troubles," I answered.

"Such a sad story," murmured Queen Euphemia. I fancied that the queen looked at me with pity as my tale concluded. But it was in truth a sorrowful story, and most everyone appeared touched by it.

"Sir Johann," declared the king, who also appeared much affected by the tale, "you should be thankful your wife died of her injuries. For I would have hated to hang such a beautiful woman. Or to burn her. For she was guilty, not just of murder, but of sorcery. What did she tell you of the slain falcon, Muirteach?"

I repeated that part of the tale; how Ingvilt had declared she needed the falcon's blood for her sorcery. Sir Johann looked sad and grim, and seemed to have aged many years since I had last seen him. He thanked the king for his wisdom and bowed deeply. His sovereign dismissed him and gave him leave to go. Sir Johann walked with faltering steps out of the chamber, followed by his squire.

"Your Majesty, what of these two men?" Cruickshanks asked, gesturing to Duncan and Gudni.

"They are at liberty," the king replied. Duncan's face relaxed a bit and Gudni almost smiled. "As is the squire. It is

clear they had no part in the murders. And I will have that
tercel," King Robert added, handing a heavy purse to Duncan.
"It is a shame about the remaining female."

"Yes, Your Highness," agreed Duncan. "She may never fly.
But we thank you for your wise judgment in this case, and
your generosity." Duncan and Gudni both bowed and left the
chamber, free men once more.

The king and most of the party also withdrew, and I was
then left alone with my wife and her father.

"And so, that is the end of that," Fearchar said. "Tawesson
and his son are released and free to go."

"I heard Henry Sinclair seeks to enlist them into his
service," Mariota said. "But I am not sure they will accept. They
may well not wish to spend more time in Scotland; it holds bad
memories for them. As this time does for me," she added.

"I am sorry for all of it," I said. "*Mo chridhe*, I was a fool."

"Yes." My wife did not say anything else for a moment and
I felt my heart freeze. Her next words did little to thaw it. "Yes,
you were, Muirteach." Fearchar stood up to leave and my wife
turned to go with him.

"Mariota, wait. Please. I must speak with you."

Mariota nodded reluctantly to her father and Fearchar
left, shutting the door quietly. My wife stayed behind. She
seated herself in the vacant chair near my bed, with her hands
in her lap. I watched her twist her fingers together for a minute
before she spoke. "Well?" she finally asked, her voice sharp.
"What do you want to say?"

"Forgive me, Mariota," I begged. "Please." Then I waited, my chest tight, barely breathing, until my wife raised her sapphire eyes to look upon me.

"My father advises me to forgive you, Muirteach. And the queen herself tells me that I should, as I am your married wife and such is my duty. But I am not sure that I can forgive you. For I lost our child, Muirteach, my very own child."

"It was my child too," I retorted, a sinking feeling in my gut as I spoke. "Do you think I feel no grief for it? For all of this?"

"God knows I have been in danger before, many times," my wife continued as though she had not heard me, "but you were there by my side. Always. Yet this time you yourself gave me the poison. How can I trust you again? Ever?"

Ingvilt's cold, dead fingers reached out from the grave to stab at my heart with sharp splinters of ice. *Your wife will never trust you again,* she had said. And now that prophecy came true.

"I can only beg you to let me try again. I cannot bear to lose you, Mariota."

"I am your sworn wife, Muirteach. And those bonds cannot be undone. Certainly not simply because my husband is a fool. But when we return to Islay, I perhaps will live apart from you, at Ballinaby." With that she turned away from me and left the room.

CHAPTER 24

For some weeks after that we lingered at court, waiting for my leg to mend well enough for me to travel. His Lordship departed after some days for Islay, his business concluded, but Fearchar remained behind to tend me, which he did with more kindness that I deserved. My wife also remained at court but I saw little of her. She spent her days with the queen and her ladies, and rarely visited me. When she did she said little, and we sat in awkward silence, ill at ease with each other.

I grew querulous and fretful, both from the inactivity and from the fear that things could not be put right with Mariota. I think her father understood, although he said little of it to me.

One afternoon I listened to the rain drumming outside the wooden shutters of the tiny room, thinking I would go mad with worry and boredom, when I heard the door open. I expected Fearchar, but saw with pleasant surprise Henry Sinclair walk into the room. He had a pitcher of ale and two glasses with him.

"Fearchar told me you might want some company," he said, shaking the rain from his fur mantle. He set the pitcher and glasses down on a table, and seated himself on the stool next to my bed. "How are you faring, Muirteach?"

I said only, "The leg is mending well enough, Fearchar says. And the burns are almost healed." I held out my hands to him, showing Henry the tender pink skin.

"Well, that is fine news indeed." Henry reached for the pitcher and poured me a glass of ale, then handed it to me. He poured a glass for himself and took a swallow. "And here is more fine news," he continued. "You'll not even be able to guess."

I did not feel much inclined toward guessing games, and sourly told Henry that. But he appeared undeterred by my poor mood.

"Duncan has sold me the *Inventio*," Henry finally announced, after I refused to make a single guess. His hazel eyes gleamed with excitement. With a flourish he pulled the small leather-bound tome from his mantle and held it towards me. "Here, look at it."

The leather cover was stained with salt water and blackened with soot. I remembered saving the volume from the flames in Ingvilt's chamber, but I made no move to reach for the book now and took a swig of ale instead. "I've seen enough of it. I've no wish to look at it," I protested.

"It is fascinating, Muirteach. Duncan sold it to me, he had need of funds, despite the pretty price King Robert paid him for the tercel."

"Indeed? And where is Duncan now?"

"He and Gudni have set sail. Two days ago. Duncan spoke of wintering in Kilmartin, with family if indeed any remain there. Although I believe his older brother still holds the lands, so Duncan will find a welcome there for a time. He told me that he and Gudni plan to sail to the north again next spring."

"Seeking more falcons?" I asked.

Henry shrugged. "Seeking something. I am not sure what exactly. I offered him service with me, but he refused. Still, I'd welcome him back, should he want to return. I could use a man with his knowledge of the seas. But now, Muirteach," Henry continued, after taking a drink from his own cup, "it's clear you've a need for diversion, cooped up in this small chamber. Listen to the marvels in this book." Henry opened up the volume, and began to read from the handwritten pages within.

In my sour and self-pitying mood I had little desire to hear of lands to the north that I would never visit. But as Henry read, his hazel eyes gleaming with excitement, I found that the wonders he recounted did distract me a little, both from the pain of my healing hands and broken leg, and from the demon of worry that haunted me.

The writer described four in-drawing seas, or channels, which divided the lands of the north. Following these channels led one to a hidden sea, in which roiled an immense whirlpool. The friar claimed that over four thousand hapless souls had perished in these oceans, drowned by the insistent force of the frigid waters. I thought of the Cailleach, that much smaller whirlpool near my own home, and shuddered, remembering the time some years back when I had thought Mariota lost in its vicious waters. I had no desire to see the ferocity of these greater, northern torrents; my blood chilled to even think of it. The horror helped distract me from the pain in my broken leg, if not from other aches.

Henry did not notice my shudder but, still intent upon the text, went on to describe a massive lodestone of black, bare rocks, said to be over thirty miles in diameter, reaching to the heavens, so high one could not see the top of the peak. This apparently was located at the very center of the earth, at the farthest North. Around this rock the whirlpool surged, beating against the stone until the waters were sucked down into the belly of the earth by the magnetic force of this immense stone.

The fantastical tale made me think of Ingvilt, and Mariota, and myself. Of course I thought of little else, imprisoned in that small room. Whether that terrible attraction I had felt for the Norsewoman would lead to the wreckage of my love and my hopes, I did not yet know. But I pondered the image often after Henry left me, imagining myself adrift in turbulent waters, unsure if my feet would ever touch solid land again.

❖   ❖   ❖

My body healed. I began to bear some weight on my leg, and finally one afternoon, Fearchar gave me permission to go outside my chamber. Fitted out with wooden crutches and grimaces, I hobbled out of my room and with his help made my slow and tortuous way down the narrow wooden stairs to the outer world below. Even my worry for Mariota could not completely dim the pleasure I took in smelling fresh air and seeing a pale sun shine through the patchy clouds. The late October day felt chill. I paused to wrap my *brat* more tightly about me, and nearly lost hold of my crutch, but Fearchar steadied me.

"You won't want to be overdoing it," he cautioned me, his blue eyes glinting in the wind.

"How am I to gain strength if I do not tax myself somewhat?" I responded. Fearchar did not reply. We set out walking down the path leading towards the Great Hall. "Let us walk as far as the gardens," I suggested, wanting to make amends for my ill humor and sharp tongue. "I can manage that far, surely. Then I shall sit and rest on one of the benches, and then return, as meek as any lamb." Fearchar nodded his assent and although I confess I found the going hard, I refused to admit as much to Fearchar. We reached the gate and entered the gardens.

Most of the leaves had fallen from the trees and the place

had a deserted look to it. A few scraggly Michaelmas daisies still fought their way up through the dead leaves, against the oncoming winter's chill. The sere, dead-looking garden little resembled the sunny, pleasant space I remembered. I found, rather than cheering me, the prospect saddened me.

"I've rested long enough," I muttered, and made to stand, but a glimpse of someone at the far end of the garden stopped me. I recognized both the blue *brat*, and the way the woman had of standing, stubborn and determined, as strong as the wave-battered rocks on the island coast. She was with another lady, the Lady Isobel I think it was, but Mariota did not see me until the other woman pulled at her sleeve and whispered something to her.

Fearchar caught my glance and followed it. I do not think he had known we would see his daughter here, but I might well be wrong in that surmise. Fearchar Beaton is an uncommonly wise man. "I will leave you to rest," he said smoothly, "and return in a bit to help you walk back." He left before I had a chance to tell him not to go.

Mariota saw me and, although I could tell she was taken aback, she approached.

"Muirteach. So you are about and walking," she observed.

"With these." I gestured towards the crutches that lay beside the bench. "But it feels fine to see the sun shine again." An awkward moment passed. "And you?" I dared to ask. "How are you?"

"I do well enough, Muirteach. I came here to see if there were roots of mallow. This is the time to pick them, for the vital force has retreated back into the root. Queen Euphemia herself asked me to gather some. I am to make some lotions and creams for the queen before I depart, and show Lady Isobel the receipts, as mallow is known to be helpful for the skin." Mariota's voice trailed away, leaving an uncomfortable silence between us.

"You are going away, Mariota?"

"Eventually." My wife gave a short little laugh. "Do not look so woebegone, Muirteach. My father and I will leave with you when he deems you can travel."

My relief must have shown in my face, and I felt unreasonably happy at my wife's words, as though the sun were shining down upon me with full summer's warmth instead of the weak light of a cloudy October afternoon. But my wife's face, I noted after a moment, did not look so sanguine.

"Mariota," I ventured to ask, "have you thought more about . . ."

"About what, Muirteach?" my wife responded, with a note of sharpness in her voice.

"Och, let it be," I replied, too cowardly to pursue the subject. "It was nothing. No doubt the queen herself will be calling for you soon enough, and you must be ready to get your herbs together and leave."

"Nothing! It was nothing!" exclaimed Mariota. "What are

you saying, Muirteach? Are you saying all this between us is nothing?"

"I was not meaning that," I said, trying to make amends. "You are misunderstanding, jumping to conclusions."

"And why should I not be? Wasn't I right before?"

"Mariota, stop! You are putting your own words into my mouth, aren't you, then! I just was not wanting to speak of what is between us now; not if it would be distressing you."

"If it would distress me! As if I am not distressed every instant of every day! Muirteach, how can you be such an idiot?" My wife bit at her lip nervously and I feared she would burst into tears.

"Mariota," I begged, frantic. "Listen to me. I was a fool, I am still a fool. Yes, you are right, I am an idiot. But I love you, Mariota. You are my sworn wife, and I love you."

My wife turned away from me, and gestured to the Lady Isobel who loitered awkwardly at the far end of the garden. The lady picked up the basket of herbs and walked towards my wife. "I must go, Muirteach." My wife gave me one last look, and then joined her friend. "The queen waits upon us."

❖   ❖   ❖

I slowly gained strength. On most days I would walk to the garden for exercise and at times I would find my wife there. We spoke superficially. I was afraid of what she might tell me and so I did not press her. Mariota, for her part, spoke

of desultory things: the weather, the salves and creams Queen
Euphemia wished her to make, the fashions of court ladies.
I noticed she wore her hair differently and had replaced her
white kerch with a veil of fine lawn, like those worn at court.
But as the days passed we grew a bit more comfortable with
each other, and the awkward silences diminished.

Finally the day came when Fearchar deemed me fit
enough to travel and I anxiously made ready to leave. I think
I feared, up until we left the castle, that my wife would find
some reason to stay with Queen Euphemia and her ladies at
the court, far away from me. But as I descended the stairs I saw
her, attired for traveling, wrapped warmly in her blue wool
mantle, standing next to her father, supervising the servants
who loaded the baggage on the cart. I also saw, with surprise,
a cage with the wounded gyrfalcon in it sitting atop the pile of
luggage. We climbed into the cart and left Edinburgh Castle
behind us. I breathed deeper with relief as we descended the
hill and the noise of the burgh and castle faded. We headed
towards the coast and His Lordship's galley, sent to fetch us
home at last.

As the cart trundled through the green hills I heard a
squawk from the back, and then thought to ask my wife of the
falcon.

"Gudni gave her to me," Mariota answered. "He fears she
will never fly, and Duncan vowed they could never be selling
her now. So I took her. But she gains strength every day. I shall

keep her at the farm near Ballinaby," she said when she saw my expression, and she gave me a tentative smile. "Perhaps she may yet fly."

I did not deserve to hope, but when I took Mariota's hand she did not pull it away.

THE END

AUTHOR'S NOTE

The research for this book led me far afield. When I started, I intended to perhaps do something with the Knights Templar and their purported presence in Scotland, and I knew I wanted Henry Sinclair as a character. However, my research on Henry led me to the Norse settlements in Greenland, and I grew fascinated by that story. Where did the Norse settlers go? Did they attempt to colonize the western lands? Did English pirates enslave them? Were the colonists adopted and merged into the Inuit populations? Perhaps all of these are true, to some extent, and future DNA studies may provide more information. But what was it like, living on the outer edges of the European world?

In the course of writing this book (and unfortunately it took much longer than I had planned) more archaeological information has come to light about Norse finds in the high Arctic, with discoveries of more trading sites and archaeological evidence suggesting that trade between the Norse and the Inuit and Arctic natives was on a broader scale than the few stories detailed in the Norse sagas suggest. Other new theories and speculations about the Kensington Rune stone, the Spirit Pond stones, and the discovery of bison fur and North American arrowheads in Western Settlement ruins lead one to suppose that there was more traffic between Greenland and the western lands than was previously believed.

Among the fascinating discoveries in Greenland's abandoned Western Settlement (actually north of the more southerly Eastern Settlement) was a knife hilt, engraved with a gyrony of eight, a symbol of Clan Campbell in the 1300s. Reading of that find inspired the character Duncan Tawesson and his story.

The discovery of carefully placed walrus jaws buried in the Garder churchyard in Greenland leads one to suppose that, despite the European-style jet crucifixes recovered from archaeological digs, some of the beliefs of the Greenland Norse may have been less than orthodox. I've extrapolated this and some of Ingvilt's machinations are the result. I've had her sail with Ivar Bardsson on his return voyage to Norway in 1364, and I've placed his visit to the Western Settlement at about the same time, although it may have been earlier.

The *Inventio Fortunatae*, or "Fortunate Discovery", is one of the more intriguing of the world's vanished books. It purportedly tells of a voyage made in the 1300s to the far north by a mysterious "monk with an astrolabe", who told of others of his voyage at the Norwegian court in Bergen in 1364. It is possible that this monk traveled back to Bergen from the north with Ivar Bardsson, the Norwegian agent of the church who finally returned to Norway in 1364 after many years in Greenland. The book has long been lost, but Jacobus Cnoyen made a summary of the contents in the 1490s. Even this text had vanished by the late 1500s, but a letter to John Dee dated

April 20, 1577, tells of some of the supposed contents. The information was incorporated into maps by Mercator in the 1560s and influenced concepts of Arctic geography for many years.

The possibility that sightings of lost Inuit kayakers may have led to legends of the selkies and Orkney's Finnmen added spice to the creative soup. Orkney folktales tell of strange mermen, the Finnmen who live in palaces under the ocean. As well, many Scottish folktales tell of the selkies, the seal men and women who would sometimes marry humans, if their sealskins were stolen and hidden away from them. In fact, the McDuffies are reputed to have descended from selkies. But there may be an even more curious story behind these myths.

A kayak purportedly hung for years in the Nidaros Cathedral, in Trondheim, Norway, supposedly brought back from an expedition King Haakon made in the 1360s. Near Aberdeen, in the 1600s, an Inuit in a kayak appeared off the northeastern coast of Scotland. When he finally was found, he was ill and exhausted, and died shortly thereafter. Did he paddle all the way from Greenland? Or was he captured by sailors and somehow escaped from their ship? Whatever this mysterious sailor's story, he proved part of the spark that led me to Gudni Skraelingsson.

With all these intriguing trails to follow, the Knights Templar and their treasure got left by the wayside. Which leaves other intriguing possibilities for Muirteach's future.

Readers wanting to know more about the Norse in Greenland might enjoy Kirstin A. Seaver's books THE FROZEN ECHO and THE LAST VIKINGS. If you would like a more detailed bibliography, please don't hesitate to get in touch. I'm always happy to hear from readers!

ABOUT THE AUTHOR

Susan McDuffie has been a devotee of historical fiction since her childhood, when she believed she had mistakenly been born in the wrong century. Her historical mysteries set in medieval Scotland are partially inspired by tales she heard as a child about her own clan's role as "Keeper of the Records" for the medieval Lords of the Isles. Previous Muirteach MacPhee Mysteries include A MASS FOR THE DEAD, THE FAERIE HILLS (2011 New Mexico Book Award for "Best Historical Novel") and THE STUDY OF MURDER (2014 New Mexico/Arizona Book Awards Finalist). Susan lives in New Mexico and shares her life with a Native America artist and four cosseted cats. She loves to hear from readers and can be contacted through her website www.SusanMcDuffie.net or her Facebook page http://www.facebook.com/SusanMcDuffieAuthor

CPSIA information can be obtained
at www.ICGtesting.com
Printed in the USA
FFOW03n1211250218
45221576-45806FF

9 780984 790098